I0822336

THE WORLD BEYOND THE HORIZON

THE WORLD BEYOND DUOLOGY
BOOK 1

ANGELA FUNK

ISBN (paperback): 979-8-9898506-2-4

ISBN (hardcover): 979-8-9898506-3-1

Cover design by @OnyxCatArt on Etsy

Planet artwork by @Akarstudio on Fiverr

Character artwork by @SYKOSAN on Instagram

To those who saw no future
Yet still found a way

AUTHOR'S NOTE

While this novel is largely a sci-fi romantic adventure full of rich world-building and witty banter, *The World Beyond* duology also covers topics that may be uncomfortable for some. This story contains depictions of anxiety, depression, mention of a parent's suicide (off-screen), and grief and loss (extensively explored).

The overall message of the series aims to be positive, however, these themes are explored throughout, so please read at your discretion.

ALSO BY ANGELA FUNK

The Forsaken Destiny Trilogy

The Heroic Facade

The Heroic Fallacy

The Heroic Fall

The World Beyond Duology

The World Beyond the Horizon

The Stars Above the Hill

THE WORLD BEYOND THE HORIZON

THE END
Sundar
Noah's Planet

Fortun
Celeste's Planet

1

UNDER THE SHATTERED MOONS

THE PLANET WAS CRUMBLING.

No one could say for sure when it started. While Sundar had always been flat, it hadn't always been cracking at the seams. The Ancient Texts hadn't predicted such from happening, either, cementing the phenomenon as an utter anomaly, right along the southern border of the planet. Whole one moment, then fractured the next, drifting off into the limitless nothingness of space.

It had been decades since the crumbling began, yet scientists had yet to discern how gravity could shift so suddenly, a thin layer between Sundar's atmosphere and the edge of the world. Above, a bright orange sky; below, a black void of darkness.

There were multiple ends to a flat planet, and each was simply labeled, 'the end,' much like the sign a few feet behind him. And beyond 'the end' was Sundar's surface, slowly floating away, piece by piece. Noah's town was behind him and one day, it too, would drift into space. Everything he knew and loved would break away, and the spectacle would come and go as life went on.

When he was younger, his mother would bring him here to play. He imagined jumping from rock to rock, traveling through the boundless beyond. It was beautiful and terrifying, but he had so many questions that only he alone could find the answers to.

Where was the land going? Why was it drifting away?

When had *she* started drifting away?

He couldn't remember the first time she became distant, but he could remember when he sensed the end was near. Though he should've known something was wrong the day he learned that passing this very sign was illegal, and his mother had taken him somewhere dangerous to play his entire childhood.

He'd long since wondered if she'd brought him here all those times to fall, but she never gave a push. Perhaps some questions were better left unasked.

Noah released a deep sigh, peering up at the two moons on either side of Sundar—Tivinis and Lynoli—showering him in light. The sun and moons were crumbling, too.

For this, he felt at ease. If everything else around him was breaking down, even nature itself, then it was okay if he broke down, too.

The crumbling must've been quite the sight to behold when it first began, the feeling of fear when life started decaying right before humanity's eyes. But for him, it was just another Monday night, looking over the edge while walking home from a string of fruitless job interviews.

His short blond hair was stringy with sweat, and he ran a hand through it to push the stray strands out of his light green eyes before staring down at his hands, wondering when he would feel whole again.

Now, when he stopped here, all he could wonder was why everyone was so alone, and why the universe pulled everything apart. No matter how hard one tried, the other was always out of reach.

Noah shook his head—it was too sad a thought to ponder on a Monday night—and tried to think about something more concrete, like his interviews. No, they had filled his entire day, and he'd stuttered through them all. There were no positive thoughts to behold today.

With another heavy sigh, he turned and walked the familiar red cobblestone road home.

It was just another Monday without her.

2

SOMETIMES HE STOOD ON THE EDGE OF THE WORLD AND PICTURED himself in the circus, high up on a platform, about to dive into a tub of ice-cold water. All he had to do was jump, and he would be greeted with a standing ovation and grand applause, recognition for a feat everyone witnessed him bear alone.

Other times, he envisioned himself falling off, like a leaf drifting from a tree on a crisp fall day. A leisurely descent into darkness, until nothing remained.

But then he remembered—even if no one else needed him, Henry did.

And that was enough to make him turn and walk home each night.

3

FAMILIAL TIES

HENRY'S MEWS FILLED THE SOMBER SCENE IMMEDIATELY UPON entry, and Noah couldn't help the smile that crossed his lips. Dimples formed on each cheek as he scooped Henry up and cradled her. Her light orange and white-lined face scrunched as she released a lackadaisical yawn, and he gave her a twirl for extra measure with a chuckle before plopping her down on the couch.

She became restless, as she often did when he returned home, and jumped down to rub against Noah's feet. He shook his head at her in exaggerated exasperation. "What am I going to do with you, Henrietta?"

Henry was short for Henrietta, because sometimes Noah had to think quickly, and shortening names he could easily permanently change was inexplicably less complicated to do. He knew one thing for certain: she wouldn't stop until she got what she wanted—attention and food. She didn't even care about the fresh bowl of water he placed in front of her, instead sniffing at it before turning her head away, nose up.

Noah sighed and provided her with a cup of kibble as a call came. The phone system had recently evolved from only working in one's home to broadcasting around the entire side of the mountain—but only the side one lived on. Which meant the north side—where the majority of Sundar citizens lived—was unreachable for Noah.

Like many apartments, his had built-in wires running along the ceiling to a small cone-shaped device connected to the wall. This either went up to his ear or his mouth, depending on who was doing the talking.

Many phones were now connected to a wall and elongated with a series of buttons, but this apartment was worn with age, and such an installation may cause it to collapse.

This phone system—which was, again, old—allowed for a sharp jab of high-pitched squeals to ring throughout the small, two-bedroom enclosure, bouncing off the walls and reverberating back into his eardrums. If he didn't pick up after the third ring, a neighbor from the complex would come knocking. It was a rather pervasive noise, and if someone wasn't home when it rang, chaos broke loose in the hallways, and an angry note would be pinned to the door.

But it was a cheap apartment, so he stayed.

Thankfully, he was in luck and picked up after the second ring. It took a certain level of effort not to grit his teeth at the grating noise. "Noah Everlow speaking. Who is this?"

There was a crackle of static before a muffled voice broke through. "Yes, this is Katalina. Your cousin—t-that Katalina."

He raised a brow. Her name was familiar, her voice even more so, yet he couldn't quite place what she looked like. She continued before he had the chance to inquire, "We met at the funeral."

Noah tried to skim through the loose files of people in his head, but failed to identify her. His family was rather large, but they weren't particularly good at keeping track of each other, and his mother had a knack for cutting others off. He hadn't seen most of his aunts and uncles until her funeral, and he certainly hadn't seen any since. It was an in-and-out mission for them. Easy. Another event marked off the calendar; another chore with a checkmark next to it.

No one stuck around to help him clean up and sell the house. No one asked him how he was doing. He'd started and ended the funeral as he was—alone.

"I'm sorry," he said, trying to play it off casually and get the conversation over with quickly. "But I met a lot of people that day. Your name doesn't ring a bell. Was there something you needed?"

More static followed, and he briefly wondered if the next noise would be a soft click as she hung up. He'd grown straightforward over the two months since his mother's passing; there was no point in appeasing the feelings of the living when everyone would one day perish. There was hardly any point in remembering people's names, either.

"Right. Well, I live in Kern—that's two hours from you—but my fiancé and I are in town to do some food tasting for our together ceremony."

She paused. He waited for the question, but there wasn't one, so he said, "Okay."

"A-and today is Aunt Relma's birthday, right? I looked it up in our family records. She would be fifty-one."

"Yes, I'm aware it's my deceased mother's birthday. I fail to see the point you're making."

"My point is—we should get dinner together. It's been two months, and from what mom says, you don't have any family up here, and mine has been so scattered lately, and it's been a bit lonesome so... why not meet someone new who also happens to be family?"

Her words were rushed and questioning, as though she were uncertain of herself. Noah couldn't deny the surprise he felt. Of course, he knew today was her birthday, but he hadn't thought to do anything special. Another day with more interviews, but no job. An apartment he could barely afford with a cat as bored as he was, and hobbies pushed to the wayside with sudden disinterest. He used to love a good book or game; now he could hardly sit still. Talking to someone, anyone—especially *family*—was probably an excellent idea, but...

"Unfortunately, going out for dinner is not within my current budget, but I appreciate your offer. Perhaps call again with a free event and—"

"Oh, no," she blurted. "It's on us. My fiancé and I, I mean. He'll be coming, too. Please say yes. We won't be in town for much longer. We're family."

It was both an incredibly daunting yet enticing offer, and he couldn't ignore the growl of his stomach at the prospect of a restaurant-quality meal. All he'd recently had were small spheres of chicken extract, which were neither filling nor healthy.

But why was Katalina reaching out now? What was the catch?

He didn't care enough to ask, and his salivating mouth decided for him. "Okay, then. Sure, why not? Where would you like to meet?"

This time, Katalina did not hesitate, nor did she contain the excitement lining her voice as she said with unrelenting, out-of-place glee, "Aunt Relma's tombstone, 6:00 p.m.! Can't wait to see you there!"

Noah winced.

What a dark thing to sound so happy about.

4

WHERE THE STARS ALIGN

Noah meandered down the rows of tombstones like he was on a stroll through a flower garden. Instead of bright, beautiful lilies and the smell of freshly cut grass, he was surrounded by drab slabs of stone, the smell of rain lingering against the much stronger scent of manure.

This is fun, he thought dryly, scanning the names and inscriptions entangled in moss and vines. He never liked to visit memorial parks, whether it be this one or the next, and now he was remembering why. Even when history was written and read, it would one day be forgotten.

The memorial park was rather expansive, holding centuries of generations within hills lined with sidewalks, swooping green trees, and the occasional bench. Nearly no one left town, though Noah was one of the 'lucky unlucky few' who got out while he could, but, like everyone else who left, eventually came back.

One day, he'd probably be buried here, too.

The thought sent a shiver down his back as Noah made his way toward the familiar star-shaped monument of Sister Ellen and took a sharp left where, five stones down, his mother rested.

A clap of thunder rumbled above, and he glanced up at the forever haze of the dim sky, closing his eyes to focus solely on the splattering of droplets against his skin. He found it oddly peaceful—though he knew the tears would come later. They always did.

He'd forgotten an umbrella, but he didn't mind the rain. It made him feel like the sadness and the anger could one day wash away. His body was freezing, bones shivering, but it reminded him he was alive, and that it was okay to live.

Noah shifted his attention to the inscription on his mother's tombstone; it'd been almost completely covered with overgrown moss. This plot of land was situated along the river bank, a rather comical choice given the amount of times the river overflowed, and the headlines that always followed about caskets washing up miles away.

Was his mother one of them? He wouldn't know—the town made a law to keep such information hidden. 'The Grievance Clause' or something like that.

Noah read her inscription again and again, mulling over words he hadn't read in months until his heart hurt and his hands were raw from his clenched fists.

She spent her life looking for the Great Beyond, and there she rests.

The quote filled him with unequivocal rage, and he tightly

clenched his uneven nails into his palms, the soft shock of pressure and pain bringing him back to a world he didn't want to be in. Is this how she felt before she took her life?

Today was her birthday, and he hated being reminded of it. How cruel it was of Katalina to call him on this day, of all the days, and to meet here, of all the places. Why'd he say yes again? For some free food?

He was suddenly reliving her past birthdays, the ones where they went hiking or out to dinner, and then he remembered their phone call a few nights before she passed about how excited she was for him to visit. How excited she was to turn fifty-one. At what point had she started lying?

Was it all a lie?

His vision became blurred as the thought of what today was supposed to be sent tears to his eyes. Noah contemplated jogging back to his bicycle, or better yet, jumping into the stream where he could sink to the bottom and stay.

The darkness wedged itself further into his thoughts, his skin becoming cold with the pricks of loneliness clawing up his spine. He needed to leave, and fast. It was a mistake to meet here; Noah hadn't visited his mother since the funeral, and he'd intended to keep it that way. Who wanted to carve time out of their day to experience such sorrow? It was self-inflicted torture, and it infuriated him so much that his nails drew blood from his palms.

Noah stared ahead, determined to stay, though every ounce of him longed to leave. He took a deep breath and held it, willing his heart back to a steady pace.

As he released his breath and the fight-or-flight drifted

away, the sound of frantic footfalls caught his attention. The splash of each puddle filled the misty air, and he could hear them near, but he was too scared to look. After all, who would run in a memorial park?

What if they'd just committed a crime? Or were on a mission he couldn't disturb? No—he couldn't look. *But he wanted to.*

Curiosity got the better of him, and he turned his head as a woman ran past, catching only a glimpse of her heart-shaped face. Her long, wavy black hair trailed behind her with dark blue highlights peeking out from underneath. She was certainly in a rush, but what confused him further was the clothing she wore—it hardly aligned with someone who was here to mourn.

He could hear his heart beating in his chest as he shouted, "Hey, wait! Where are you going?"

The woman paused. She must've been close to his age, in her early-to-mid twenties, her skin silky smooth and sun-kissed. For a moment, he was nervous she wouldn't turn around. He shifted uncomfortably in his spot as he turned fully to face her, waiting with bated breath for her to either keep running or acknowledge his existence.

When the woman turned, it took everything in his power not to gasp. She was beautiful. Her eyes were speckled with purple and pink and blue. Light freckles dusted her cheekbones, highlighting the soft blush lining her features. It wasn't particularly hot out—the damp, dark rain clouds were parting, making way for the shining, silver moons—which meant she must've been running long before they ran into each other.

She took a deep, shuddering breath, as though what she said next would be detrimental, and she wasn't sure if he was prepared. "Our planets are set to collide in two months, and everything you and I know will be gone."

Noah stared at her, a pool of dread filling him despite knowing her statement was absurd, and he desperately tried to push it down. "Why would you say that?"

The most widely accepted theory was that the planet would one day crumble away, but to be destroyed by another planet altogether? In two months? That was unheard of.

But he couldn't deny her eyes and attire felt... otherworldly. He didn't know a thing about women's fashion, but most dresses he'd seen were one dark color, bare and flat. The one she wore was a faint, frilly blue, with layers of fabric and light, puffy long sleeves. Lining her midsection was a mini corset separating the top and bottom half of the dress, and the flowing fabric on the bottom half stretched to her knees.

Her clothing was captivating, but it scared him to see something so different from what he usually saw.

"You asked why I was running," she said with a shrug. "And maybe I'm tired of trying to figure it out all alone."

Her eyes met his, and even from this distance, he could've sworn he saw an entire galaxy hidden within them. He could hardly contain the pounding of his heart. She was so certain, too, that another planet was coming to collide with theirs.

Though it was absurd, part of him wanted to believe her.

"Do you want to help me save them?" she added with the cock of her head, almost as an afterthought. She outstretched her hand for him to take.

Noah stared across at her offer but ignored it. "That doesn't explain why you're running through the memorial park in particular. Do you know someone buried here?"

She nodded, dropping her hand with a soft, seemingly reminiscent smile. "My brother loved your planet while he was researching it. He was part of a team that came here, you see. They wanted to find a way to stop the collision."

"And did they?"

She pulled around a bag he hadn't noticed was wrapped around her shoulder. Unzipping it, she revealed a small notebook no bigger than her palm, and a watch. "They did. The next step is in this notebook. And while I do find memorial parks fascinating—my hometown never had one—this is the fastest way back to my planet. I already said goodbye to my brother back there."

He blinked at her blankly; the amount of information she spewed was overriding his thoughts. He opted to raise a brow. "I'm sorry for your loss, but I'm not sure if I can believe you. I mean, what kind of town doesn't have a memorial park? I think there are more people buried here than living these days. It's the natural course of places like this."

She smiled softly. "*That's* what you took from what I said? Not the colliding planets part? Or the fact I might be the last person alive with the answers? Look,"—she held up the watch, which was ticking away faintly in the light breeze—"this is counting down to the end. If you look closely at the very top, it says 'end' where the 'twelve' should be."

Noah gulped, having no choice but to walk over to her and examine the watch closer. She smelled like lavender—sweet and inviting, and he blushed at their sudden closeness. He saw the word 'end,' but he couldn't decipher how she got two months from the big hand on 'ten,' and the little on 'six.' "Maybe it's broken."

The woman handed him the notebook next, and he leafed through it as she said, "Your town is only so small compared to the park because you live close to the crumbling. Haven't you been to the other side of the mountain?"

She made a point of looking around; the small buildings of his town were visible in the near distance along the mountain dividing Sundar. Though the climb up the peak was treacherous, there was a path leading around the base of the steep mountain that could be passed with a small toll.

He nodded. His university and job interviews were on the other side, and it was indeed packed with people. As if turning away from the crumbling land would make it reassemble itself. "It's all the same, just more crowded. Not much more to do except markets and fairs. A tad more interesting than this side, though."

The woman tapped her chin in thought. "I find the simplicity in your town to be refreshing, personally, and there must be *some* meaningful ways to spend the time if someone like yourself chooses to stay."

Someone like himself? He couldn't help the pink hue that climbed to his cheeks. Such a reaction made no sense, of course. They didn't know each other beyond an awkward two-minute conversation, though she must've been drawn to him enough to stop running when he called.

"I don't know whether I should be flattered or disturbed

about being hit on here." Noah paused on a page in the research notebook with a drawing of a deep teal, majestic eel. Next to the drawing appeared to be words, but in a language he couldn't read.

The woman cocked her head. "Who says I'm hitting on you? I could merely be taking a guess. You don't look the type to stay somewhere you don't want to be."

While she wasn't wrong, her ominously on-the-nose words made him nervous. What was she getting at? The stranger looked down, and he noticed she was running her thumb along her knuckles. Was she nervous to talk to him, too?

Silence filled the spaces between them as he considered what to say next. It was as though he suddenly got whiplash from the conversation, and he found it difficult to follow. He'd grown so used to being alone that he hadn't a clue what to say after a certain point. Even at job interviews, which were supposed to be a choreographed dance of questions and answers that he used to perform flawlessly, he now fumbled each time.

"Where are you from?"

A smirk slowly crept onto her features. "I'm from where one world begins, and another ends."

Huh?

"I could show you if you'd like to come with me."

What an absurd thing to offer, and even more so for him to contemplate. He thought of his cat, Henrietta, who would be fine if he left for a few days. He had an automatic feeder set up, and a friend who would hopefully notice Noah's absence and check on her. Granted, he no longer spoke regularly to said friend, a product of drifting away from society. A product of a loss so deep he couldn't get out of bed most days. Other than a cat and a friend—what did he have here? Was there any reason to stay?

What if this woman was telling the truth, and the end of the world was approaching? He had to do something about it, right? He'd be a fool not to. Noah didn't know his cousin or her fiancé, so it was okay if he bailed and they went to dinner without him, right?

Finally, Noah sighed and said, "What have I got to lose?"

He held out his hand this time, but quickly retracted it before their palms met. "I don't think I can take the hand of someone without knowing their name."

"Knowing my name won't make me any less of a stranger."

"No, but I can trick myself into trusting you better that way. You could lead me to my death, for all I know." Noah stuck out his hand again. "I'll go first—Noah Everlow."

She smiled, taking his hand firmly. "Celeste. Short for Celestial. My parents have a knack for picking silly names for their children."

"I wouldn't call it silly at all. *Celestial.* I like it," Noah said. "Alright, lead the way."

Celeste's eyes widened as she looked between his hand and his gaze. Confused, he asked, "What is it?"

"Nothing. I—I just didn't expect you to say yes."

"Well, are you telling the truth about our planets colliding?" It was such a weird sentence to utter.

"Of course."

Noah smiled while handing back her research notebook.

She placed it and the watch into her small bag before swinging the pack to her back. "Then I think anyone would take your hand. If only to check that you're well. Now, where to? A secret dungeon?"

She laughed. "I promise you, you're safe—unless the planets collide sooner, of course. Or if my brother's research is wrong. Or if I fail... *but* I promise it's something you'll only see once. I think you'll like my planet."

With their hands locked together once more, Celeste dragged him along, and he let her. Over the rush of the wind and the air escaping his lungs with each pump of his legs, he called, "This is an odd place for a meet-cute, is it not?"

"Who's to say that's what this is?" she called over her shoulder. "I could be very passionate about saving the worlds."

"With a stranger?"

"Someone who looks so sad can't possibly be someone to worry about."

Noah nearly released a laugh of his own; the naivety in her voice was as clear as her actions. He thought of bringing up that a lot of sad people did heinous things, but wandered into wondering if he should be flattered by her words or offended. He deduced he felt a mixture of both.

They wound through twisting sidewalks, up and down hills, past empty benches under lonely, billowing trees. The world seemed slower, as though it could simply stop at any moment.

He was so used to the long days and nights of solitude, of sadness mixed with alcohol and comedies on the radio, of using anything to distract himself from the spare room in his apartment where his mother's things were stored, where pictures of the past stared back so aimless yet cruel. Anything to get away, but not too far away, so as to not feel guilty.

Noah wasn't one to psychoanalyze himself, though he could guess why he took Celeste's hand—he was tired of the solitude, and he knew he couldn't stay here, surrounded by the dead any longer. He had to get out.

Even if he didn't know what 'out' was, he knew it was this way, with her, and this way he would go.

5

FREE FALL

"Hey, Noah! Sorry, we're late—" Noah recognized her from the funeral as soon as he saw her. His cousin, Katalina, who was currently very late with a tall, dark-haired man in tow. Noah stopped, as did Celeste, though she took her interlaced fingers out of his when the other two approached.

Katalina looked between the two of them, pausing a beat too long on Celeste. She eyed up Celeste's attire while asking, "Where are you going?"

He met Katalina's pale brown eyes with a meek smile, though he could tell by her expression that he looked more broken than happy, more distant than present. He could hear the disappointment in her voice, too. For some reason, she needed this dinner. Why reach out now? Why on this very day of all days?

Katalina and Noah shared some similar features; oval-shaped faces, and slim figures. Their styles had similarly sleek aspects as well. Her dark brown dreads cascaded over her black turtleneck, and her jeans were high-waisted and tight until they reached a flare at the bottom. Noah, too, wore neutral colors; a long-sleeved white dress shirt and a red tie paired with trousers.

All these commonalities, yet they were borderline strangers. Having any similarities at all, and the potential to bond over them with Katalina, irked him.

"I'm afraid I'll have to cancel on dinner, but thank you for such a kind offer. We're going this way. To"—his head was on a swivel between Katalina and Celeste, looking for an answer to give. He didn't want her to think he was being sarcastic—"somewhere."

Celeste turned with a beaming smile, and it was so bright that he knew he should tear his eyes from her, yet he couldn't. She almost looked happy, if not for the sorrow tucked beneath her gaze. He knew that look well. Some were better at hiding it than others. What was going on in her head? "You're more than welcome to join us."

"But to where?" Katalina asked. "To what?"

"To save the planets!" Celeste tugged at the strap around her shoulder with a sudden nervous crinkle of her brows. He could've sworn the bag disappeared and reappeared, but there was no way to prove such a thing, so he kept this observation to himself for now. "We should get going. There's no time to spare in these circumstances."

Katalina cocked her head before sharing a confused and uncertain look with her fiancé. It occurred to Noah then that he had yet to learn the man's name. "I'm afraid I don't understand."

Celeste nodded for them to follow before she began

walking away. He watched her go for a moment before turning back to his cousin. "She's explained to me that another planet —*her* planet—is colliding with ours. And, I mean, look at her clothes! She's definitely not from around here."

Katalina was watching Celeste as well, whereas her fiancé's eyes were glued to her, waiting for her to make the final decision. Finally, Katalina scoffed. "That's ridiculous—"

Noah turned to follow Celeste, not bothering to wait for Katalina to finish. "I'd rather help if it's true than turn the other way. I hope you have a splendid dinner."

Celeste was jogging now, so he jogged, too. When he looked behind him, he was surprised to find that Katalina and her fiancé were following, their fingers intertwined. He'd rather they stayed behind.

"I didn't know one needed saving," Katalina yelled between huffs.

Noah's legs were growing heavy, his chest tight as they passed the last of the tombstones and began weaving in and out of streets and houses and cyclists. He sensed a familiarity about the way she was leading them, a path he took at night when the job interviews ended and he had nowhere else to go. But no, she couldn't be taking them *there.*

He hadn't run like this since his youth school days, and it was one of the worst pains he'd ever felt, even then. His chest was on fire, and he thought for a moment that being on fire must've been better than this.

How much farther did they possibly have left to go? He was about to raise a complaint when they passed 'the end,' the lopsided sign standing where it always was. As in, the end of the *planet* and everything he knew and, perhaps, the most important parts, gravity and oxygen.

"Trust me," Celeste yelled. "Or don't. But if you care to come with, grab onto each other's hands, and stay in a single file line, please!"

They were getting closer now, to the edge where gravity decided to bend and splinter and break, and Noah could hardly contain his fearful elation. She was either leading him to his death or... well, that was probably it.

And yet, not once did the thought of stopping cross his mind.

"You can't be serious?" the fiancé yelled, his voice a low rumble. He'd been wearing a thin jacket over his dark purple polo, but when Noah looked back, the man had discarded it.

"Might as well, right?" called Noah, reaching behind him for Katalina. He looked back, and they locked eyes. "What have we got to lose?"

Something shone behind Katalina's gaze, a recognition he couldn't quite place, and then she smiled and took his hand.

"You've met my mother, Mark," she called back to her fiancé. "You know our family is eccentric. Now come on."

There was no logical explanation for what they were doing. None that Noah could place, anyway. He was as broken as this land, and Celeste looked far too tired for how young she was. Katalina and Mark, well, who knew why they would want to come? It didn't matter, because this was the path Noah chose, and he was *excited.*

"Last thing," Celeste yelled over her shoulder. "You need to jump as high as you can while keeping a tight hold on each other's hands! In three..."

His stomach fluttered with anticipation, and he took the deepest breath he could to prepare for what they were about to do. "Two..."

Celeste looked back at him only to give a nod of encouragement, her brows furrowed in concentration. When her eyes snapped back to the front, the edge of Sundar was there, and she was shouting, "One!"

They jumped.

And then they fell.

6

THE GREAT BEYOND

HIS MOTHER OFTEN SPOKE OF A WORLD SHE WANTED TO SEE. ONE beyond their own, far away from the people going places and the places selling things. She wanted freedom, but there was no freedom, was there? Wherever she was, he wondered if it was the mystical place she dreamed of within the great beyond.

That was the first thing he thought as he jumped off the edge of the world.

The first thing he felt was a nauseating pain, followed by a gasp as though all the air had been pressed from his lungs and he could finally fill them again.

His surroundings were blurred and blotched until they slowly came back into focus, and his eyes widened. The sky was an impossibly bright purple, speckled with dashes of oranges and pinks and a smear of blue so light it was nearly undetectable. The clouds were bulky and violet, an unusual color when he had only ever known a bright red and orange, wispy horizon.

Noah's thoughts were hazy. He remembered jumping hand-in-hand with a stranger and his cousin—which sounded like the start of a bad joke—and hearing the high-pitched screams coming from Mark. But then everything went black, and sound was squeezed from his ears until he couldn't hear at all, and now he was here. Awake and staring up at an impossible sky.

Despite the agony crawling up his back and along his arms, the ground beneath him was surprisingly soft—softer than the softest sheets he'd ever laid on. He must've been dreaming, because the sun didn't look quite like the sun, and there was a reflective sheen along the edges of the clouds that shined when he tilted his head.

Groaning, he remained on his back while scoping the area to check that the others landed safely. His heart sank as Celeste's pinkish-purple eyes stared back at him, her mouth slightly parted, and pupils still. Noah sat up quickly with a gasp and rushed over to her side. The closer he got, the worse off she looked—her poor, twisted body wasn't moving, her legs contorted atop each other.

A scream bubbled within his throat as he reached down to tap her awake—he'd made it a point to learn CPR after his mother passed—when Celeste's head snapped to face his, and she blinked. Noah paused, one arm on either side of her head.

She blinked again, a goofy smile crossing her lips. Heat rose to his cheeks as he glanced between his arms and her eyes. "This doesn't look good, does it?"

"No."

"Right." Noah pushed himself up and onto his feet without a second to spare. Running a hand through his thick, blonde hair, he added abashedly, "I-I'm sorry. I thought—I thought you weren't—"

He couldn't finish the thought or the sentence, his heart ricocheting off his ribs in an unharmonious cry for help. He hardly knew Celeste, yet doom permeated the air at the thought of her existence being erased so soon and suddenly.

"It's okay," she said, her pupils focused on him and him alone. He wanted her words to be enough, but the air was getting harder to breathe, and his racing thoughts were getting harder to control. He ran another hand through his hair as he paced. Thinking. Always thinking. Always lost in thoughts to the point he wondered when he would simply never return.

Celeste stood and found a place in front of his path before grabbing him by the shoulders softly. She gave them a light squeeze, and his thoughts dissipated as he stopped walking and stared back. The stillness of her hands made him realize that his body had been shaking, too.

"It's okay," she whispered, as though his soul was made of poems and she could decipher every line. "I'm okay. We all are."

Her words reminded him that his cousin and her fiancé had come, too, which spurred the reminder that they'd all *jumped off the end of the world.*

As if on cue, a startled gasp sounded beside him. "Where—what—"

"Who, when, why?" Celeste finished Katalina's exclamation with a chuckle and a smile. He supposed he should've been terrified of someone so unafraid of doing the unthinkable, yet he was intrigued. "You did what most wouldn't. You trusted me."

"If the roles had been reversed, we'd still be back home..." the fiancé—Noah remembered Katalina calling him 'Mark'—said under his breath. Ever the life of the party, Mark was. Though Noah couldn't deny he was right. If the roles *were* reversed, Celeste would probably decline in fear of being murdered. Yet here he was, following a beautiful stranger off his planet and onto the next.

Unless they were dead, and this was—

"This isn't the afterlife," Celeste interjected, and Noah jumped back in surprise. Could she read his thoughts? But no, surely she couldn't. She chuckled again. "I can see it in your eyes. You look terrified. Relax, we aren't here nor there."

"So then, where are we?" Katalina asked with a look of awe as she ran her fingers along the grass beneath her. He hadn't realized the strands were a light teal until then, and when he pulled on them, the blades came out in a tangled clump. He began mindlessly unwinding the clumps, only to find the grass wasn't made up of individual strands, but merely one incredibly long one.

"You saw we passed 'the end' sign, no? We're everywhere and nowhere all at once. We're at the beginning and end of life and death and everywhere in between."

"Could it be?" Katalina met Noah's gaze. They'd spent no more than five minutes together, yet he understood her expression perfectly; they were in a wonderland, and it was terrifying. "We're on another planet?"

Celeste gave her a knowing smile and nod.

"This is ridiculous," Mark yelled, his thick brows furrowed in anger. "I don't know what you've done to us, but you need to take us back to Sundar immediately. We have a kickball game tomorrow!"

"Have you been here before?" Katalina blurted, her wide eyes bouncing from Noah to Celeste.

Noah shook his head as Celeste said, "I should hope I've been here before—this *is* where I'm from, after all. And of course, I know the way back to your planet, but we can't leave yet. Like I've said, your planet needs saving as much as mine does."

Katalina turned to Noah, her brows scrunched in worry, as though she hadn't willingly taken his hand and jumped off the world. "Who is this girl? Do you know each other from school or work or something?"

"I'm unemployed," he said, and his brows shot up when he realized Celeste said the same thing at the same time. She may have claimed otherwise, but it truly felt like she was reading his mind. "And no, we met a few minutes before you arrived. While I was visiting my mother's memorial site."

"*What?*" Mark's voice boomed, a dash of fear interlaced within his growing anger. He was scared, that much was certain, and Noah supposed he should've felt the same. But, strangely enough, he didn't. He was finally away from everything holding him down, and he had no way of knowing how to get back up. While Mark probably felt trapped, Noah felt free.

"I'm sorry, Noah, but I must agree with Mark here," Katalina said, placing a hand on her fiancé's shoulder. "What were you thinking, following a stranger down here?"

"Isn't that what you did?" Noah challenged.

Her eyes grew wide, and he almost regretted his words. Noah knew his tone was harsh, but it was *real*. He had an extensive list of family, yet no one spoke to him beyond one hour-long service, and Katalina was just one more of *them*.

Though, of all the people to be abrasive toward, it probably shouldn't have been the one person reaching out *now*.

"We're family." A phrase she felt the need to keep saying when she must've known it meant nothing. Her voice was soft and wavering.

The meekness she portrayed—as though he were the bad guy for being mad at something she did—frustrated him further. It was enough to make him roll his eyes before he could think about what he was doing. "Does that make a difference when we've spent a total of ten minutes together? We hardly know each other's names, much less anything else."

She looked hurt, shriveling away from him like a wilting flower. Noah tried to remind himself that Katalina had lost an aunt during this entire ordeal, an aunt who had cut off most of the family when Noah was younger. Katalina was trying to help. He repeated it over and over in his head, but the anger had yet to fully fade.

"How is there a sky?" Mark's voice rang out, changing the subject so effortlessly it was as though they'd been talking about their surroundings this entire time. His eyes met Celeste's before bouncing to Noah's. "If we fell off the world, then there shouldn't be a sky. We should be in space, looking up at our planet. Frozen, probably. Land hardly makes sense, but it does a little bit more than the sky."

Celeste shrugged. "There isn't the nothingness of space underneath your planet, exactly... there's a black hole. It's what separates our planets... among other things, but this isn't anything new. Jumping off the end of the world is discouraged, but it's not like it hasn't been done before. "

"But I thought those chewed you up and spit you out?" Noah asked, astonished at the illogical logic. She said it all matter-of-factly when it was, in fact, nothing of the sort. "Or you get stuck in them."

"Forever space," Mark agreed. It was something widely taught in early education.

"Is this like... a pocket of reality? A different dimension?" Noah continued.

"A dimension is a pocket," Katalina corrected, pinching the bridge of her nose. Which, in turn, frustrated him. She could've stayed behind. "It *is* a pocket of reality."

"Don't convolute things even further when it's hardly necessary." Celeste looked between the three of them as she spoke, her eyes wide with uncontainable vigor. "We're on another planet with the same oxygen as yours, luckily enough, and travel through black holes is so instantaneous that you probably didn't even realize you were holding your breath until we landed."

"You said you're from where one world begins and another ends. This is it, isn't it? You grew up here on—" Noah nodded for her to provide the name of her planet.

"Fortun."

"—Fortun. Okay. Huh. I thought the name would be cooler." Noah was expecting something a bit more... pretty, to match his surroundings and the woman he followed here.

"So, the planets are going to collide," Katalina repeated to herself, an index finger to her chin in thought. "Do you have any idea *how* to stop whatever's happening?"

Celeste cocked her head. "Your world has been researching ours for half a decade longer. It's much harder to go up than down."

"I don't think that answered her question," Mark said hesitantly, taking in the world around them once more. Noah was inclined to do the same—trees appeared to engulf their surroundings with tall mountainous peaks in the dazzling distance.

"Few things will."

A smile crawled onto Celeste's lips as he caught her gaze from the side, and he blushed before looking away. His attention drifted to the sky; all he saw were violet and pastel-pink clouds splashed against a purple backdrop. There was no telling where they'd initially fallen from, no end or beginning. He was starting to understand why Celeste told them they weren't here nor there.

"Were you truly on Sundar to visit your brother?" he asked suddenly, curious to see how she would react. After all, they didn't truly know her.

Celeste gave him a raised brow and a playful rolling of her eyes, as though it was absurd to ask. "Of course. He was one of the original researchers of your planet. From his decade, anyway. It was there he stayed."

"Um, excuse me?" Katalina asked with a hesitant hand

partly raised. "You said the black hole separates our planets 'among other things.' What did you mean by that?"

Celeste put her hands on her hips and sighed. "It's sucking both our planets in. The theory is that they'll both reach the black hole at the same time and collide. Your planet is made of a stronger rock than mine, so at least seventy-five percent of the land should survive the impact, whereas this planet, my planet, will explode."

Mark's jaw dropped as he took a long, hurt step backward. "You took us to your planet *knowing* it could be destroyed while we're here? Do you know when?"

Celeste moved toward a tree with thin branches and fresh red berries hanging off the tips. She ran a hand along the bark. "The research suggests we have two months left, but there is no knowing. Perhaps only the sky knows, and it's never shared any of its secrets with us before."

"Fuck, Noah. Your date led us here to die," Mark said, rubbing a hand over his eyes before addressing his fiancée. "I love your kind nature, my love, but some family members aren't worth knowing."

Katalina shook her head and crossed her arms with a huff. "How dare you, after I put up with your stepsister adding hair dye to my—"

"And have we seen her since? I don't know how many more times I can apologize for what *she* did."

"Neither of you *had* to come," Noah said as he cocked a brow in an accusatory nature. "Why did you, Katalina? Mark obviously followed you here to keep you safe, but why did *you* come?"

Katalina gulped, taking a step back as all eyes turned to her. Her gaze bounced between everyone before landing back on Noah. "It was like you said. If what she's telling us is true, I'd rather try to save the planets than turn away and hope someone else figures it out."

Noah didn't believe her, not fully, but something told him he shouldn't press further. Not here, anyway. Not with an audience. His gaze flickered to Mark. What was she hiding?

"I didn't lead anyone here to die," Celeste chimed in, taking control of the conversation. "Quite the opposite. At first, I brought you here because I saw how sad Noah looked at the memorial park, and I wanted to cheer him up for an hour or two and maybe request a small hand in this minor task—"

"Who calls saving the world 'minor?'" Noah asked. He was trying his best to gulp down his nerves. If he hadn't seen this with his own eyes, he wouldn't have believed her, but the ground felt solid, and the breeze was cool.

He was on a different planet with a woman who claimed that two worlds were going to end, and above it all, he was chosen by her out of pure pity. *How romantic*, he thought dryly. *A stroke of fate, chemistry, and pity.*

"—But now, I'm hoping the three of you will stay a little longer and help me save them."

Celeste was met with three pairs of wide, nervous eyes.

7

A PROPOSAL

"I KNOW YOU SHOWED ME YOUR BROTHER'S RESEARCH, BUT YOU never explained how you propose we save the planets?" Noah finally asked as he went back to pacing the lawn like an animal trapped in a cage. He gestured at Katalina and Mark, then at himself. "We aren't exactly the smartest people you could've invited. Why us and not someone else from *your* planet?"

"Hey—speak for yourself," Mark said as he crossed his arms, brows furrowed, and gaze narrowly pointed at Noah. Noah looked away, avoiding eye contact for as long as he could.

Celeste's focus was still directed toward the branches of berries, her voice airy. "Like I said; I didn't choose you for any rhyme or reason aside from simply wanting to spice up both our days. You looked much too sad to be standing there alone, and I thought it would give *you* a fresh perspective while keeping *me* some company."

His mouth fell open; he was utterly speechless. What was

he to say? As if it hadn't hurt once to hear, she doubled down on the pity he apparently exuded. "What perspective would that be? And what would the point be when Sundar will supposedly be destroyed soon, anyway?"

"Only twenty-five percent," she added brightly, her eyes aglow with enthusiasm. Noah grimaced; her hopefulness was a beam of light that burned his eyes. None of this made sense. Who picked a stranger to aid in such a monumental task? There had to be more behind her reasoning than what she'd already claimed.

"*Theoretically*," he countered. "Why aren't more people trying to save both planets if they're going to be destroyed?"

She nodded solemnly. "There are some research teams out there now, but most gave up ages ago. The colliding of the planets has been known for quite some time now—since your planet started crumbling—but no one can seem to figure out a way to reverse it. It's gotten to where the public either doesn't take it seriously since it's been so long and nothing has happened yet, or they think it's a ruse to spark fear and increase spending."

"Why doesn't anyone on *our* planet talk about it, then?" he asked.

Her gaze was sharp, cutting into the very fabric of his being. "Our worlds are different. Yours has a system of elite men and women who know how to keep tight lips. My world is far more... open with knowledge like this."

"They probably didn't want everyone world-hopping," Katalina pondered. "Since you said it's easier to go down than up."

Celeste gave another small nod. "That, too. People tend to disappear when they world-hop incorrectly."

"Disappear?" Katalina asked quietly, her dark skin paling. Mark wrapped a protective arm around her shoulders, and she leaned into him with trembling hands.

"You really think you can save the planets?" asked Noah.

"Sure, why not? My brother's team was far more innovative than most of the others."

"And you signed up for this all on your own? If Noah hadn't been visiting his mother, you'd still be alone right now, right?" Katalina cut in, stepping up to stand beside Noah; Mark followed suit. "Isn't that a bit... risky?"

"Someone's gotta do it. We all die. May as well try to not die a little longer."

If he'd known he'd wake up today and be asked to save the world, he would've stayed in bed. But that wasn't an option anymore, was it? How frustrating it was to be put in such a compromising position.

Noah took Celeste in and realized the simple fact that if she'd been asked to save the world, she'd shoot out of bed and *do it.*

For some reason, the knowledge of this worked. "Okay... but is there anything we actually *can* do?"

"There's someone who can help, someone with the answers we may need... but he doesn't always like the questions being asked of him, nor the people who come asking."

"And you need us here because...?" Mark tried again, pushing for freedom that wouldn't come. They hadn't a clue how to get back home without her, and Noah doubted Celeste would provide that information any time soon.

And what did it matter if they went home when the planets were going to be destroyed?

Celeste shook her head. "I don't know how many more times I can explain the same thing, Mark. You need better comprehension skills."

"Excuse—"

"I don't *need* any of you here. I simply saw a sad fellow, asked him if he wanted to help and you happened to tag along."

"Things don't just happen," Mark continued to contest.

Celeste folded her arms over her chest with the look of someone who knew they'd already won the argument. "Look around, Mark."

He let out a frustrated growl as he provided her with his signature pointed glare. "Stop talking to me like you know me."

"Relax." Noah placed a hand on Mark's shoulder. The man backed away with fury burning in his blue eyes. Clearly, telling an enraged person to relax was not the most astute way to de-escalate a situation. Noah gulped as he added, "If we hadn't met her, we wouldn't have known about any of this, which means we would've been home, possibly being destroyed along with the other twenty-five percent of Sundar in two months."

"That *does* seem like fate, does it not?" Katalina muttered to herself, barely loud enough for the other three to hear. Noah's brows rose—he'd never particularly thought about fate, likely due to how his mother viewed the world and life itself. It felt cruel to suggest they were the only ones destined for this knowledge, though. Perhaps there was something out there beyond both nature and fate, but who was he to wonder when he would never know until it was his time to?

Mark scoffed and gestured toward Noah and Celeste as though they were bugs that needed to be squished. "You're taking their side?"

"Um, technically, I think she's choosing fate's side," Celeste said with a finger pointed to interrupt him.

The anger flaring in his eyes was palpable and incredibly hard for Noah to look away from. Mark's voice was dark, too—was he trying to be intimidating, or was it natural for him? "*Things don't just happen*. Spare us more lies—"

"—I haven't lied."

"That we know of. Did you target Noah? Did you decide to drag him down here and ruin his life? Huh?"

"Dude." Noah stepped forward, his voice and demeanor suddenly surprisingly calm, yet filled with gusto at the same time. He lifted his hands for extra measure, to both appear nonaggressive and keep a distance between them. "If anything, she saved me—us."

"Saved us?" Katalina asked. "But what about them—what about everyone else who doesn't know? How do we know my parents are on the side of the world that isn't crushed? You may not know them, but they have names and lives. They should be warned."

"We don't know, so isn't that more of a reason to help Celeste?" Noah argued. "We'll find this person, this..."

He turned to Celeste for confirmation, realizing thusly that she'd never provided a name.

"Ruler of the Deep."

He nodded. "Right, the Ruler of—what?" His gaze snapped back to her quickly, incredulously, his mouth partially agape.

Celeste met his gaze, nodding for him to finish the title, but it was so inexplicable that he couldn't say a word. So she clapped and said with emphasis, "*The Deep.* Ruler of the Deep. Supposedly, he's a big sea snake or something."

"Supposedly?" he asked, a brow raised.

She sighed. "Yes, well, there is no record of a true human interaction with the Ruler of the Deep. There is some speculation about encounters, of course, but there is no proof to back up such claims."

"So, we don't know if this thing exists... which means we're hoping it will not only exist but also have the answers we're looking for? Don't you find this all too..."

"Unlikely?" Katalina finished, and the world felt as though it had paused, a moment for four strangers to reflect on the implications of what was being discussed. Two planets, destroyed by sheer nature, and the knowledge that no one with the power to do anything was doing a thing to stop it.

Mark pinched the bridge of his nose. "How do you suggest we find this Ruler of the Deep, then?"

Celeste nodded, putting a finger up to her chin in contemplation before exuberantly slamming a fist on her open palm. "Why, with a boat, of course."

8

WAIT AND SEE

To find the Ruler of the Deep, they needed a boat, and they couldn't get a boat without going to a city and buying one.

There was only one issue—they were in the middle of nowhere, on a planet they weren't from, and the only person who was supposed to know where they were going had terrible directional skills.

As they walked, the clearing they'd landed in had transitioned from a flat plane into tiny hills before transforming further into staggering mountains a few miles over yonder. Celeste pranced atop a hill of blue-green grass speckled with yellow flowers, the sun showering them in a faint golden glow. She stopped at the very top and shielded her eyes as she looked out at the horizon.

"Figure out which way yet, boss?" Noah asked, craning his neck and spinning in circles, hoping to spot skyscrapers off in the distance.

"Could be this way or that. Who's to say?"

"Do you treat everything like a guessing game?" Mark grumbled. "You must know the way by now if you've gone and come back before. Is this 'boat' we're looking for even a boat?"

"It is, and I know we'll find one once we reach the city. I always struggle until I find the sign within the hills, but I'll have a better grasp of which way to go next once we find it. Should be around here somewhere. Sometimes you have no choice but to trust the process, and it will lead you to where you need to go."

"I thought you said things happen around here for no rhyme or reason? How, then, is there a process to be had?" Katalina asked.

Celeste's lips pulled into a half-smile. "Ah, the type of question a scientist would ask."

Katalina returned the gesture. "I work for the Sun and Space Anesthesiology Department of... well, it's classified."

"Wow, I didn't know I had a family member who knew classified information," Noah said with raised brows. Anesthesia and space didn't sound like two things that went together, though.

"As far as you know, you don't." Mark came up to Noah with a puffed-out chest, towering a few inches over him with a menacing glare—or at least an attempt at one.

"Honey, I think he gets it," Katalina said behind him, but Mark didn't back down. Noah felt incredibly uncomfortable, but he enacted the same stance. He knew it must've looked silly by the twinkle of laughter in Celeste's eyes.

"You could've stayed behind," Noah reiterated. "No one

forced you to come with. So either man up and stop acting like a jerk or we'll leave you behind. Your choice."

Mark scoffed, but Noah was done with the conversation, so he turned on his heels and sped down the hill due north. It looked and felt incredibly steep, and for good reason—his body was tilted at a complete ninety-degree angle. From his point of view, he was walking straight toward the ground. It filled him with mild dread, but so did the idea of turning around.

When he reached the bottom, he was back to a normal angle, and a wave of nausea washed over him. It was simply inconceivable.

"Wait!" Celeste's voice called from above before she raced down the hill and reached for him. Noah's chest fluttered at her touch as her fingers wrapped around his wrist. He turned to face her, a sudden gust of wind ruffling his blond hair as their eyes locked.

Before either could say a word, Celeste paled, her jaw clamping shut. A glossy sheen of sweat was pooling along her brows and forehead, and before he knew it, she was leaning over and expelling her earlier meals right there at his feet.

Noah closed his eyes and pointed his head upward while taking a deep breath of fresh air to avoid whatever was happening below. His eyes fluttered open with the expectation of more purple skies, but now Mark was descending the hill, his body a blot on Noah's view.

Mark, too, was at a complete ninety-degree angle, looking directly down at Noah like he was an ant on the sidewalk. Mark evened out as he reached the bottom, and then he returned to a normal vertical state.

"What a peculiar way to descend a hill," Katalina said after following suit, looking over her shoulder at the steep land ahead of them and rubbing her stomach. Her lips were puckered, face pinched. He knew exactly how she felt; his stomach was throbbing in pain.

Celeste wiped her mouth when she was finished and stood up with two hands on her hips, her normal, bubbly energy seemingly back. "I'm sorry you had to see that. I forgot about the cardinal rule—don't run down hills."

"Any hill?"

"*Any* hill. No matter how small it may seem."

"How small would you say is the smallest before it is no longer considered a hill?" Katalina knelt in the grass and raised a hand a few inches above the ground. "This small?"

"Ah, collecting all the variables, are you? My brother was the same way. No matter how outlandish the question was, he asked it. And I cannot definitively say what is the smallest, but I've seen some almost as tall as me. Say, five feet high? Small to us, but a hill to others."

He wondered what 'others' she was speaking of, but he kept the question to himself for fear of looking foolish. This was followed by the abrupt and intrusive realization that Celeste had brought up her brother, which then dredged up thoughts of his mother. How she only saw a world layered with sadness; how she would never see or hear of this new world.

If only there was a way to turn off his thoughts. Noah glanced around, but his options were limited. They had to keep walking and talking. They could talk about anything, except *that.*

Words were escaping him, his throat becoming tight, the tears building, and he knew that if he thought for one more second, he would burst. No, he couldn't burst, not here. Not in front of a beautiful stranger, his cousin, and her wet blanket of a fiancé.

So, Noah went with the former and started walking onward to the next hill blocking their path. He focused on the wind brushing against his cheeks and the slight ache in his feet from all this movement in his otherwise relatively sedentary lifestyle.

The act of climbing each hill started like it did back home, yet the descent was still at an impossible ninety-degree angle. He couldn't gauge if he liked the oddities of this world or if they hurt his head. Noah landed on both and neither, which hurt his head even more.

The grass was a deep crimson on this side, so dark it was nearly black when under direct sunlight, yet it reflected a hint of red when looked at from the right angle.

And the trees, well, they didn't seem to be trees at all. They looked to be two-dimensional and smeared on a canvas, individual strokes of various greens creating a whole. When he and the other three walked by, the trees were considerably flatter than one would expect a tree to be, yet they were not completely two-dimensional, either. Like a prop set up for a play, a trick of the eyes to look real. They were gorgeous yet off-putting when looked at for too long.

He walked past another narrow tree, this one made up of splashes of purple and pink streaks, as were the rest of the trees to the left of their path. To the right, they were shades of green and blue and shaped like pines. From the front, they were narrow at the top and gradually grew thicker with bushy needles. But as they passed, these trees were the same girth as the others—wafer thin.

It was hard believing people who looked and sounded like him lived here, that this entire planet existed at the bottom of another and could be accessed so easily. He wondered how often the two planets corresponded with each other, or if the governments did extensive testing or hardly any at all. He'd never heard of anyone venturing out past 'the end' sign and living to tell the tale, so it must've been a well-kept secret—or no one had ever returned.

But no, Celeste said her brother was a researcher who'd gone to and from this planet plenty of times, and so had Celeste, and undoubtedly countless others throughout the years. Yet they all stayed silent on the matter of the planets colliding. Why?

Unless... did the government *want* to keep people in the dark? Did they *want* countless deaths on their hands?

Surely, that wouldn't be the case.

Then again, he wondered why this idea shocked him so. It aligned with the nature of humans and the government.

Theoretically, both planets could be obliterated to the point no one survived, but some citizens on Celeste's planet could be moved to Sundar, where seventy-five percent would remain intact. Right? Or did they accept the fact of man versus nature —that man hardly won, and it was futile to try?

He had so many questions that refused to leave his lips.

"This is astounding," Katalina's voice sounded above the noise in his head, and he turned to find she'd stopped beside one of the thin trees. She rubbed some of the pine needles between two fingers, and Noah felt inclined to do the same before Mark joined in as well.

Only Celeste stood back and watched, though she didn't deter them from touching the pines, either. The needles looked pointy and sharp, but they were soft, somehow maintaining their hardened appearance through a means he would never know.

"And this is real?" Noah asked, looking at Celeste for confirmation.

"It can't be possible," Mark proclaimed. "Why, everything around us looks like—"

"—a painting?" Celeste interjected. She nodded. "Yes, I thought the same after I saw the art in your world for the first time. Of course, your trees look far different from ours. I'd lived here my entire life until that point, and I'd always thought these looked 'normal.'"

"Your world," Noah added without thought, "defies logic."

Celeste snorted. "Says the man from a planet with a literal end to jump off of. Not to mention the crumbling sun and moons and land itself."

She nodded for them to keep walking, and Noah kept pace beside her as the other two trailed behind. He couldn't stop wondering why Katalina would come with them. She and Mark had friends and family back on Sundar, and neither seemed to be the adventurous type. Then again, neither did he.

"It's been crumbling for centuries," Noah said. "But if what you're saying is true about the black hole sucking our planets in, then do you think there's a chance Sundar is pulled apart before both planets collide?"

"For that, I'm uncertain, but I think things have a funny way of catching up to us, like the slow crumbling of your planet, which one day won't be so slow anymore. One moment, we're worried about all these little things throughout the day, stressed for no reason, only to come home and do it all again the next day."

She sucked in a deep breath, her words rushed yet somehow still airy, as though she knew how to stop herself from sounding sad. "Then you realize you haven't called someone in a month, then two. Eventually, one day you try, but they aren't there, and they never will be again."

That's how quickly things went from okay to not okay. The sudden shift in her tone, the aversion from his gaze as she filed through the thoughts flooding her mind. Noah paused, lightly grabbing her shoulder.

Celeste stopped walking and met his gaze quickly, a tear falling. She gasped, reaching up to her cheek where the droplet slid. Perhaps he should've let her continue—it was best to speak during these moments—but he couldn't see her cry. Not when everyone else was a beacon of misery, and she was one of hope. It would break him.

A shove came at his back, and he stumbled forward. Celeste turned in such a way that he landed in her outstretched arms, their bodies colliding. She pushed him back upright with a grunt, her face inches from his, her brows crinkled in concentration.

Noah blushed, a reflex to being so close, and turned to find that Katalina was apologetically holding up her hands.

"Give us a bit of a heads-up when you stop next time, would you?" Mark said, wiping off his clothes as though they'd gotten stained from Noah's existence.

Noah righted himself quickly. "Or you could watch where you're walking. We'd stopped for at least five full seconds before you ran into me."

"Wow, five seconds. Such an enormous amount of time."

"It is for most people, but I guess—"

A snort from Celeste cut him off, and they all turned to look at her. A moment of stunned silence passed, and then she laughed. It started as a light chuckle that she tried to suppress with her hand before it crescendoed into full-blown laughter.

She wiped away the rest of her tears, which had seemed to morph from sad to happy, and met his gaze with watery eyes. "I'm sorry. It's just—the two of you are so entertaining. I don't think I've ever met two people who despise each other so much so quickly and for so little reason."

Without another word, she continued walking. Noah almost reached out and grabbed her wrist for the sole purpose of turning her around and looking into her eyes a moment more.

It was ridiculous, he knew, but something was burning within him that he couldn't quite pinpoint. He knew the feeling of lust well, but this somehow felt like more, a flutter whenever their eyes met or fingertips grazed. He held onto that feeling, fearful of letting go.

Mark tsked. "Well, I suppose I should hate Celeste for

bringing us down here and telling us all of this. But it's easier to take it out on—"

"Another man?" Katalina asked, and the look in her eyes told it all.

"Exactly," Mark said under his breath after an awkward second, realizing he'd been cornered. He gave off an aura of perpetual anger, and Noah wondered how Katalina could live with someone like that. Noah already found it rather exhausting.

"Let's keep going," Noah finally announced, breaking the tension as though he were an egg cracking and oozing all over their bickering. "Personally, I think I'd rather know than not know about the world ending, so maybe cut her and me some slack."

"We don't even know where the fuck we're going," Mark yelled in frustration, his voice bouncing off the two-dimensional forest.

"Is swearing necessary?" Celeste called from the front. Hill after hill, they climbed. Each time was the same; the angle downward was impossible, yet there he was, staring directly at the ground as he descended before somehow becoming upright at the bottom again. How could someone live on a planet with such nausea-inducing physics? "And your pessimism will get us nowhere."

"Maybe you could have some quiet time while we're walking?" Noah suggested, looking over his shoulder and meeting Mark's annoyed gaze. There was something fun about the way the man's fists curled and the anger seemed to seep from his ears.

"Our existences are in jeopardy, and you're worried about a few swear words? What's wrong with you?"

"I'll list my flaws once you list yours." Celeste shrugged. "Besides, we're going the right way. Look—we've found the sign."

Noah followed her finger to a wooden post with multiple arrow-shaped signs pointing in various directions. Some were pinned atop each other, lopsided and difficult to read, while others were straight with bold letters.

Each arrow was labeled. 'This way,' 'That,' 'Far,' 'Near.' He was intrigued most by the signs leading to 'Go' and 'Stay,' but he was also mildly terrified by their connotations.

"This place," Katalina said with a soft gasp. "It's magical. It has to be."

"Magic?" Celeste asked, leading them down the path labeled 'Near,' to their right. "I'm unfamiliar with the concept. Our planets have different rules, that's all. Yours has boring old wooden branches, ours look painted. You walk all boring-like on one plane of reality and we can adapt to multiple. As I've said before, some things simply are."

Noah wanted to ask her that if things simply were, why would they save the planets? Perhaps this was their natural course of life, and where humanity was always meant to meet its end. That was the beauty of the natural elements, after all—they could be explained eventually but rarely tampered with.

Noah didn't ask for fear of what she might say.

Katalina tapped her chin. "I'm trying to come up with a way to describe what magic is to us, but I don't think I can. We don't have it, but it's in books. Like fantasy books—"

"Fantasy books? What are those?"

They all collectively stopped walking again, this time with three pairs of disbelieving eyes focused on Celeste. Noah once fancied himself as a literary connoisseur. Before Noah moved away, he and his mother had a routine of going to the local cafe attached to a bookshop, where they would each buy tea and a novel. They'd read it separately and report back after crucial chapters. What did one do if there were no books?

Did Fortun not have stories of fantastical worlds because it was one?

Katalina covered her mouth as her eyes grew wide; Mark put a hand on her shoulder and gave her a light squeeze of comfort. She looked up at him, and her voice broke as she said, "What kind of world doesn't have fantasy novels?"

Celeste opened her mouth to respond when an arrow shot through the air. She gasped and ducked, the arrowhead lodging in one of the nearby pines instead of her head. Katalina released a shriek as another arrow flew past.

Noah was already running when Celeste yelled, "Make a run for it! We should reach the city any second now!"

An opening in the trees emerged in the distance; his heart raced at the thought of finally being free of the forest. As they neared, the opening grew darker until it appeared to have been sealed shut. Noah took in his surroundings quickly, wondering if he could duck behind a tree. But no, they didn't provide adequate cover, so he had no choice but to keep running at full speed.

"What's going on?" Noah shouted, hoping Celeste would give something more than a confusing roundabout way to say absolutely nothing. To his surprise, she yelled, "They're the city protectors, of course! Once you leave, you aren't allowed back, and outside travelers aren't allowed in, either!"

"Then how are *we* supposed to get in?"

"You'll have to wait and see," she said with a laugh, and he could hardly wait at all.

9

THE WAY IN

NOAH'S LEGS BURNED, HIS CHEST HEAVING AS EACH MUSCLE ached. His body begged him to stop, yet he propelled himself forward with sheer will. The exhaust permeating his thoughts clouded his awareness to the point he'd forgotten to check if Mark and Katalina were still trailing behind. He couldn't maintain this speed and look, so he focused on stabilizing his breaths and hoped they were close.

"Come on," Celeste called as she diverted from the relatively clear-cut path ahead of them to one with treacherous, steep slopes. "They blocked the main access point!"

Her hard pivot led them down a denser patch of the forest, and the trees themselves became thicker, too. No longer did they appear painted in beautiful splotches of blues and greens. Now, they were a bleak brown, and the branches were gnarled and vacant of leaves.

Were they real? Was any of this real?

Would he awake from this thinking it was a dream or a nightmare?

Onward they went, but the darkness only seemed to amplify, and the arrows were flying faster and higher. It was only a matter of time before one struck—

"Duck and slide in three"—without warning, Celeste started counting down, sending his anxieties into a frenzy as he took her hand once again—"Two..."

"What do you mean 'slide?'" Mark yelled from the back, but "one" had already passed Celeste's lips, and she was ducking and sliding.

A surprised yelp escaped Noah as he was dragged along behind her, and they slid down a sharp slope.

"How many times do we have to—*fall?*" The last word to leave Mark's lips echoed against the darkened walls suddenly surrounding them as they slid.

The four landed in a heap on the ground with a loud thud, Celeste at the bottom. He let out a light groan as he hovered above her, looking down at her heart-shaped face and galaxy-speckled eyes.

She was looking back at him with a soft smile.

"What's so funny?" he asked, breathless from the fall and the ache of having Mark and Katalina piled atop him.

"I should ask you the same thing." Noah crinkled his brows in confusion at this, and she released a chuckle. "You're smiling—it's nice. I almost thought you weren't capable of it."

He hadn't known he was smiling until he felt the corners of his lips dip slightly. She seemed to mimic his expression; her smile disappeared as well. But no, the moment couldn't end now; he wasn't finished looking at her yet. He couldn't be.

What an odd thing to think, he thought, so he stopped thinking and made it a point to examine their current position pressed together, instead. "We need to stop ending up like this."

"It's said that you land on the person you trust the most. I can't say whether it's true, though."

"Time will tell, I suppose," he said, his soft half-smile slowly returning. "Is there a guidebook on the places we're heading, by chance? Or a warning we can work out so we know when we're about to experience something horrifically unusual—by Sundar's standards?"

Celeste tilted her head in thought. "I don't know all the intricacies of your world, or what is considered 'horrific' or even different, aside from some of the stuff we've already encountered..."

Noah released an involuntary groan from the shifting weight of Mark and Katalina as they maneuvered themselves off of him. Then he stood, brushed himself off, and offered Celeste a hand. She took it gratefully, her touch warm and inviting.

They'd slid into the bottom of a wide, incredibly dark cave with cracks in the ceiling to reveal enough light to lead their way deeper inside.

"Will those things attacking us follow us down here?" Katalina asked, rubbing her forearm.

Noah squinted at the area in question and noticed part of her sleeve was darker than the rest. "Is that—blood? Did you get hit?"

Celeste brushed past him as the words left his lips and reached for Katalina's arm, but stopped halfway. "May I?"

Katalina nodded tentatively and handed over her arm. Her hand covering the wound was soaked in a dark crimson. "It's just a gash—it should heal on its own, right?"

"Just a gash?" Mark asked, grabbing her arm lightly from Celeste and bending down to inspect it closer. Katalina winced, but let Mark continue. When he was done examining her arm, Noah could see the look of destruction painting Mark's features. "I've hurt men for less. You have gauze on you, don't you?"

She nodded toward her jeans pockets and he fished out a roll of black fabric. Mark worked quickly on wrapping it around her wound. "It's not much, but it'll hold for now."

"You carry this around with you?" Celeste asked, grabbing the small roll and examining it with a skeptical brow.

"Every day," said Katalina, her voice light as she grimaced. There must've been a reason, he thought, but there was no time to ask.

Whooping came from above and Noah pointed at the small opening they'd slid from—except they shouldn't have been able to see the opening from here based on the angle they'd slid down. "Uh, I think they found us!"

"They won't follow us down here," Celeste said. Noah cocked his head at the four city protectors; they were perhaps three feet tall with the faces and midsections of lizards, only they were two-legged. Their bows were drawn and aimed, yet not one took a shot.

"Why not?" Mark asked before holding up a finger to add, "There won't be an explanation that doesn't upset me, is there?"

"It's because of the draegon, but I wouldn't worry about it. As long as we're quiet, it'll stay away from us."

Mark took a deep breath, then asked with a look and tone of unwavering neutrality, "What's a draegon? And don't tell me it's that horned beast that can fly from the Ancient Myths."

Her response was simply a stare, and the stare said it all. Mark's shoulders slumped. "Fuck."

"*Please,* Mark. Your pessimism is showing again," Celeste begged.

Mark gestured toward Celeste while looking at Katalina. "And you're going to put up with this?"

Katalina looked away. "It *does* wear me down sometimes."

Mark's mouth parted slightly as he rubbed a hand over his lips. "What does that mean?"

Katalina failed to make eye contact, looking in every other direction but his—not that there was much to look at except for the damp cave walls. Noah could hear a faint trickle of a stream, though it was too dark to see much beyond what was right in front of him.

"We don't need to talk about this right now," Katalina finally said.

"Uh, I think we do," Mark's voice rose to a shout.

Celeste put a finger to her mouth with a stern furrow of her brows as she whispered, "Didn't you hear what I said? We can't wake the draegon!"

"So, what? You're saying I'm too much of a downer for you?" Mark asked, ignoring Celeste's ongoing pleas.

Katalina's fingers curled into fists as she suddenly burst from her shell in a grandiose—albeit poorly timed—outpouring of her thoughts. "Yes, okay! Sometimes I'm having a good day, and you come home, and you make it... less... good. You always find the bad in everything."

Mark looked around in a purposeful show of confusion before meeting her eyes. His words were laced with sarcasm as he said, "I'm sorry, is there a positive to this situation? Everyone we know and love is in imminent danger and we're away from them, trying to save two planets based on a hunch and a myth."

A roar erupted from somewhere deep within the tunnels, enough to rumble the walls and ground. Noah gulped and added, "Two myths."

Mark threw out his arms in exasperation. "Right. Of course."

"You aren't listening to me," Katalina yelled.

"Fine, add that to the list of my flaws you've apparently been keeping a tally of. Thank you *so* much."

"If we're all about to die, self-discovery and acceptance are pretty important, though," Noah pondered. He'd been squinting at the ceiling, watching water trickle down the edges of the rocks, and when he turned his attention back to the others, they were all staring at him. "Maybe having a list of flaws is a good thing."

"Read the room, Noah," Mark said with a sigh, the fight seeming to die within him.

"Excuse me, didn't the three of you hear that roar? If we stay in this tunnel, we're toast," Celeste yelled, running to the right with a speed he hadn't known was humanly possible. But no, it must've been, because Katalina was bursting ahead now, too. Was Noah really *that* out of shape?

He'd have to think about it more when they weren't in the middle of trying to save the planets. *After*, he reminded himself. *After* they saved the planets. Noah wiped off his arms with a grimace. "I think your negativity is rubbing off on me."

"Oh, fine, I'll shut up for now. How about that?"

"Finally," Celeste said, and they kept on running.

10

DRAEGON'S BREATH

He realized they followed Celeste without hesitation, winding deeper into the tunnels and away from the city protectors. But to where? He didn't know, and he still wasn't sure that she did, either.

Draegons were said to be no shorter than fifteen feet tall with winding horns atop their heads, though he'd yet to feel the ground rumble from footfalls. Scaly and often red—though sometimes green and blue and everything in between, depending on their mood—draegons were known for their temper, and for their ability to fly like a bird.

Another growl erupted, echoing throughout the cave, and he could've sworn it sounded closer this time, though he knew Celeste would lead them far away and into the city without running into—

Noah ducked as a ball of fire spiraled toward his head. He performed a somersault of sorts, tumbling forward and back around in a movement he'd never done nor cared to do again. He didn't stop running afterward, either, propelling himself even faster despite the pain shooting up his legs.

He'd been so focused on dodging the fireball that he hadn't realized he was running straight toward what could only be described as the draegon. Such beasts were merely myths on his planet, drawn in children's books and displayed in fantasy artwork. Yet he was staring at one, and it was staring back, and it was almost exactly as described—except it could also breathe fire.

The draegon's scales were deep red, and it stood to be at least twenty feet tall, taking up a large chunk of the spacious clearing within the cave. Surrounding the beast were abandoned old houses carved into the rock walls. The beast watched them with narrow eyes and outstretched fluorescent blue wings.

Someone on his planet must've known of the existence of draegons and spun them into tales. It was magnificently terrifying to realize how small he was in a universe that was made of one infinity wrapped within another.

He was in awe of the beast, yet so scared he couldn't stop to stare. Sometimes, he didn't want to live, but in moments like these, he didn't want to die. Goddesses, what an awful position to be in.

There were multiple smaller tunnels lining the walls, like the one they emerged from. These were spaced out and far too small for the draegon to penetrate, though a fireball would incinerate anything within the tunnels immediately.

With their presence known, it was almost better to stay out in the open.

But as another fireball flew by, it was clear nowhere was safe. Celeste pushed him out of the way, and he fell to the ground in an embarrassing display of flailing limbs. "Fire wasn't in the stories!"

Celeste cocked her head. "Really? That's what makes them different from a raegon."

"A 'raegon?'" asked Noah.

A shrill shriek rippled through the air before Celeste could respond. Suddenly, the beast was on its side, panting. Noah jumped up from his spot on the ground and started running again, glancing over his shoulder briefly. What would've caused the draegon to cry like that? Had Mark and Katalina figured out a way to disarm the beast already?

Then Noah saw—there was a scrape on the draegon's left side. He glanced above to find sharp crystalline rocks hanging from the cave's ceiling. One must've fallen, a crunch of rock scattered around the draegon while it whimpered. A piece of stone stuck out of its side as further proof.

Noah stopped running; Celeste took two more steps before skidding to a halt and turning to face him. "What's the verdict?"

Bending over with hands on his knees, Noah focused on the ground while catching his breath. He nodded toward the draegon between gasps, his legs wobbling. "I think we have to help it."

"Are you insane?" Mark asked as he came up beside Noah. The man truly had a way with words.

Celeste kept her eyes on Noah, effectively ignoring Mark,

and nodded. "Yes, I agree. We have to help him. Or her. I can never tell with draegons."

"Do you see them often?" Katalina asked, to which Celeste shook her head.

"They don't normally hang around the landing or leaving spots of the black hole, but sometimes one or two will fly over the city. They aren't normally interested in people, so spotting one is rather rare."

"But they keep one down here to protect the city?" asked Noah next, rubbing his chin in thought. The draegon didn't look to be chained, but it also didn't appear to have a way out, either, nor a source of food or water. Though it was trying to kill them, he couldn't help but feel sorry for it.

She nodded. "Yes, but I've never seen the creatures that guard the city before. I'm sneakier when I'm alone."

Celeste glanced over at Mark as she spoke. "He's going to need to get his anger in check. We've been lucky so far, but he's putting us in danger."

"Me? I'm the one putting us in danger?" Mark asked, pointing to himself with raised brows. "Not the woman who dragged us down to a planet that's going to be destroyed?"

Noah was inclined to agree with Celeste, but he was normally a pacifist when it came to talking about people he hardly knew. So, he changed the subject instead. "Do you have movies here, then, if you don't have fictional books? Or music?"

Celeste chuckled, and he winced at the pointlessness of his question. "Of course, but neither are what you'd think."

"Why do you think our governments have kept our worlds

separate all this time?" Mark asked suddenly. "Aside from the potential world-hopping?"

She sucked in a deep breath, perhaps to stall. "Who's to say? I think politics got in the way a long time ago, but my parents, well, they work for a subset of the government—you might end up meeting them while we're here. They're the reason my brother could go up and come back with his research team so often. Dad always made it seem like remaining separate was just meant to be. Natural."

"What happened to the rest of his research team?" Noah asked. *And him?* But he couldn't ask that, not at all, no matter how desperately he wanted to.

She turned back to the draegon. "They're all gone."

Her voice was resigned, a sigh hidden beneath her words, and he knew he couldn't ask more.

Up close, the beast was even bigger, and Noah had to crane his neck to look up at the injury on its side. Beside the draegon was a wooden sign labeled 'Elora.'

Noah scratched the back of his head. "Well, unless magic exists here, I don't think there's much we can do."

The draegon whimpered as Noah lightly rubbed the base of her leg. Her scales were cold and damp, and she looked back up at the destructive ceiling with a grimace. Elora was to spend her entire life condemned to the darkness with nothing and no one, never to use her wings or feel the rays of the sun. Noah found her existence relatable.

He couldn't believe what he was looking at, or how the conditions for this draegon were so poor, and he didn't know what solutions there could be. He turned to Katalina with a hopeful raise of his brows. "You're a doctor, right?"

"I'm an anesthesiologist. It's a little different from a"—she looked up at the creature—"vet."

"We could try, at least," Noah said. "We could climb her back, take out the rock, and put, I don't know, Katalina's gauze over the wound?"

Celeste nodded with brows raised in surprise. "Huh. That's a good idea. Good work!"

"Don't look too shocked," he grumbled, though it was clear by the lack of a reaction that no one heard him.

Katalina nodded dutifully and took out her small roll of gauze and a tiny circle of what appeared to be tape. "We won't have enough to wrap around the draegon, so hopefully we can tape on a small square for a temporary fix, at least."

"Celeste and I have a better shot of being lifted," Katalina added quickly.

"Do you think you have the arm strength for that, though, babe?" Mark asked. "It could be difficult to reach with only my shoulders to stand on."

Katalina crossed her arms. "Well, I can't lift you, can I? So, this is the safer option."

Mark looked her up and down before nodding, and they did as Katalina suggested. Mark grabbed Elora's nearest leg in a crouched position for Katalina to climb onto his shoulders. Noah and Celeste stood across from each other before he gave a curt nod and mimicked Mark's stance.

"I'm sorry in advance," Celeste said. Noah braced himself;

he was thin by nature, but lifting an entire person was something he hadn't thought to train for. "But please don't drop me."

With that, Celeste climbed onto his back and then shoulders, and he let out a grunt as he lifted upward with all his strength. She used two hands on the top of his head to push herself into a standing position before awkwardly reaching for the wound with one hand, tape in the other.

Katalina had a more difficult time finding her footing, but once she did, she and Celeste maneuvered the rock out of Elora's side with relative ease. They tossed it to the floor with simultaneous grunts, narrowly missing Noah's head. Thankfully, he'd noticed in time and clung to Elora's calf as the rock flew past and shattered into pieces below. He didn't dare look at the damage, however, instead remaining focused on keeping Celeste steady and upright.

Katalina unraveled the gauze and placed it over Elora's wound. Celeste followed next with the tape, and he thought they were good to go—until Celeste wobbled.

Noah's breath hitched as he scrambled to find his footing, but gravity took hold, and they were falling backward. All he could do was pray to the Goddesses of the Moons that Celeste's head didn't crack open upon impact.

The ground never came. Something rough pushed against his back and lightly guided him back to his feet, Celeste still secured around his shoulders. With a gasp, he turned his head to find it was Elora's tail, protecting them from the fall.

Celeste quickly climbed off his back before they turned to Elora. The draegon was staring at them with her chin on the ground, yellow eyes glazed and lids fighting to stay open. She appeared tired from the wound, yet she saved them.

They couldn't leave her down here, could they?

But the tunnels were too small for a draegon to fit, and the entire ceiling was made of crystalline rock that could fall at any moment.

"How'd they get a draegon in here?" Noah asked, perplexed.

"They must've raised it here as a child. That's the only explanation I can think of. I don't see a way for it to leave," Celeste said with a stretch; her hands were shaking. Did she realize he would've dropped her if Elora hadn't noticed? The thought made him feel inexplicably useless.

Katalina jumped off Mark's shoulders, rubbing her hands together with a look of satisfaction. "We have to save her, right?"

Noah and Celeste agreed in unison; Mark was rubbing his chin in silent thought, though he didn't argue.

"Any ideas?" asked Noah. Silence followed for a moment more, and then Mark snapped his fingers.

"Think fire could melt some of those spikes? She could angle the fire toward one corner until it melted. Or is that dumb?"

They all mutually glanced at Celeste. "No, that's good. That's *really* good. See where positivity can lead?"

Mark rolled his eyes as Noah asked, "How do you think she'll react if we wave her down? Think she'll listen or burn us to a crisp?"

Celeste leaned forward and whispered, "We could have Mark do a test run to find out."

Noah opened his mouth to agree when Mark scoffed from behind. “I heard that.”

“Good, then you know your assignment,” Celeste said. “Go ahead then, wave the draegon down.”

Katalina shook her head frantically. “No way. I can’t let the father of my future children risk his life.”

“Okay,” Celeste drew out the word as she continued to think. “Then that leaves you, Noah. Unless you have kids we don’t know about?”

He shook his head. “I have a cat.”

“Close, but not close enough. Go on.”

“And why can’t you?” he asked.

“Because I’m the only one who knows the way back to your world, and around mine. I can’t be sacrificed.”

“And I can?”

“Well, no... of course not, but I think you’ll be fine.” He stared, and she sighed. “Fine then, we can do it together.”

Celeste reached out a hand, and he noticed she was still shaking. So there were things in her world that even she didn’t know or understand. He supposed that was true for everyone, though—no one knew everything, and there was always something new to be scared of.

He took her hand, and they stepped forward. His heart felt as though it were going to burst, and he attempted to calm himself with a held breath as they neared. The draegon was still resting her head on the ground, her eyes dazed, and Noah looked to Celeste for direction on what to do next. Celeste shrugged before waving for Elora’s attention.

Noah mimicked her actions, brows crinkled as nervousness

coursed through his limbs. Elora cocked her head in confusion while Celeste transitioned between popping her hands and pointing toward the ceiling. Then she did the same motion, again and again, and Noah mimicked her, again and again.

Elora stared blankly ahead, occasionally following their fingers toward the ceiling before resting her head back on the ground. Celeste's hands dropped to her sides in defeat. "It's useless."

A loud smack came from somewhere behind Elora, near her tail. She let out a roar and Noah's heart dropped, his body reacting with sheer adrenaline and instinct. He pulled Celeste by the wrist as Elora's mouth erupted with fire. They stumbled away, Elora transitioning back to standing on her four powerful and clawed legs.

She released another roar before directing a round of fire at the ceiling a few feet ahead. Noah gasped, turning to see what had caused such a shift in her behavior.

Behind Elora's tail was Mark, and he had part of the thick rock that had fallen in his hand. They made eye contact as Mark used the stone as a paddle, striking Elora's backside. Again, she released a wave of fire toward the sharp rocks above.

Noah covered his eyes with his arm, sweat lining his face and limbs as heat rose in the closed-off cavern. "Why would you hit the draegon?"

"I thought it would give her an extra push to shoot her fire," called Mark.

What an absurd plan—but it was working. The rock was melting. Had the beast never thought to melt its way out before?

Mark jogged over with Katalina close behind, tossing the rock he used to the side. "Looks like she's going all on her own now."

Noah watched in astonishment as Elora continued to breathe fire at the ceiling until finally, the night sky peeked out from above and a soft breeze drifted through, cooling the sweat soaking his body.

Elora looked at the four of them, cocking her head a second time before stretching her wings and taking flight. In an instant, she was gone.

They stood silently for a moment before Celeste put her hands on her hips. "Huh. I thought she'd take us with."

"At least one of these tunnels will take us toward the way out… right?" Katalina asked, glancing around and wringing her hands nervously.

Celeste nodded, yet held a grimace, and he couldn't help but think she looked beautiful even when she was frustrated. He wouldn't mind seeing that furrow of her brow every day.

Noah shook his thoughts away; they were replaced with words she spoke when they first met—*knowing my name doesn't make me any less of a stranger.* Right. He'd have to keep reminding himself of that.

Celeste's words came out with a disappointed sigh. "Yeah, but it would've been super cool to ride a draegon. My parents would've been so impressed."

"Would they have believed you, though?" Katalina asked, inspecting the hole Elora had burned and escaped from.

"No, probably not." Celeste kicked a stray rock in further dismay.

Noah prepared to offer agreement—who wouldn't want to ride a draegon, after all?—when a shadow fell over the opening. His gaze snapped up; there was the draegon, lowering herself back into the cave. Katalina tossed a fist in the air with a delighted jump. Elora gingerly dipped her head and wing. Her scales were now a deep orange, the color of gratitude, if he remembered correctly.

She'd come back for them.

Noah couldn't help the smile that crossed his lips.

11

INTO THE CITY

THE WIND WHIPPED THROUGH HIS SHORT BLOND HAIR AS HE desperately clung to the draegon's back. His cheeks rippled with each flap of her wings, and he didn't dare try to peek over Elora's broad shoulders at the far-off ground below. They sat in a straight line with Noah third, between Katalina and Mark. Naturally, Celeste was in the front, her arms wrapped around half of Elora's thick neck.

The world was fading in and out slowly, as though he were stuck between a dream and reality. It was a feeling he had little experience with but dreaded all the same—faintness with a dash of dizziness to round it out. The ascension to a thinner atmosphere was far too overwhelming, and his heart ricocheted off his chest as Elora flew through another cloud.

"Is this real?" Katalina shouted over the rushing wind. He looked over his shoulder and met her gaze. "Are we really here?"

Her words brought him back to the present, and he took a few deep breaths to rid the lightheadedness plaguing his thoughts.

"I—I think so!" Noah called back. The reaffirmation of this created a deep pit in his stomach—if they were to lose their grip, even for a second, they would fall to their deaths. Which, as the only people seemingly interested in saving the planets, would be very, very bad.

But, *wow,* it was beautiful up here in the sky. The clouds were dark violet wisps dancing around each other. When he wasn't thinking of his imminent death, the thinness of the air ripping at his lungs became refreshing. As though at any moment, he could stop breathing. He lived for it, longed for it. The flutter in his chest made way for an excitement he found rare, even before his mother passed.

Since he was in the center of the draegon's back, he was given no indicators as to where they were on their journey until a harsh jolt rocked his grip clean off. Noah released a gasp, his body hanging off the side as he clung with all his strength. Mark wasn't able to stop himself in time, and a yelp escaped him before he slid off and down the rightmost wing.

Noah watched Mark tumble down the arched wing and roll to the ground with a grimace. There were no easier ways down, so Noah clamped his eyes shut and let go. He slid down Elora's wing and brushed himself off once he stood. Celeste and Katalina quickly followed suit.

Crimson grass was replaced with a wide paved path, and when Noah looked up, the silhouette of a city dotted the scene. The skyscrapers were tall, silver, and shiny, and many had billboards connected to their sides with advertisements too small to read from where he stood.

He glanced back at Elora, who released a soft huff as she dipped her head. Noah squinted, certain he could make out a smile, though it was impossible to tell. He was staring at a myth, after all.

The paved path they stood on was surrounded by sparse trees and clear sand. Noah stopped to scoop some up, but as his fingers neared, Celeste slapped them away. He withdrew his hand with a frown, rubbing the area she smacked, but Celeste merely shook her head. "It's not worth it."

He prepared to ask why when a low thump sounded ahead, followed by a pained and frustrated groan. Noah's attention shot toward Mark, who was a few feet ahead and now rubbing his forehead with a face scrunched in sore surprise. "I—I ran into it! I ran into the city! I—what the hell is going on?"

Noah jogged up and stopped beside him; the skyline was closer than it had appeared. He ran a tentative finger over a silver building that looked like nothing more than a series of paint streaks up close. Running his finger down the painting further, he noticed a crease in the wood. Following it with his eyes, he realized it was an outline of a door. A few inches down was a doorknob.

He cocked his head as Celeste clutched the knob. She turned back to him. "Ready?"

"But what about—" Katalina began, turning back to Elora. Except she wasn't there.

Celeste waved Katalina's words away before she could finish

her thought. "Draegons are meant to be in the wild—she'll be fine."

"I thought this was the city?" Noah asked incredulously.

"It is. Trust the process, right?" With that, Celeste pushed the door open with her shoulder and disappeared onto the other side. He caught the door with his foot, fearful it may close, never to open again, and nodded for the other two to follow.

Before he stepped all the way through, he turned to Mark. "Are you okay?"

Mark continued to rub his forehead with a grimace and a nod, his black hair matted with sweat. Katalina stood behind him, rubbing his back softly with her long nails. "The pain will pass. But I must say, Noah, this is the longest dinner date I've ever been on."

"Hopefully everything gets sorted out soon and we can get back home to our... to your families," Noah said before running a hand through his hair. "Look... I'm sorry for dragging the two of you along. I honestly didn't know where she was taking me. I can only hope we save the planets and go on that dinner we were supposed to have."

A small smile crept onto Katalina's lips. "I'd like that."

"I will admit, riding a draegon *was* pretty fun," Mark said. "I think I'm getting too old for this, though."

"You're twenty-four," Katalina said, a single eyebrow raised.

Noah laughed. "Come on, best not to keep Celeste waiting."

With that, he stepped through the camouflaged door of the city skyline, and his mouth dropped open.

On this side, the skyscrapers were impossibly tall, some

disappearing altogether in the clouds high above, and each building was outlined in bright neon purples and blues. While it wasn't as outlandish as it could've been, he supposed the city had a certain charm to it.

The nearest building was covered in light blue and green neon vines crisscrossing around a cone-shaped top. Small yellow flowers blossomed along the way. Bright pops of color seemed to be the standard here, whereas his home planet was filled with drab, tired architecture. Rundown buildings made of red brick or gray steel ran rampant on Sundar, many with small rooms and windows. Some were polished and new, but most were a blot on the horizon in need of erasing.

The more he thought about his planet, the more he realized how decrepit it was compared to how stunning *this* one was. There were so many things to do here, too, whereas there was nothing but staring at walls and words back home.

Now, the four appeared to be standing on the outskirts of the city, with pavement leading up to a small river and a bridge running over it. Beyond the bridge began the makings of medium-sized buildings before the larger ones took over. There, he could vaguely see people milling about, though they were too far for him to catch faces or clothing.

He, Katalina, and Mark found Celeste at the edge of the river, peering below at the moat-like structure. Her wavy black and blue hair billowed in the breeze along with her dress. She looked like she belonged inside the landscape. Like she was part of a painting.

"What's this city called?" Katalina asked, coming up beside Celeste. Mark took up the spot next to his fiancé while Noah stood on the other side of Celeste. He couldn't help but notice the closeness of their arms. He wondered if she noticed, too.

Celeste turned to Katalina. "Mermain City. There's also Merside City and Merup City—which is still in development."

"Is it really... up?" Katalina asked, pointing to the sky for emphasis.

"Now you're getting it," Celeste said, snapping her fingers with a goofy grin. "The way to get up is by climbing a vine. It takes forever, so not very many people choose to live there. But it's growing, I've heard. Merup City is overseen by the Ruler of the Sky, though. She's... well, I don't swear, but you can guess what she is."

Noah looked up to the sky, too, wondering how an entire civilization could live in the clouds just out of reach. Was that where most of the draegons stayed, too, he wondered?

"How many 'rulers' are there?" he asked.

"Four, but if we're lucky, we'll only need to deal with the one."

"And all these cities start with 'mer' because...?" Mark asked, extending the word 'because' before trailing off.

"They all worship mermaids."

"Naturally," he responded dryly, before taking a few steps closer to the water-filled moat around the city. Noah followed, and when he looked down, his eyes met the crystal clear water, and his reflection stared back. Fish resembling the orange and white koi from back home swam leisurely around each other. It was surprisingly peaceful.

A clock dinged, and he jumped as small pellets tumbled from the sky. The pellets landed directly into the water despite the wind that should've pushed them onto the surrounding land. Not one strayed from its path as they fell from a source he couldn't see, and the koi-like fish nibbled happily.

"Should we ask mermaids where the Ruler is, then?" Katalina asked. "If they're worth worshipping, they could—"

"Mermaids won't help," Celeste continued coldly, her tone curt. "They aren't worth the trouble, and they're brutally honest. Which means they aren't very nice."

"Bad experience?" Noah asked.

Celeste did not respond and instead turned away with curled fists. She didn't appear mad, however, more so focused as she attempted to de-stress before emotion took hold. Yet more questions built within him.

The furrow of her brows only increased as the silence prolonged. He was growing uncomfortable, but he hadn't a clue what topic was appropriate to jump into, so he kept quiet for much too long.

"Should we find someone to buy a boat off of?" he finally asked, and he saw the hint of a thankful smile tug at her lips as the conversation changed.

As if on cue, Mark's stomach growled, and he patted it with a solemn nod. "I think food should be at the top of our priority list, if you ask me."

"Perhaps we could split up?" Celeste suggested, and his heart nearly stopped. He reached for it, making sure it was still beating. It was, and that surprised him most of all.

Celeste reached into her pockets and produced a few bills with a language and numbers he couldn't read, though he could deduce what it was. He tilted his head; the symbol in the top left corner was a square with the lower line missing. He'd never seen anything like it before.

She must've caught him staring, because she added, "It's the equivalent of fifty dovas in your world, give or take. Called quentiles, named after the late Queen of Tiles. Should be enough. All the food places will have displays of what to eat, so you can point to what you'd like to order. Mermain city gets a lot of marine folk traveling through, and this solves the language barrier of deep sea and mainland folk."

Noah wished he could pick a bench somewhere, anywhere, and sit and talk and take it all in. But there was no time, was there? If they didn't save the planets, then hers would be completely gone. All of it. Elora the draegon, this city, Celeste's family. They would all be gone, and twenty-five percent, if not more, of his planet would be, too.

There were so many places here to explore that he would probably never have the chance to see, and the thought was so heartbreaking that he had to stare up at the sun to stop tears from falling. Even as they crossed the bridge into the city, he couldn't bring himself to look anywhere but up.

Why was he like this, mourning a moment while he was in it instead of relishing in the splendor of the brief life he had? Perhaps it was because soon there would be no more moments to have for anyone, anywhere. Or perhaps it was because he was born with a brain naturally set to self-destruct, no matter where he was going or what he was doing.

"How will we know where to meet up later?" Katalina asked as she and Mark prepared to embark.

Celeste waved her hand in dismissal. "I'll find you. Don't

worry about that. Go on, have some fun. We'll find a boat seller and get you when we're done."

She said it so confidently that the pair took it as fact instantly. It appeared when Mark was hungry, complaints drifted away, and suddenly he and Katalina were lost in the crowd.

Celeste turned to Noah, and he held his breath with each second their eyes remained locked. It occurred to him then that this was their first time alone since they'd met at the memorial park, which wasn't exactly the best place to have a one-on-one.

"Ready to explore?" she asked.

"Shouldn't we be preparing for our journey to save the worlds?"

"We have a little time to spare. Besides, we'll find someone to get that boat easily enough. If anything, I can borrow one from my parents. They should be in the city right now."

"You have an answer for everything, don't you?"

"I wouldn't know who I was if I didn't have at least most of the answers," she agreed with a chuckle. "Now, let's go! I've always wanted to be a tour guide, and we only have so much time left before the shops close."

He knew he should insist they look for the boat as soon as possible, but he couldn't get himself to. Instead, he followed, and he supposed that if they took too much time, and they were too late to save the planets, then at least he got to experience this with her.

12

THE SEA IN THE SKY

MERMAIN CITY WAS MUCH LIKE THE CITY ON HIS HOME PLANET, with just enough shops to spend all day in, and restaurants to keep hunger at bay. There may have been the occasional floating performer from the Sky Kingdom, or a fish walking around on two legs with darting, aimless eyes, but other than that, it was a lot like home. In a way, he appreciated that.

The day had long since passed, and the sun had set. Noah walked alongside Celeste, a cone filled with pink ice cream in hand. When he licked it, there was a hint of flavor he'd once smelled but couldn't place.

"They can't trap a smell within a taste here, can they?" he asked, smacking his lips together while breathing in deeply. It definitely tasted like a smell, but what?

Celeste chuckled, eyeing up her standard chocolate ice cream. "The two go hand-in-hand, don't they?"

"Yes, but I imagine it's usually the other way around." It

tasted divine, reminiscent of a warm summer day, and he basked in the moonlight as they walked, surrounded by other pairs eating ice cream. Some were merpeople, who stood out against the rest with their blueish-green scaly skin and gills where hair would be, while others were human, or a mix of everything in between.

He and Celeste stopped under a tree with long, pastel pink vine-like branches that cascaded down to their ankles. Noah pushed the branches to the side as he led Celeste through. It was vacant, a sliver of seclusion from the busy world outside.

"So, you eat sugar for dinner here?" Noah asked, examining his ice cream that didn't seem to melt despite the slightly warm breeze. "Are there no limits?"

She raised a brow as she licked hers, which he'd tried and had deduced tasted like a bitter, wintry day that curled toes and made eyes wince. It reminded him of how every time he almost made a friend, he would find a way to turn the conversation stale and fractured, as broken as his mother until he drove them all away.

"Even the limitless have limits," Celeste said. "We can't have too much meat or starch or we'll get sick. But sugar is surprisingly nutritious according to our data."

He considered this. "Is this data coming from a trusted source? Because if this is all the three of us eat while we're here, I think we'll become malnourished."

She held his gaze for a moment longer and then nodded for him to follow her out. His shoulders slumped; he'd hoped for a few more seconds alone, and time to talk about something more than ice cream or Fortun. "That's good to note. I'll try to find somewhere to eat next with plenty of meat."

Something in her voice pointed to disdain toward the idea, but Noah was too invested in finishing his ice cream to ask. Whatever this flavor was, it was the best thing he'd ever had.

He became starkly aware of their closeness as they continued down the walking path, their shoulders firmly pressed together. Words dwindled from his mind; he had so many questions that he didn't know where to begin.

Noah finished his cone, and she handed him hers as well. "I'm full. Please, would you mind finishing it? We find it rude to waste food here."

He stared down at the half-eaten ice cream with a gulp, his stomach protesting. His vision seemed to blur at the edges, creating a tunnel around the offering. He couldn't do it. He couldn't endure the memories the taste would dredge up.

But it was too late, wasn't it? Because now he was thinking of his mother's voice, and how tired she sounded whenever she called his name for dinner or to get ready for the bus or to get out of the snow or—

"Noah? What's wrong?"

Celeste's voice cut through his thoughts, and he jumped, reality coming back into focus. The ice cream in his hand was gone, though he couldn't remember throwing it away, and there was no spill at his feet.

Noah shook his head, eyes darting around and away from hers. He'd thought the moment would be romantic, yet he'd ruined a mood that had barely been there.

He let out a startled gasp, leaning forward with his hands on his knees. A pair of women holding hands walked by, glancing at him with nervous whispers and a quickened pace, as though he were a disgrace to see. Maybe he was.

Noah shook his head, but his throat felt like it was closing in. Panic crashed over his bones as his muscles grew rigid. "I-I'm fine. It's the... that ice cream... I know it's dumb, but it reminded me of my childhood and my mother..."

He trailed off, unable to finish his thoughts. Celeste didn't inquire further as she rested her forehead against his, her eyes closed. He stared at her; her face was impossibly close, her breath warm against his cheek.

"It's okay. It's okay." She rubbed his back, then filled her lungs and released a deep sigh. "A month after my brother died, I walked past a tea shop on your planet. It wasn't even one my brother talked about. It had no significance whatsoever, but it reminded me he loved tea, and I cried the rest of the day."

He soaked her words in silently, miming her calm breaths. Once he got his breathing to a reasonable speed, he pulled away from her forehead, only enough to see her entire face. It felt like they were the only two people there, breathing each other in and making each other whole.

But then their surroundings bled into his line of sight once more, and he spotted another glare from a couple as they passed. Noah blushed, his hands in hers while she lightly stroked his palms.

"I take it people don't show affection in public often here?"

She smiled and looked up at him, her eyes alight with joy. How did she do it? How could she possibly be so positive all the time? "It's very taboo. But follow me—I want to show you my favorite part of the city."

Celeste took one of his wrists with both hands and tugged him forward. He stumbled, and then they started running at full speed, weaving in and out of buildings. When they stopped, he was out of breath, but she was standing tall and mighty. Proudly, she stated, "I love running."

"I can tell," he said through heavy gasps. He couldn't say he felt the same.

There appeared to be a barrier between where they were and where they were going, murky and wavy with a sheen when hit in the right light. He couldn't see past the rippling water-like barrier, but it intrigued him enough to take a step closer. For some reason, he did not feel afraid.

"What's on the other side?" he asked, though he could guess what she may say.

"You'll have to step through to find out," she said, confirming his suspicions. She nodded for him to follow further and poked the barrier with her finger. A ripple began where she touched it, starting with small circles before expanding into much larger ones. "You first."

Noah gulped before taking the plunge without a second thought. She'd taken him to another planet, after all—he trusted her fully. The sensation was odd and freezing, but over in less than a second, and suddenly he was looking at the same city but with fish swimming around. Fish. Swimming in the air.

His mouth dropped open, and Celeste laughed beside him. He jumped, having not realized she'd gone through the barrier already. The fish swam linearly, disappearing through buildings only to resurface again on the other side nearly instantaneously. They were oval-shaped with a triangle for a tail, made up of bright oranges, reds, purples, and blues.

He didn't know what to think, but he had to admit—he loved them. "How do they—"

"—breath?" she finished. He smiled and nodded, a faint reassuring thing to indicate his appreciated comfort in this odd new world. "They don't."

He weighed her words. "So they just... live?"

She tilted her head in contemplation before nodding. "I suppose so."

"But... well, do they procreate?"

"Nope. They don't need to breathe, so they don't die. And they don't reproduce or sleep or eat. They simply live in this self-contained section of the city, swimming aimlessly. We don't even know if they have thoughts. They're simply here."

"Aren't we all?" he asked under his breath, once again faced with the feeling of insignificance within an endless universe.

Noah turned in circles, again and again, before his eyes caught a fish swimming directly at him, only to disappear as it hit his forehead and reappear from behind. He spun around quickly to make sure the fish made it, and Celeste laughed again with the back of her hand covering her mouth.

"So," he continued, wracking his brain with ways to fill the silence. "Why go on this journey with a stranger instead of someone you know from home? Like your sister, or parents, or friend, or... boyfriend?"

He winced at the obviousness of his question, his pause

before 'boyfriend' a beat too long. If she noticed, she didn't comment on it.

"Sometimes I wonder what compels me to do things," she admitted. "Sometimes, I think it's completely random, but I don't know how random it could be, running into you."

"You chose to stop and talk to me out of pity," he said, undermining his existence with a single sentence. "But you must've asked others to help before we met?"

She tsked and gave him a playful glare before she lightly pushed her shoulder into his. "No, I didn't ask anyone else besides my step-sister. She declined. Doesn't exactly believe me or my brother's research. Honestly, when I first saw you around that corner, I was going to take a different way. But... you looked like someone I had to meet. Have you ever felt like that before?"

He gulped—he couldn't say that he had, but there had to be a reason he called out to her as she rushed past. There had to be a reason he took her hand.

Celeste nodded, her shoulders slumping slightly at his reaction, as though it wasn't the one she was hoping for. "I hadn't before, either."

A moment of quiet washed over them until, finally, he asked, "Do you believe in fate?"

Her smile turned sad, and he regretted how the topic changed and the mood dissipated—if there was ever one to begin with. "No—I can't imagine my brother's death was fate. Sometimes things just happen. But I do believe in gut feelings, instinct, and that's what made me gravitate toward you."

"Oh, wow. Well, I—" He had no clue what to say, his mouth

sputtering, words failing. His face was becoming exceptionally hot as he scratched the back of his head with a blush.

Noah knew when he was being flirted with and when the waters were being tested, but he couldn't think of a coherent sentence. He wasn't one to flirt in his life back home, though he'd had two girlfriends in the past. In recent years, he almost always kept to himself. Needless to say, his skills were... rusty.

He opted for the most classic of techniques—changing the subject altogether. "How are we going to find the other two? It's getting late, wouldn't you say?"

Celeste cocked her head. Heat rushed down his body before climbing back up, and he couldn't deny the insatiable desire to lean in and kiss her. Despite this, he also wanted to run away, the embarrassment of such a steadfast attraction making him shudder as he awaited her response.

She nodded, her face growing serious as she held out her hand. Somehow, he knew she was going to drag him along to somewhere new. "You're right. It's time."

He put his palm on hers without question, and her features transformed into a slight smirk riddled with elation. "This'll be fun—I haven't used the horn in ages."

13

THE HORN

SHE PULLED HIM ALONG, WEAVING IN AND OUT OF THE CROWDS like they were being chased for a crime they definitely committed. He let the burning in his lungs consume him this time instead of weighing him down, and he held his breath to feel the extra pain. His muscles ached, but the ache was always worth it in the end, wasn't it?

It was certainly better than feeling nothing.

Celeste slowed to a light jog until they reached the center of a large clearing; the ground was made of metallic, square paneling. In front of them stood a tall fountain, gurgling as water cascaded from the top, where it began with a small bowl. At the base was a wide fountain basin two feet tall and filled with water. Purple and blue neon lights lined the rippling water, much like the neon lights lining the buildings.

Noah gawked; it should've been impossible for the water to stay within the perimeter of the basin below, yet it did. The bright neon lights provided an aura of magic within a magicless world. He peered over at Celeste to find she was already watching him. He blushed as her smile transformed into a beam of light.

"This was Altair's favorite place to go when we visited the city," she explained, and Noah nodded along, knowing that although two years had passed, the pain from the loss of her brother would forever remain.

"I can see why," Noah exclaimed. "It's gorgeous."

"Oh, no," she said with a defiant shake of her head. "This wasn't his favorite part."

She stepped up to the fountain and used two hands to push herself up and onto the outer edge of the basin. Celeste made quick work of the climb and stood triumphantly with her hands on her hips as she stared into the water.

Noah looked up at her, astonished and terrified, yet she nodded for him to come up, and so he did. They stood side-by-side, inches from the rushing water. The only thing separating them now were decorative rocks level with the ledge. "In my world, this is a crime."

She shook her head. "Everything is a crime in your world."

Without another word, Celeste jumped through the cascading water. Noah nearly yelped, jumping back in surprise. He slipped, his arms propelling as he felt the inevitability of gravity take hold—he was about to both royally embarrass *and* hurt himself.

A hand popped through the water fountain and secured itself around the top of his shirt. He shut his eyes before he was pulled through the water. The droplets were heavy against his skin, yet not an inch of him was wet when he reached the other side.

When he opened his eyes, he released a deep breath—he'd been holding it in without realizing it—and examined his surroundings. Here, there was a spiraling set of stairs leading upward. He looked at her for confirmation, and she nodded. "We're almost there. Trust me."

Up they went, his fingers tracing the walls decorated in beautiful stain-glass mosaics. Depictions of galaxies and gods and goddesses dressed in the planets and clouds and stars. Brilliant bright blues and pinks and purples he could get lost in forever.

The detail of each image was immaculate, and he despised how everything was moving in such a blur. He wished he could pause time and walk step-by-step to explore every element of everything here. Even the stairs, he noticed, had patterns pressed into them he couldn't make out at their current speed.

At the top of the stairs was a platform with a closed, bright white door.

"Always a door," he murmured with a raised brow.

"Doors and falling from great heights," Celeste agreed, turning the knob and exposing a square platform no bigger than ten feet wide each way. Attached to the platform was a large horn far bigger than he, beginning with a small tube he could blow into before winding into a large metal opening facing away from them.

The mouthpiece stopped an inch away from where the platform began, and he took a step closer so he could see over the edge better. It appeared to be completely open on each side, miles up from the ground, though they hadn't climbed more than two stories. Noah gasped, taking a step back and glancing down the staircase, wondering if he should retreat.

"It's okay," Celeste said, nudging him forward until he stepped up onto the platform. "There's transparent glass along the edges. We're safe."

"This is someone's worst nightmare."

"And someone else's dream."

"Which one is it for you?" He was still trying to determine this answer for himself, but knowing Celeste, she already had one.

"Neither. And both. Depends on who I'm here with." She drifted toward the mouthpiece and tapped it with her index finger. She didn't give him time to form a response, and he was too flustered to think on his feet. "Think of Katalina or Mark, and then blow into this horn. It'll show you exactly where they are, but you have to think clearly about a specific face."

"Used this before?"

She nodded. "Like I said, it was one of my brother's favorite places. We would try to trick the horn and play hide and seek around the city."

Right. He'd forgotten she mentioned Altair merely minutes ago. Celeste was busy flirting, and he was busy putting his foot in his mouth. "H-hide and seek, huh? Now that's a game I could play."

Celeste raised a brow, and her lips pinched together in a wavering half-smile and frown, as though she were using everything in her power to stop herself from laughing. He was trying to flirt, and she was trying not to laugh. This was going well.

"I'll keep that in mind. Now, go on, and think about one of them. Picture their face, mostly, and hair. Then blow."

Noah nodded and stepped up to the mouthpiece, rolling his neck before bending to get a better angle. He closed his eyes and released a nervous breath, trying his best to picture his older cousin. It was odd, the feeling of knowing exactly what someone looked like, yet forgetting immediately when asked to remember them.

Still, he tried, beginning with Katalina's dark brown hair pulled back into dreads. He imagined his uncle must've had similar features, but he hadn't seen his uncle *or* aunt since he was a child, not even at the funeral. They'd long since become estranged, though he couldn't recall when or why despite knowing it was his mother's doing. He wondered if he should ask Katalina, but this wasn't the time.

He pictured Katalina's slightly crooked nose that drooped ever so slightly at the tip, and her golden-brown eyes that were always so wide and questioning.

The image of his cousin was drawn in his mind's eye like a sketch before colors were filled in, and when he thought the image was clear enough, he blew on the horn. A low rumble shook the tower and reverberated through every bone in his body. It was terrible, yet soothing all at once.

He jumped back quickly after an image of Katalina and Mark sitting on a bench flashed through his thoughts. "I know where they are. Tea shop. Three streets down."

Noah paled as nausea coursed through him. Celeste's smile dropped as she grimaced. "Oops, I forgot to warn you. You should hum. It'll help get rid of that horrible feeling in the back of your throat."

"You really need to work on warning us of these things," Noah said. He did as instructed, but it was too late, and he doubled over.

14

THE SISTER

"WHAT WAS *THAT*?" KATALINA ASKED AS CELESTE AND NOAH rounded the corner. She came up to Noah, her nose inches from his chin, and he had to narrow his gaze to look down at her. Was she always this short?

He took a step back. "What was what?"

She began pacing, her brows furrowed. "Like a—a loud ringing cut through my thoughts, and then your face appeared in my head, clear as day!"

The trio's attention snapped to Celeste in unison and she provided a shrug, suggesting she knew exactly what Katalina was talking about. "The horn works both ways. It can be spooky. Sorry, I forgot to tell you."

Did he bother reprimanding her again?

"The horn...?" Katalina's voice was as meek as it had been the first time she'd called him. It was only yesterday, though it'd felt like months since they'd met and ended up here. They'd jumped from night to day and now it was night again, yet they hadn't found a time to sleep. Thankfully, adrenaline kept him wide awake thus far.

Celeste shook her head. "We'll have to tell you about it another time. It's far too late to be traversing the city any longer —it can get scary at night in certain parts of the city. Like *this* part of the city."

"Do they have an inn here?" Mark asked, rubbing the back of his neck with a yawn. "I would kill for a shower right now."

"Would you?" Celeste asked with a squint. "Who would you kill?"

Mark's eyes widened. "It was—it was an expression. I, well —" He looked over at Noah, who nodded in agreement. He'd probably pick Mark out of the three of them, too. There were no hard feelings; Mark wasn't as interesting as Celeste, and Katalina was family.

"I'm joking. *Anyway,* we have inns here, but my family lives close, so I think we should head there for the night," Celeste suggested. "My stepmother and father have a sizable house— we should be able to get some peace in our own rooms."

"Wow, introducing us to your parents so soon?" Noah asked, touching a hand to his chest, feigning shock. In reality, he was trying to hide the excitement gnawing at his core. "I didn't know we reached this stage, but I'm touched."

Celeste rolled her eyes in such a beautiful way that he almost asked her to do it again, just for the sake of it. But the moment passed, and she stepped forward. "Their house isn't too far from here. We should get there right at the start of the city curfew."

"A city curfew? For what?" Katalina asked.

Celeste only shook her head. "It's not worth knowing. You wouldn't be able to sleep."

THE DOOR to her parent's estate swung open, and a woman wearing a revealing crop top and incredibly short shorts stood on the other side with one hand on the door and the other on her hip. Oh, and she was blue. A merperson, like the many other scaly, hairless merpeople walking about the city.

From what Celeste described, merpeople originated from cities in the ocean as mermaids, but they could become land citizens to grow their legs, with the caveat of being forced to go back after five years without a shot of ever returning. A one-and-done deal. Fortun was not without flaws.

"Are you a... half merperson?" Noah whispered to Celeste with wide eyes, looking her up and down. Was she wearing a disguise, perfectly crafted to look like the woman of Noah's dreams?

She shook her head with a chuckle. "Oh, no, my parents are both human, though I've been told we have five percent 'hare' in my bloodline." Celeste appeared proud of this, her chin tilted notably higher. She gestured to the taller blue woman with gills across from them, who was still blocking the doorway. "This is my step-sister, Lu—"

"—na Tide," her step-sister, Luna, finished with a bluish-green hand outstretched and a bold smile. Her voice sounded bubbly, as though she were talking underwater, and it was difficult to decipher what she was saying. "Have you finally learned how to make friends?"

Celeste rolled her eyes and stepped around her sister and through the front door. Noah hesitated before nodding at Luna awkwardly and barrelling past her. The house, though incredibly pointy, misshapen, and seemingly inhabitable from the outside, was quite mid-sized and quaint within.

Noah stepped into the living room, where two black couches faced a canvas above a fireplace. Quilts made up of dark reds and blues lined the couches, and two fluffy, red chairs took up the spaces in between. A red candle was lit on a black center table, an aroma of pinecones filling the room and calming his senses.

"Tide?" Mark asked under his breath. "That's a very... on-the-nose last name for a sea person."

"Every merperson has the last name of Tide. It's what connects their species," Celeste said before disappearing around a corner and reappearing with a chocolate-glazed donut. She took a bite of it with a moan of satisfaction. He was beginning to question if there was truly data backing up her sweet tooth, or if she was merely trying to justify a bad habit. Either way, he was bummed she didn't offer him a donut.

There were no electronics to be seen, and Noah watched the canvas mounted to the wall with a look of scrutiny and confusion. The colors appeared to be moving incredibly slowly, red and blue swirling in the center to create a murky and muddled brown.

Katalina and Mark stood beside him, taking the painting in

as a whole, their heads collectively tilted to the right and brows furrowed in thought.

"Are mom and dad ho—" Celeste stopped mid-sentence as her eyes met the painting. She folded her arms over her chest with a huff, her happy exterior melting away, replaced with displeasure. "Really?"

"What? What does the painting mean?" Katalina asked.

"They're making love," Luna called from somewhere down the hall. When Noah turned, the front door was closed, and she was gone, though still close enough to hear and to be heard. He wondered if it would be rude to ask her to bring a donut for him.

"That's what this means." Celeste gestured to the canvas with a look of disgust, and his appetite disappeared at the implications.

"They... paint what they're going to do?" Mark asked, taking a step closer to examine the painting further. The red and blue began on two separate ends of the canvas, yet met in the center. Noah supposed it showed exactly what 'making love' would look like.

"Two colors merging," Noah murmured to himself. "Interesting. Why red and blue? Do you know who is who?"

"My stepmom is always blue, but she's never told us why. I've always associated red with anger or pain, but my dad is the kindest person I know."

"Maybe he's not as kind in the bedroom," Mark suggested with a side eye and smirk. He chuckled to himself as Katalina lightly shoved his shoulder with a tsk, though Noah could see she was trying not to smile, too. It must've been the first time he'd seen either of them look happy since they'd landed on Fortun.

Her smile turned to laughter. It was surprisingly light yet loud despite her timid demeanor, and she covered her mouth with a hand in an attempt to stifle her chuckles. She was failing spectacularly.

"Disgusting," Celeste said, but her tone was carefree, and he could tell she was both entertained by their reactions and ready to move on. "Their souls are connected to this painting. Each husband and wife receives one after their official forever ceremony—it comes from the ritual."

Something about the sultry sweetness in her voice made him gulp down his anticipation and racing heart at the way she said 'ritual.'

"Most people decide to put them in a closet," Luna said as she entered the room and sat on one of the long black couches with a scaly blue arm resting on a decorative pillow. She didn't bring food along with her, and his stomach grumbled in protest. "But no, not our parents. They hung it up in the middle of the living room for everyone to see, instead."

"It never gets better to look at," Celeste said with a shudder. "I used to have nightmares about the colors moving."

Noah couldn't help but stare at the gills along Luna's forearms and on the top of her head. She had no hair to speak of, and her eyes were sunken in and hard to see. But when he looked closely, he saw the light blue of the sea, speckled with darker shades of teal. Suddenly, he thought he could stare into them forever.

He was so enamored with her appearance that he hadn't

realized she was glaring at him with a prominent dark blue blush across her cheeks. Noah rubbed the back of his neck with a look of shame and a bright blush of his own. "Sorry, I—I've never—"

"Seen a merperson before?" she asked, her voice soft and full of unexplained defeat. He'd seen merpeople on their walk over, but he hadn't looked long enough to catch the glimmer in their gazes. Did everyone on this planet have beautiful eyes?

"It's okay," Luna added swiftly. "People always stare the first few times. You eventually get used to it."

"It doesn't look like you've gotten used to it," he said, and he could swear her blue blush deepened. "I'm sorry. Now I know—only look at you for a normal amount of time. Got it."

Luna nodded with a small smile in thanks. He glanced over at Katalina and Mark to find they were staring at her as well. They turned away quickly; Katalina pretended to examine a family photo hanging on the wall, and Mark took to whistling and looking around at nothing and everything.

"They'll probably take all night," Celeste exclaimed with a sigh. The group allowed silence to fall, but not a sound erupted from above or below. "We'll have to wait until tomorrow to ask about the boat. We'll be having a morning lunch."

Yet another contradictory statement. He expected Katalina or Mark to comment on such an absurdity—the morning was meant for breakfast, and lunch was meant for midday—but they all remained quiet. Mark's eyes drooped as he struggled to keep them open, and Katalina was leaning against his side softly.

The journey was taking its toll.

"No offense, but the four of you look terrible. What have you been doing?" Luna asked, reaching underneath the couch and pulling out a long box. On the cover was an image of a fish and a kingdom beneath the water, and it looked to be a puzzle. When she opened it, the pieces were incredibly small and seemingly infinite.

Luna's shoulders relaxed as she ran her fingers over the mound of pieces and released a sigh. "I think I'll need to visit home soon. These crafts you make me can only do so much."

Noah grabbed the box and flipped it over. "Is this what it looks like where you're from?"

Luna nodded. "Beautiful, isn't it? Now, tell me. What have you been doing, and don't tell me it's—" She cut herself off when she saw Celeste's bashful expression, and Luna's mouth dropped open before she scoffed. "You need to let that go. He was wrong. Our planet is perfectly fine."

"Let me tell you what I fou—"

"No, Celeste. I'm sorry, but no. Altair and his team thought they were onto something, but they weren't. There have been no articles about the so-called end of the world. Everything is *fine.*"

"What do you mean, his research was wrong?" Noah asked.

"He worked with a well-renowned spaceologist as the co-leading researcher," Luna said matter-of-factly. "His team thought they discovered an abnormality in space that was pulling our planet closer to it. But other species and countries caught wind, did their own tests, and it was determined their team was wrong. It was a ripple in spacetime from the bursting of a distant star."

"Just because the majority believes in lies doesn't make them any more true," Celeste said through gritted teeth.

"I know you looked up to Altair, and the two of you were close, but please stop. The existence of another world close enough to collide with ours is impossible, or it would've happened by now."

"But we're from that world," Noah blurted, and Luna's gaze snapped to meet his.

She scoffed. "Come again?"

"We're from that other world, on the other side of that 'abnormality' in space. I don't know if it's what we'd classify as a black hole back on our planet—*but* our planet is crumbling and we jumped off the edge with Celeste and traveled through the black hole. Landing here."

"You... jumped? Off the edge of your planet? Is it not square or round?"

Noah was taken aback by such a question, but he eventually found it within himself to nod. "It's flat. I think whatever your brother, er, step-brother was looking into was a very real threat to both our planets."

Luna stared at him before shaking her head incredulously. "No. There's no way. *Our* planet isn't crumbling, and certainly, *someone* would release such news if it was serious." She turned her words to Celeste. "I don't know how you found people crazy enough to believe you and follow you around, but it's time to stop. It's time to move on and grow up."

"And if I told you my mom and *our* dad were the reasons Altair and I could go up to this planet?" Celeste asked, her words coming out hot and heavy. "Or if I told you every government knows and they're all collectively keeping it quiet? What if I told you they all think it's inevitable, so it's best not to cause a panic before both worlds end?"

Luna crossed her arms and leaned back with a roll of her eyes. Something told Noah they'd had similar arguments before, and Luna was never swayed. "I'd say you're delusional."

Celeste balled her fingers into fists, showing a feeling she'd yet to expose in front of them—absolute anger. Now he understood why she'd told them mermaids—and by extension, merpeople—wouldn't help their cause. He was watching the proof unfold.

When he was certain Celeste was going to explode, her shoulders relaxed, and she released a deep sigh instead. She held the gazes of each person in the room, respectively. "Alright, well, this conversation isn't leading anywhere new tonight. I think it's time we found you three somewhere to sleep, don't you?"

And with that, the discussion was over.

15

SHARED SPACE

There was a brief moment when every bone in his body was aglow with wishful optimism. Katalina and Mark would be placed into a room together since they were engaged, and he would have no choice but to share a room with Celeste. It was perfect. They didn't have to share a bed or *do* anything. As long as there were a few more minutes left to simply exist together.

Noah finished his shower and made his way down the hall, swiping his towel over unkempt and wet blond hair before pushing his bedroom door open. He stopped in the doorway, the towel still half over his head as Mark came into view.

Mark turned around, wearing nothing more than his checkered briefs. If their roles were reversed, Noah would've jumped out of the way from the open door so no one else could see his nearly naked body, but Mark stood tall and proud, his minimally hairy chest on full display.

Noah raised a brow and tossed his towel onto his bed—

which now had two towels on it. Great. The other was probably wet with Mark's post-shower sweat, which had now undoubtedly seeped into the sheets and bedspread Noah would be sleeping on and under.

He also couldn't help the disappointment coursing through him that Celeste was nowhere to be seen, though he tried his best to hide it. "Am I in the wrong room? Is Katalina...?"

Mark shook his head. "She's rooming with your newfound crush, so I guess you're stuck with me tonight. Tell me, do you always do whatever you're told by women you think are pretty?"

"Isn't that exactly what you did?" Noah countered.

Mark considered this before responding with a shrug. "Sure, but I know Katalina, and I know once she has an idea, she tends to stick with it. And, if she jumped off a ledge, I'd follow. There'd be no point in living without her."

Mark pulled a fresh maroon shirt over his head and plopped onto his navy blue bed before continuing. "What I want to know is why *she* basically followed a stranger. You, I can understand. No support system, no close family, and your mom recently died. I can see you feeling like you have nothing to live for."

Noah winced, and Mark's brows raised in the smallest of amounts. "Sorry. But as I was saying, what could Katalina have going on in her head that led her to follow you? Unless you've met before? Or you're not her cousin at all and this is all some weird fantasy the two of you concocted."

"Goddesses, dude. No." Noah cringed, taking a step away from Mark's bed to maintain a distance between them. Glancing around, he noticed the pastel blue walls and navy blue carpet matched the blue shades of the beds. Even the abstract pictures pinned to the walls and bedframes were various shades of blue. It was very… bright. He couldn't tell if it was pretty or the worst thing he'd ever seen.

"We're cousins and she felt bad for me, like everyone else," Noah added, his voice lined with defeat. "Yes, she took the extra step of reaching out, but I don't know why she came. And why'd you have to ruin my mood like that? First, inviting me to dinner on my dead mom's birthday…"

"Hey." Mark held up his hands in defense. "I think she thought it would be a good way to get you out of the house on such a sad day. But don't come after me about it. I'm not the one who made the plan or agreed to go. You could've stayed home."

Noah clenched his jaw, annoyed that Mark was right. The cherry on top was that if Noah *had* stayed home, he wouldn't have met Celeste. So should he be thanking Katalina for her invitation, even though he perceived it as cruel?

"And, to be fair, I was only stating a fact," Mark said, doubling down on his stance, as though it was acceptable to casually bring up the recent passing of someone's parent. "I would've thought it'd be easier for you to talk about by now."

"Well, it's not easier, Mark, and there's no winning, ever. The second you're reminded—it's game over," Noah said, his voice riddled with defeat as he plopped onto his rough mattress rather harshly. He wanted a day when he didn't have to think about his mother and feel so… unbearably hopeless. "It's better to not bring it up."

Silence fell.

"I haven't lost someone close to me," Mark said, lying on his back with his hands clasped over his stomach, eyes glued to the ceiling. "Aside from my childhood dog, Piggle. I think I cried about it."

"You think?" Noah lay with his hands tucked behind his head as he glanced over at Mark. The beds were shorter than their bodies, and their feet were dangling off the ends and slightly out of the blankets. It was uncomfortable, to say the least—and cold, with the addition of Mark's wet towel germs.

Mark rolled on his side, tucking his fingers under his cheek, eyes on Noah. Noah kept his gaze locked on the ceiling as Mark said, "I suppose I block those things out. Compartmentalization works wonders."

"Aren't you afraid of... exploding?" Noah asked, wondering if Mark had enough self-awareness to know he exploded numerous times throughout the day. Noah was hard-pressed to think of someone who got so irrationally angry over nothing so quickly. It looked to be both a blessing and a curse.

"There's no point in fear," Mark said. "Except for when it comes to the end of the world, I guess."

Noah was surprised to feel a smirk form on his lips. "Until you compartmentalize that, too?"

Mark nodded. "The beauty of the human brain is that you can manipulate it however you want with patience and practice."

"Huh." Mark's words carried oddly terrifying implications, but by now, he knew Mark well enough to know he meant well—even though it came out wrong every single time.

Eventually, Mark stood and turned off the lights, but it was increasingly difficult to fall asleep.

"Do you think we can do it?" Noah asked the dark room. "Save both our planets?"

There was another lull so long that Noah began to drift off to sleep. But then he pictured two planets crashing into each other, and his eyes shot back open.

Noah attempted to take Mark's advice and compartmentalize all the highly likely ways this adventure ended. But there were good outcomes, too—they could all survive, and he could take Celeste out on a proper date. He could pick up Henry and show her this world. He could go to the dinner that started this all with Katalina and Mark.

He smiled. Was Celeste rubbing off on him? He was genuinely excited about what was to come. Hopefully, it wasn't a fluke designed by lust and exhilaration.

Right when his last round of moonlit thoughts hit, Mark snorted and said, "How the fuck should I know?"

Noah let out a sharp laugh, wholly unprepared for the emphasis Mark put into every word. Such vigor and passion in each syllable. If he didn't take Mark too seriously, the guy was pretty funny. Noah was starting to like him.

For the first time since he could remember, he didn't want the conversation to end. A few hours ago, he'd wished he'd had tape to put over Mark's mouth, but now he *wanted* Mark to keep talking.

"You know," Noah tried. "What you said about Katalina was lovely—that'd you jump if she jumped. But, I wanted to say earlier... that while the sentiment is sweet, you shouldn't. Someone would miss you."

"Eventually we're all missed. And then, one day, we won't even be known anymore. One day, we'll all be... stardust."

"Stardust," Noah repeated, letting the word rest on his tongue as he stared into the darkness. Mark's words sounded strangely like something Celeste would say, and he was surprised Mark had it in him.

The shadows were twirling in on themselves the longer he stared at nothing, his mind filling in the gaps that his eyes couldn't.

A lump formed in his throat as his thoughts were brought back to *her*, and he couldn't go there, so he closed his eyes and took a deep, shuddering breath to stop the sob begging to break.

He wondered if anyone knew him well enough to miss him. *Truly* miss him. Noah tried to shake the thought away and remind himself of the things he had. Henrietta. Healthy lungs and liver despite his awful university days. This world. Knowledge. Celeste. Mark. Katalina.

But did anyone *know* him?

He was afraid of the answer.

"Celeste is right," Noah said with a yawn, turning over to face away from Mark while tucking his feet underneath the blanket. "You need to be more positive."

"It's not that easy," Mark said, his voice growing distant as he, too, slowly drifted to sleep.

Noah closed his eyes, the words leaving his lips in a whisper. "No. It's not."

16

THE PERFECT MORNING FOR LUNCH

Noah stretched as he reached the bottom of the spiraling black staircase. He'd hoped for a moment of peace where he could explore on his own before inevitably making his way to the kitchen to stave off his hunger, but peace evaporated the second his foot left the last step.

Katalina, Celeste, and Luna walked up in a line of giggling girls. They were dressed in fresh clothes—jumpsuits matching in style, with short sleeves that dangled off their shoulders, though each wore a different color. While Katalina was in a deep green reminiscent of the forests of home, Celeste was in a bright pastel pink, and her sister was in baby blue.

Next to each other, Katalina's green contrasted so heavily with the other two that it looked like they intentionally left her out, but she didn't seem to mind. In fact, she was beaming from ear to ear as she breezed past Noah.

Noah turned in time to watch her jump into Mark's arms,

who released a grunt upon collision and landed on the stairs behind him. The impact was rough; his brows creased in pain, but he wore a half-smile.

"You look beautiful this morning," Mark murmured, grabbing Katalina by the waist lightly. His lips grazed her ear as he placed one hand on the small of her back and the other behind her head. He pulled Katalina in, and they kissed, right there on the stairs for everyone to see.

Noah looked away and at the one person he wished to be entwined with. Celeste's long, blackish-blue hair was decorated with pastel flowers. Each pink petal looked like the stroke of a brush, and he reached out to touch one before stopping short, worried he'd ruin the artwork.

"Wow." The word escaped his lips before he could stop himself, and he winced at how obviously in awe he was. He attempted to backtrack, adding swiftly, "That looks... comfortable."

He should've stayed quiet.

Noah was in a standard black t-shirt that hugged his body just enough to make him look slim while still providing room to breathe—and jeans. The shirt and pants had arrived at his bedroom door along with a pair for Mark, though there hadn't been time for Celeste to collect their measurements while they were awake.

"The three of you look like sisters," he said, referring to their outfits.

"In one way or another, we're all sisters," came a sing-songy voice worn at the edges with age. A woman he could only classify as a 'free spirit' rounded the corner. She was three feet taller than her daughters, and her scales were the same deep blue as Luna's. Noah could tell immediately who designed the room he and Mark slept in.

"You must be the stepmother. I'm Noah." He stuck out a nervous hand with a warm smile. He wasn't sure what compelled him to be so forward this morning—perhaps he was merely excited to meet an entirely new species.

Or, realistically, because he wanted to impress Celeste's family, even if it didn't matter in the slightest.

Noah glanced over at the canvas Celeste's father and stepmother were connected to. No longer were the colors mingled in such a grotesquely brown way. While they were separated on the canvas as a blue and red dot, some paint still lingered in the center, bleeding over to the other. If he squinted, he could swear they were moving.

"That's the symbol of love, my dear," the woman said with a pat on his head as she passed. His hand was still outstretched for her to take, and he looked down at it before slowly placing his hand back at his side. She chuckled, presumably saying her name as she passed. "Pevelyn, darling."

Gills hung from her arms and neck, and she had what could only be a dark blue wig covering the flap lining the top of her head. Her eyes narrowed as she looked over at the stairs where Mark and Katalina were happily entangled. "Please, tell your friends that love-making is strictly off the to-do list for our morning lunch."

Katalina appeared to snap out of her lip-locked daze immediately and jerked away from Mark. Mark remained on the stairs, his eyes glazed over as he looked up to Katalina and then to Pevelyn. Snapping back to reality, Mark scrambled to his feet and took Pevelyn's hand with a bright red blush. "S-sorry about that! I'm Mark, and this is my fiancée, Katalina."

"And this is Noah," Celeste said as she gestured toward him with a small smile. His name on her lips sent his heart throbbing, and he blushed, pushing down the embarrassment regarding the need to be introduced twice.

Pevelyn turned with a knowing look he didn't quite understand, and she came over to scrutinize Noah further. When she was finished circling him, she said with a disappointed half-frown, "Just another human boy, huh?"

"Just another?" he asked, perplexed and put off by the tone in her voice.

Pevelyn gave him a stern look, the kind with a raised brow and hands on her hips. "Oh no, dear, I didn't mean it like *that*. I only meant there are other subhuman species to explore, you know?"

He did not know, because he came from a world where these sorts of things didn't exist. A question regarding the number of subspecies here rested on his tongue, which he promptly gulped down. He couldn't disclose any information that may lead to Pevelyn learning he was from the other planet —right?

Celeste's eyes bore into him, the tension in her shoulders noticeable. Whatever he said now would make or break their entire morning.

Noah supposed he should've been offended by what Pevelyn implied, but feathers needn't be ruffled today, so instead he went with, "Ah, I understand. Well—have no fear. We're only friends. Katalina and Mark are engaged, though."

He hoped that would be enough to steer the conversation away from him, but when he looked at Celeste again, her eyes were wide and nervous, and he noticed she was biting the inside of her cheek. Had he said something wrong?

Pevelyn reached out to Katalina. "Splendid! Oh, do show me the mark, dear. It's my favorite part."

Noah, Katalina, and Mark blankly stared at Pevelyn, her words lost on them. Katalina's eyes panned to her own hand, tracing the edges of the diamond-studded ring on her finger, the band a swirl of more diamonds.

"Um," Celeste tried. "They used a ring as a symbol of their love instead of the mark."

Katalina released a nervous chuckle. "Yes, we decided it would be too difficult to constantly hear jokes about Mark's name being... Mark."

She went along with the lie. He filed this information away for later.

Pevelyn raised an unimpressed brow before grabbing Katalina's hand, pulling the ring closer to inspect before unceremoniously letting go. Katalina's hand fell to her side, and she grabbed her forearm with an anxious glance away.

With a condescending sigh, Pevelyn said, "You'd be happier with a man who isn't afraid of the mark, darling."

"*Lunch,* mother?" Luna cut in, breezing past and out the back door without another word, her head held high as though she knew she had the power to make everyone else follow.

Pevelyn clapped. “Right! I hope you’ve all brought your appetites!”

“Actually—” Noah meant to ask for a quick glass of water—his mouth was unfathomably dry—but Pevelyn waved his words away.

“Nonsense, boy! You *must* eat! Come, the table is set outside.” Pevelyn led them through the back door, bending under the threshold because of her height.

Outside, the dining table was long, with a white tablecloth underneath various dome-covered plates. Fifteen chairs and respective plates were set up on each side of the table, with one more placement at both ends, but there was only enough water in the middle for four.

“This is an absurdly long table,” Mark remarked under his breath as Celeste led them to the center seats. Noah glanced behind them, hopeful that Pevelyn hadn’t overheard. “Wouldn’t you say?”

“I find it is not quite long enough,” Celeste responded, pulling out a chair as her eyes found his. Noah had fallen through a universe within a black hole, and yet nothing both terrified and amazed him more than her eyes. He stopped in front of her, and she added with a nod toward the seat, “For you.”

He nodded his thanks, hoping he didn’t blush too hard in front of her family. “Shouldn’t I be the one to pull out your chair?”

“Next time,” she whispered into his ear before taking up the seat across from him. Much to Noah’s dismay, Mark plopped down beside him. He understood not sharing a room with

Celeste, but they could've sat together for lunch. Was Celeste avoiding him on purpose?

Even more curious was Celeste's stepmother and sister sitting at each end. They felt so impossibly far away when surrounded by plates and chairs and haughty decorations. The domes seemed to disappear as he sat down, replaced with a glorious spread of fine, buttery pastries, eggs, and bright fruit salad. At least, he thought they looked like fruit, though they were neon greens and blues and strangely pointy.

His mouth watered. It'd probably been a full twenty-four hours since he last ate. At that moment, he desperately wished they'd discussed the customs regarding table etiquette and when one could partake once the food was presented.

"Now," Pevelyn began as a server approached her with a single plate full of food, though none of it matched what was on the table. Celeste added a biscuit, cheese cubes, and some strips of green beans wrapped in bacon to her plate. "Where did you say your friends are from? Tertiary school?"

Celeste kept her head down and her eyes on her plate, moving around the small cubes of yellow and green cheese with her fork. She released a timid chuckle but didn't respond, and he thought this may be the first time he hadn't heard her give an overzealous explanation with an unwavering smile. It was the first time she didn't immediately have an answer, either.

Noah looked between Celeste and Pevelyn in quick succession; Pevelyn's chewing slowed as she realized something more was going on.

"It's okay," Pevelyn announced to the table, her words aimed at no one in particular. Then her gaze shot to Katalina, and she gave her a shrewd smirk. "She gets like this when she knows I won't like an answer."

"We met from there," Celeste said under her breath.

"From where, honey?"

"From *there*." The emphasis she placed on a single word was the nail in the proverbial coffin, and Pevelyn's smile dropped. The table went silent; Luna cleared her throat awkwardly, opening her mouth with a finger pointed upward before she clamped it back shut.

"What?" Pevelyn's voice boomed as anger boiled from her ears and burst from her eyes. "You *WHAT?*"

Her voice somehow became higher, a screech unlike anything he'd ever heard from a human or otherwise, and Celeste shrank away. For someone with so much light, he hadn't thought she'd find any situation as equally uncomfortable as he. Her limit appeared to be here with her stepmom.

Noah took a drink of the water set at his spot to alleviate his discomfort. He gasped as the icy substance trickled down his throat, but the cold wasn't what made him gasp. The taste transported him to a memory. There he was, aged fourteen, getting onto their tandem bike—the sole ground transportation on his planet—and pointing out the shapes in the clouds above.

The flashback was so sudden that tears slipped from the corners of his eyes and the glass fell from his fingertips, shattering to the ground. A deafening crunch rattled his ears, and the present slipped back into focus as suddenly as it'd gone.

Why must he be reminded of her everywhere he went?

"What's wrong, Noah?" Celeste asked, but his attention turned to the stepmother.

"H-how did you make the water do that?" he asked, his voice breaking.

Pevelyn waved his question off. "It's water from our estate's Remembrance Well, darling." Her eyes remained locked on Celeste. "You promised you would stop this nonsense, following your brother's research around. Can you not be trusted to do the bare minimum and behave?"

"Your father said I can have the final say in this matter if it were to arise again," she continued. "Since he's gone for business, I have no choice but to forbid you from leaving our estate."

"Don't you understand our planets are going to be destroyed?" Celeste asked. "You're condemning us—"

"Wait," Luna yelled, throwing out her arms as she stood; the legs of her chair got caught on the uneven dirt, the chair tipping backward. All heads turned to her, the argument ending abruptly.

Luna's blue gills had knocked over a centerpiece, and a candle encased in glass spilled over the white linen. He grimaced at the crunch of more shattering glass, and he couldn't help the burning desire he felt to leave the table and tension behind—with a plate full of food in hand.

Noah grabbed Mark's cup of water—best to spare him from *that*—and prepared to throw it onto the small fire that the candle started. His hand stopped halfway when the flame sprouted legs and ran the other way.

Dumbfounded, he turned back to Luna, and Mark snatched the drink out of his hand with a brow raised in annoyance.

Pevelyn finally turned away from Celeste and asked from across the table, "What is it, dear?"

Luna's pitted blue eyes were daggers as she squinted at her mother. "Don't you smell that? It's rancid."

Noah turned up his nose and sniffed, but he couldn't smell a thing aside from the crispy, buttery bread sitting in front of him. He eyed it up suspiciously, wondering if it would give him emotional whiplash, too.

He reached down and took a tentative bite—hunger was more powerful than fear—before releasing a soft moan from the way it melted in his mouth. The smell alone was intoxicating and sure to rid him of the thoughts about his mother. The taste was so overwhelming he nearly forgot that Luna was in the middle of a sudden outburst.

The last bite of his biscuit was hovering inches from his mouth when Luna's voice cut through the air. "Something's off. There's a shapeshifter here."

17

A SHAPESHIFTER AMONG US

"IMPOSSIBLE," PEVELYN SAID, THOUGH SHE WAS EYEING UP THE rest of the table. "We have unpeckable security here, and shapeshifters don't come this far north."

"Don't you mean impeccable?" Katalina asked, ever the one to find a way to sound smart. While they hadn't known each other long, and they hadn't met very many new people, he'd noticed the subtle ways she pushed her intellect onto others.

"Nothing's impeccable, darling. The home is *unpeckable*—that's how they break in, you see. They peck their way through the wood of a home, nasty little shi—"

"*Mom,*" Luna said at the same moment Celeste said, "*Pevelyn.*"

"Theoretically," Noah interjected, amused by their joint reaction to a simple swear, yet mildly terrified about what a 'shapeshifter' could entail. "If one were to be here, why would you think that is?"

Celeste pointed a thumb at him and looked around the table with an accusatory squint. “He’s right. Don’t they only take on bounty jobs?”

Pevelyn’s expression remained neutral.

“Is your family into dark stuff?” Mark asked under his breath. “Because that would’ve been good to know before we jumped off the end of the—*our*—world.”

Celeste glanced at him from across the table and whispered back, “No, actually, it’s probably because merpeople aren’t supposed to live above ground for more than five consecutive years, and Pevelyn has been up here for at least a century. She has a business agreement to stay topside for as long as she wants, though.”

“So a bounty makes no sense,” Noah concluded.

She nodded, crossing her arms and sitting back with a squint directed at Mark. Their eyes locked. “Are you the shifter?”

His mouth opened and closed in a way that made him look inexplicably guilty—but also too nervous to *actually* be guilty. Mark shuffled uncomfortably in his seat and avoided eye contact at all costs as he finally said, “O-o-of course not.”

Celeste turned to Noah. “You?” He shook his head, and she turned to Katalina last. “Then that leaves you.”

Katalina pointed to herself. “Me?”

Celeste nodded. “It adds up. A shifter would pretend like they don’t know what they’re capable of doing.”

“She’s right,” Pevelyn said.

Noah’s heart pounded as he gestured toward his newfound

friend and family member, his words directed at Celeste. "How could you suggest that?"

"It makes sense. And she went to the bathroom a little while ago before lunch, no? She must've gotten attacked and switched with the shifter then."

"Yeah, but so did I, and Mark, and you, and your stepmother. It could be any of us. It could be you." He held his breath after the words tumbled out, a twinge of hurt lining his features. Noah knew it was logical to keep the investigation open and look into everyone there, but making the accusation stung, nonetheless.

Noah peered over at Katalina and Mark, but neither looked any different from before. None of them did.

Katalina must've sensed his gaze, because she gave him a look that said she was disappointed, and said, "I know you don't remember me, but we played together for a time when we were younger. And I remember thinking, even then, you were a deeply lonely person. And your mom... she never had a nice thing to say about you or anyone or anything. There, does that prove I'm me?"

Noah's fingers curled into fists as a sudden anger flared from within. "Can we stop bringing her up for one goddamn day, *please*?"

"Language!" Celeste and Luna yelled in unison before Celeste added, "And that doesn't prove a thing, Katalina. Unfortunately, since shapeshifters feed on the conscious and subconscious of their victims, they know a lot about a person. It's pretty hard to differentiate, honestly. Some people never realize their friend or coworker or lover was... exchanged."

A shudder passed through Noah at the thought, yet he was still exhaustively angry that the memory of his mother had to be jogged so early in the day.

"I don't think I've brought up your—" Katalina began, her attention never leaving him.

"Enough!" Luna shouted. Again, the bickering stopped, and all heads turned to her. She pointed to the head of the table. "It's you."

Pevelyn laughed with a hand to her heart. "Oh? And why would you think that?"

"Easy—you never agree with Celeste. On anything. Ever. Honestly, sometimes I think you hate her."

Noah's brows shot up in surprise as he tried to focus on the topic at hand and not his endlessly swirling thoughts. What an incredibly sad thing to say about another family member. Though, he supposed he said and felt certain things toward his mother—and the rest of his family—sometimes. And while his mother wasn't the pinnacle of every standard out there, he still felt bad for saying and feeling such things.

Moments like this chipped away at his soul.

Celeste crossed her arms, making it a point to turn and settle into her seat with an accusatory smile directed at her stepmother. "Ah, good catch. Very good. Tell us—what are you doing here?"

"And what did you do to my mother?" Luna added, giving Celeste a pointed glare at the lack of regard for Pevelyn's true whereabouts and subsequent safety.

"Girls, I don't know what you're talking ab—"

Luna jumped onto the table. It rattled, each half-filled glass tilting to the side while various foods catapulted across the table. The Remembrance Well water now drenched the tablecloth. He tried to save a cup as it rolled off, but the glass slipped from his fingers, and the water soaked the ground.

He watched the cup fall, noting a plant growing in its place —though the bud was a single music note instead of petals. Beside it, where his original glass had long since fallen and shattered, was another music note-shaped flower. Noah supposed he should've watched the events unfolding on the table instead of the flowers, but he had the inexplicable urge to pull the nearest one from its roots.

If he'd been watching, he would've heard Luna call for a duel, and Pevelyn accept as she, too, jumped onto the table.

Noah reached down and wrapped his fingers around the blue stem. He was immediately tugged elsewhere, the table and backyard dissolving like ink splattered on a page. The world around him drifted into a galaxy of tiny stars. Not just any stars, but ones drawn exactly as he and his mother drew together and stuck on his bedroom ceiling when he was younger. Echoing overhead was a distant melody. One he recognized but couldn't place, though it seeped into his soul and soothed it.

His heart thundered in his chest, and he clamped his eyes shut. When he opened them, the world seemed to zoom out until he was back in his body and sitting at the table, and he leaned away from the flower with a gasp.

When he finally looked back at the table, the fight was reaching its end. Luna had a hand wrapped around the neck of something that was no longer her mother. Noah grimaced at the sight—the shapeshifter could only be described as having feathers made of continuously flowing sand, creating a look akin to melting ice. Its colors were a deep brown and red, and its face was made of a large beak with two dark beady eyes above it. The creature was a tad fascinating but mostly grotesque; he couldn't look at it for long.

"Shapeshifters don't think like us," Celeste tried to explain as Luna tossed the body to the ground. "They're basically like big animals, except instead of a cat eating a mouse for energy, shapeshifters knock out their hosts and feed off their consciousness."

"Until the person they're feeding off of dies?" Mark asked as he paled, taking an extra step away from the shapeshifter's body, though he was already the furthest compared to the rest of them.

Celeste scrunched her nose. "No, of course not. They aren't heartless creatures. They could kill, but they choose not to."

"'Take what thy need,'" Luna said. "The question is, why did they need to come here? Why us? Mother had a pact with the nations so we could stay topside..."

Luna trailed off as she continued to mutter to herself, too softly for anyone else to hear. She glanced up, realizing the group was still there, and gave them an awkward smile before nodding toward the shapeshifter on the ground. "That one is out for now, but we should find my mother. Hopefully, she's still unconscious on the property somewhere."

Celeste nodded dutifully. "We'll check her bedroom and upstairs first."

Noah, Katalina, and Mark had no choice but to follow along and help. Up the stairs they went, passing by the living space and the respective canvas. It was now simply painted a single dash of blue covered with a single slash of red. And while that brought about a sense of unease within him, Celeste hardly seemed fazed by the current situation at all.

"How did it get inside, you think?" Noah asked as they reached the master bedroom door. It was closed; Celeste's hand rested on the handle as she turned to him.

"As Pevelyn—or the fake version of her—said before; the house may be unpeckable, but that does not make it impenetrable. While I can't say I know how or why, I'm guessing there is another one somewhere. They tend to travel in pairs."

"What if they were after you?" Katalina asked.

Celeste crinkled her brows. "Me? Why?"

"Your brother's research. It sounds like it's incredibly divisive, and there are probably plenty of others who knew of what he and his team were doing, right? Maybe that's what—"

Celeste opened the bedroom door before Katalina could finish her thought, her expression unreadable. Noah tilted his head as he followed. It was a good guess, yet Celeste didn't dignify it with a response. But she always had a response—she prided herself on being someone who knew almost everything. And although he hated to admit it, Katalina's guess lined up.

On the other side of the door was Pevelyn. She was lying on her bed with her hands neatly placed on either side of her body, her eyes shut and her hair perfectly combed. Not a detail was out of place, and the only thing noticeably different about her was her skin tone, which was now a much paler shade of blue.

"She lost a lot of her life force," Celeste said with a sigh as she ran a hand through her hair and paced the room. "But she'll be fine after a few more hours of rest. What should we do in the meantime? We didn't get a chance to ask about the boat..."

"We could go back to eating?" Mark asked.

Noah snapped his fingers and pointed. "We could go back to eating. Is everyone else in agreement?"

Katalina patted her stomach. "That fruit was both delicious and incredibly unfilling."

"So that's a yes?" Mark asked with a hopeful tone as he looped an arm around Katalina's neck and pulled her in for a side hug.

She looked up at him with a grin. "That's a yes."

Noah and Celeste made eye contact as he smiled at her bashfully, and she smiled back. They turned for the door, the day saved, when she leaned into Noah's ear and said rather seductively, "You did amazing today, honey. I'm so proud of you."

He stopped mid-stride, his face still turned away from Celeste and toward the hallway. His eyes widened, his foot hovering over the threshold as his body grew rigid. The air went stale, and time seemed to stop.

Noah was certain by the way the word rolled off her tongue—there was another shapeshifter in their midst.

18

ANOTHER

"HONEY?" HE ASKED, HIS ARMS FALLING TO HIS SIDES. HE LOOKED into her eyes, and they looked the same, yet felt off, sucking the energy from his spirit. There was a face and a voice and a smile that looked like hers, but there was nothing really *there*, a spark gone.

Though, in all honesty, it was hard to tell if it was her or not. Part of him wondered if he was wrong, and this was a new, bold flirting tactic he'd yet to encounter. After all, she'd expressed a mild interest in him before, right?

Celeste's smile slowly fell as she looked up at him and cocked her head. "Of course, honey. Why wouldn't I call you that?"

She—*it*—doubled down on this supposed fact. If the shapeshifters fed off of their victims' consciousness, then *it* should know that Celeste has never called him 'honey' before. His confusion was mixed with an agonizing fear as he took her

—*it*—in and debated on what to say. Luna was nowhere to be found; he was alone with Mark and Katalina to come up with a plan.

He needed to trick the shapeshifter back into its original form, but how? It was either an incredibly intelligent species that he wouldn't be able to fool, or one that would fight or flee the moment it was discovered.

Noah sifted through all the ways he could get the creature to revert to its original form and landed on the most surprising yet daring of acts—a kiss.

He'd kissed three girls and dated two in his lifetime. First, Evia, in the ninth grade. It was a dare at a birthday party meant to be a joke, but she'd taken it seriously, and she'd gotten tears all over his cheeks because she was embarrassed everyone was going to know they kissed.

Second was Allei, a girl who moved between towns often because of her father's business. They'd been best friends the summer before junior year and wanted to see what it truly felt like to date and kiss when there were emotions attached. Unfortunately, they weren't the same emotions meant to make a kiss mean something, and they drifted apart shortly after.

And lastly, he'd dated Tory during the twelfth, and final, year of lower education. Tory was a kind soul, a bright star, and utterly destructive. Two years later, he learned she was in jail for stealing. Upon reaching out to her, Tory admitted she staged a robbery at his mother's home when, in actuality, *she* was the one who did the stealing. He supposed there was trauma interlaced within that experience, but there was no point in drudging it up now, with the end of the world and all.

The point was that he didn't have any memorable experiences with women that hadn't ended horribly.

He didn't think twice—if he did, he wouldn't have been bold enough to follow through—and planted his lips on hers—*it*. He knew this was a risky move, and would come across terribly if he was wrong, but he knew in his gut that he wasn't.

This kiss was no better than the rest.

Stiff, unmoving, ungoddessly awkward and dry.

But it worked.

19

YOU DID WHAT

WHEN HE OPENED HIS EYES, HIS LIPS WERE NO LONGER PRESSED against human lips, but the pointed end of a bird's beak, instead. Two beady eyes stared back, black pits that instantly made Noah's skin crawl. He backed away with a startled gasp, pressing himself against the nearest wall as Mark yelped and jumped away.

"Who could've predicted shapeshifters would look like *that*?" Mark asked, his voice suspiciously calm despite the unraveling situation. At what point had he and Noah switched roles? "It's hideous."

The creature released a shrill squawk, much like a chicken would back home, and Noah winced at the thought of what he'd done. He opted to push the disgust down. Deep, deep down where it couldn't be reached.

"Where's Celeste?" Katalina asked, her voice shaking as she forced each syllable out. Her demanding tone sounded unnatural, and his stomach dropped. What if everyone had been taken? What if he was the only one left?

Katalina took a step toward the shapeshifter. It turned its head slowly toward her, black pits providing a never-ending stare as it squawked again. The sound was lower this time—primal.

Katalina shrank away, her meager demeanor returning instantly. Noah was far too stunned to say or do a thing. He could push down the disgust, but he couldn't shake the initial shock of it all. While he was certain it was a shapeshifter all along, the sudden morphing from one face to the next, from human to something so *inhuman*, left him speechless.

A yell came from behind the shapeshifter, and suddenly a candlestick was being bashed into the side of its head. The shapeshifter fell to the ground in a heap, and Noah couldn't help but feel bad for it. At the end of the day, it was just another living thing, and now it looked lifeless at their feet.

"Why do you always end up hitting things?" Noah asked. First, Elora the draegon, and now this. He supposed it wasn't the worst action to default to in moments like this.

Mark dropped the candlestick beside the creature, panting slightly as he looked down at the mass of sandy feathers. He started pacing while muttering obscenities under his breath. At least Noah wasn't the only one in shock.

"Wow," Katalina exclaimed as Mark made his way back to her. She grabbed his muscular arms with a squeeze and a loving smile. "You look like an action hero."

"Guys, the issue at hand here?" Noah interrupted. Katalina

was right, of course, but now was no time to point out Mark's good genes. "Our tour guide is missing?"

"I think the actual issue was that plan of yours," Mark said with crossed arms. Katalina held onto his forearm like a barnacle as they both looked at Noah. "Was that *really* the only way you could've found out it was a shapeshifter? You couldn't have done anything else *aside* from kissing it?"

"I wanted to catch it by surprise without resorting to a fight," Noah sheepishly explained as he grew increasingly embarrassed. "My plan worked, didn't it?"

"What will Celeste think?" Mark tried again, hammering in the point: Noah's plan was stupid. But it *did* work.

"Maybe we won't tell her?" Noah suggested, his voice rising at the end.

He could tell by the deadpan expression Mark held that he wasn't about to entertain this idea, even if he nodded tentatively and said, "Sure thing."

Luna appeared around the corner. "Father is still out of the house. Where's Cele—*oh my goddesses!*"

She gasped, stepping away from the doorway and clear into the hall and against the wall. "There was another one?"

Noah nodded. "It was pretending to be Celeste."

Luna gasped again, harsher than the last, a hand over her mouth in a dramatic overture. "Did it say why?"

"I didn't know they could talk—"

"Did it squawk?" she asked. He nodded. "Mimic it."

"Mimic what?"

"The squawk. What else?" Luna's eyes bulged as though she

were speaking to an absolute idiot. Which could be true—he could never gauge his intelligence. "Mimic it."

"I believe I can help with that." Mark stepped up and cleared his throat before releasing a series of squawks that sounded incredibly fake, yet somewhat similar all at once.

When he was finished, Luna's eyes widened. "My stepbrothers...research? It was *that* important?"

"Squawk?" Mark said again with a raise of his shoulders and brows. Noah would've laughed if not for the wheels turning in his head. The shapeshifters wanted the planets to collide? Or was there something more sinister lurking within Fortun than at first glance?

"I'm sorry," Katalina said, gesturing between Mark and Luna. "Did you understand what he said? How?"

"He mimicked it pretty well." Luna rubbed her chin. "The shapeshifter version of my mom didn't seem too surprised about Celeste going to another planet... is it true? Are the three of you from another planet?"

Noah nodded. "And they're crashing into each other in a little less than two months."

She stared at them before nodding dutifully. "I'm guessing Celeste is in her room. The shapeshifters must've come this morning. I'm surprised Father and I hadn't gotten energy-drained, too."

"Yes, that is... odd..." Katalina agreed.

"Maybe we shouldn't count you out yet, though," Mark added, squaring his shoulders and raising his chin slightly as an intimidation tactic.

"Let's find Celeste," Noah said, much too tired for how early in the midday it was. The sun was shining, the sky was spotless, and he'd slept... well enough, yet he was exhausted. Perhaps it was because he'd fallen onto another planet... though a more likely explanation was that he could now scratch 'make out with a shapeshifter' off a list he didn't know he needed to have.

"You don't care if she—" Mark began, gesturing toward Luna.

Katalina cut him off. "No, Noah is right. We should find Celeste first before dealing with the rest of the family."

"Or better yet, we could leave and never come back," Mark grumbled, which was preceded by a glare from Katalina and Noah. Luna didn't seem to care, instead darting to Celeste's bedroom door.

Noah stayed close behind her, craning his neck to see around Luna's broad shoulders as she pushed the door open. There Celeste was. She was in a similar state as her stepmother; her arms were laid out on each side of her body, and her eyes were clamped shut.

"Well, that was easy," Mark said, turning back to Luna. "Now, back to the question at hand—are *you* a shapeshifter, too? Best to tell us now than face the consequences of your fellow brethren, yeah?"

"News flash, asshole." The words were hot on her breath. "I'm the one who pointed out our lunch smelled like a shapeshifter. Do you think it would make any sense *at all* for me to announce that if I was one of them?"

Silence.

She nodded with a smug smile. "That's what I thought."

Noah raised a hand, and Luna's brows furrowed as he said,

"Um, language?"

Luna tsked and brushed past them to her sister's side, pulling out a small black bag from her jumpsuit pocket.

"What's that?"

Luna glared at them with a roll of her eyes. "I thought it was ridiculous that Celeste claimed you were from another planet. But if you truly don't know what this is, then you must be."

She reached into the bag and pulled out a pinch of sparkling violet powder. She sprinkled it over Celeste's mouth and nose. He thought Celeste would inhale or ingest the powder, but it appeared to dissolve into the skin of her face instead.

A sudden, deep inhale erupted from Celeste as her eyes snapped open, and she burst from her bed in one sweeping motion before landing upright on two springing feet. She bounced a few times before stretching, her eyes wild as they darted from person to person.

"Howsitgoinghowlongwasloutwowwhatisthatsmellisthere-ashapshiftersomewhereorsomething?"—she took a deep breath and then—"OrwasitmewasItheshapeshifter?"

Her words were incomprehensible, sentences running into each other with no clear beginning or end. Noah grabbed her by the shoulders to stop her from moving.

"What did you give her?" he asked. "Adrenaline?"

Celeste cocked her head with a playful smile, then released a light laugh as she continued to bounce despite his growing effort to keep her still. He looked at Luna for an explanation.

Luna smirked. "UnSleep Powder. Usually, it's used in medical centers, but, well, I have a connection. It'll pass in a few minutes, and she'll be back to her usual, equally annoying self." She put her hands and her hips and added, "I should've known something was off. Celeste hates putting flowers in her hair."

Noah's brows rose. She was right; the shapeshifter version of Celeste had pink petals sprinkled in her dark waves, but now her hair was untouched. He found himself mildly disappointed by this.

Celeste held her stomach as she threw her head back with a hearty laugh. "A classic, sisterly joke! Man, I love you."

Luna rolled her eyes again but patted her stepsister on the back with a knowing smile. "UnSleep Powder also makes someone incredibly overjoyed and interested in everything around them. It can be quite addicting—hence the lack of over-the-counter varieties."

"Why do you have some, then?" Noah asked.

Luna sighed. "Altair always wanted it around in cases of emergencies. I never understood what he was so paranoid about, but... well, maybe he knew someone would be after him one day."

"But I don't get it," Katalina said as she folded her arms over her chest and leaned into Mark. "Do you think there are people out there who *want* the planets to end?"

Celeste nodded avidly as if she was about to spill the biggest secret in the city. Thankfully, at the very least, her words now came out smoother and easier to follow. "There are always bitter people—and subspecies—with bitter solutions. Altair always said it was only a matter of time before shapeshifters infiltrated."

"Mother may not have believed him, but she still put up the fail-safes to appease him," Luna added mindlessly.

"He was always her favorite," Celeste agreed longingly, and Luna nodded.

Noah meant to ask why they would both think such a thing, but Mark pointed a finger at Noah before he had the chance to speak. Somehow, Noah knew exactly what Mark was going to say, and he squirmed in his spot before the words were out and the shame took hold.

With a voice that truly carried, Mark exclaimed, "He kissed the bird thing disguised as you!"

20

CONFESSION

Celeste's eyebrows shot up as she turned to Noah with a mouth parted in surprise. "While it was still me or after?"

Noah quickly put his hands up in defense, his heart threatening to break out of his chest. "While it was still you, of course. I mean, what kind of question is that?" Sweat trickled down his forehead, and he wiped it away with a nervous chuckle. "After I deduced it was a fake, I thought it would reveal its true self if it was surprised."

She squinted, her face scrunched with skepticism. "How'd you figure out it wasn't me?"

Noah hadn't known a blush was coming, yet his cheeks suddenly felt as though they were on fire. "Well, uh, you—*it*—called me 'honey.'"

He hoped the story could end there, but he could tell by the piqued interest in her eyes that the topic wasn't dying anytime soon. "So you kissed me? Simple as that? I've heard shapeshifters can put on quite the show..."

His blush deepened, and he debated turning around and leaving the room altogether. "It was quick and effective."

"Tongue?" she asked.

He felt an odd sensation crawl up his spine at the specificness of the question. "No tongue."

Her shoulders slumped slightly before her features perked up once again. "You—you—wow, Noah. I didn't know you had it in you... Was I—was I good?"

"*That's* what you ask?" Mark exclaimed, incredulously slapping a palm against his forehead.

Noah sucked in a deep breath, and her brows fell as she seemingly realized what he was going to say before it left his lips. "I—No. I'm sorry, but no. It's on my list of the top three worst kissing experiences of my life. But not number one, so that's something, right?"

She folded her arms with a *humph*. "Well, I suppose they can't get everything right." Her gaze snapped to his. "What would you have done if you were wrong, and I was always me?"

"I knew," he said definitively. "It was pretty obvious, so I took one for the team. But if it *was* you... I suppose I would've felt bad."

"That's it?"

He shrugged, unable to control his eager thoughts as Celeste inched closer. Her gaze held onto his in a way no other had, a hook reeling him in. With her lips so close to his, she whispered, "You wouldn't have felt... anything else?"

There was a beat of silence between them as tension built

within his gut. His throat became tight and the amount of sweat he was producing seemed to triple. Suddenly, he was forcing himself to picture grotesque images to keep his mind off the arousal eating away at him.

It was agonizing to have his lips inches from hers, and he wondered if she felt the same, or if she was toying with him. At the rate at which life was going, he wouldn't be surprised by either.

Mark whistled with a single clap, disrupting Celeste and Noah's moment together. He stepped between them and placed a hand on both their shoulders. "As much as I love the sexual tension unfolding here, do you think it's about time we leave?"

"There is a lot more ground to cover," Celeste agreed, before leaning over and whispering in Noah's ear, "Unless you'd like to take a detour."

Noah took a step back then, unprepared and unwilling to continue. Mark was right for once, and there were planets and lives to save, as crazy as it sounded. "W-we'll need a boat and the coordinates to get to the Ruler."

Celeste slammed a fist into her palm, and declared in a rallying war cry, "Right! To stepmother, we go!"

"If she's awake," Noah added with matched fervor, an arm and finger pointing toward the door.

"If she's awake," the other three cried in unison.

"MOTHER HAS SOME GASTROINTESTINAL ISSUES, so I couldn't use the UnSleep Powder, but she's awake now," Luna said as she led them down the hall to a set of double doors. They followed her inside, and there was Pevelyn, resting upright on the bed against a pillow.

"If she's been a shapeshifter this whole time, then..." Mark started.

"We haven't met yet," Katalina finished. She squared her shoulders and held out a hand for Pevelyn to shake.

Pevelyn was still rather pale, her scales a dash lighter but returning to their full, true blue, and she looked down at the offer with a faint smile. She didn't take Katalina's hand, however. Katalina briskly pulled her offer away, her gaze darting around the room in embarrassment.

"She's still a little loopy," Luna whispered to Noah, and he nodded. "Shapeshifters can drain a lot of energy from their hosts."

"I'm happy you're all okay," Pevelyn interjected, her voice airy, her attention directed at nothing and no one in particular. "Oh! And we have company! Goodness me..."

"I think we'll need a moment alone," Celeste said, turning to Noah with an apologetic look. "If that's alright."

Noah nodded. "Of course—take your time. We'll just be... somewhere. Doing... something."

With that, he, Katalina, and Mark left the room. He pressed his ear against the door in an attempt at eavesdropping, but he couldn't hear a thing through the thick wood. They'd just have to wait. He was so very tired of waiting.

21

FOR NOW GOODBYES

AFTER CELESTE, LUNA, AND PEVELYN SPOKE, THEY CAME OUT OF the bedroom with puffy red eyes, smiles, and side hugs. All of these appeared to be good things, and he allowed himself to smile after the craziness of, well, everything within the last forty-eight hours.

"My darling, *of course,* we'd let you borrow the boat. Why didn't you ask sooner? You could've called on the wire."

Noah was under the impression this world didn't have any technology, yet calls existed. When he looked around, he couldn't spot the familiar wires along the walls connected to a device like the apartments and homes on Sundar. Peculiar.

This world fascinated him endlessly, and he wondered if that's how Celeste's brother felt about Noah's planet, coming back each time with a discovery to jot down, and a new adventure to take. This place was so unlike anything Noah could've imagined that he was hard-pressed to believe Celeste and Altair found Sundar as interesting as Fortun.

"I know—it's been such a busy few days," Celeste exclaimed. She was leaving information out, and for good reason; they'd seen how the shapeshifter version of Pevelyn reacted to the news Noah and the others were from another planet. It was supposedly incredibly accurate to Pevelyn's true thoughts.

"I'll go fetch the coordinates of the ship and find the license card so you can be on your way," Pevelyn said, leaving the rest of the group in the living room. Noah plopped down on the couch across from the canvas and stared ahead. The canvas hadn't changed, and he found himself thankful for this.

Noah cleared his throat; the awkward silence following her wake was too much to bear. "So… where is your father?"

Celeste took a seat next to him and looked up at Luna with confusion. "That's a good point. Wasn't Father supposed to be off of work today?"

"He's away on business," Luna said. Her voice was distant as she peered out the patio's closed double doors, arms folded over her chest. The sun was hidden behind clouds that looked like they might pop. "'An urgent matter,' he said."

She kept her response brief, and Pevelyn walked back in, disrupting the questions on the tip of his tongue. "*Every* matter is urgent to him, darling. Even when it shouldn't be."

What kind of job did someone have on this planet? It hardly felt like a job could exist at all, at least not on the same level as back home, though he supposed someone *had* sold him ice cream. Did that mean they had drab offices here, too? The neon lights of the skyscrapers outside led him to believe they did not, but something had to be boring about this place.

Pevelyn dangled a pair of silver keys connected to a ring between her fingers. With a bright smile, she exclaimed, "My only request is for you to bring it back by tomorrow morning, darling. Your father hates to come home from business and find it missing."

NOAH, Celeste, and Mark waited outside the estate, scrunched beside each other on the narrow, deep red pavement leading up to the black and misshapen house. Pevelyn provided each of them with a black backpack full of water bottles and small bars made of oats for their travels, but packed little else. There were no roads for bikes or other modes of transportation. Instead, there were winding sidewalks with enough room for two to walk side-by-side. He found it... aesthetically displeasing... but in a pleasing way.

"About time," Mark said as the front door slammed shut and Katalina came clamoring down the stairs.

Katalina rolled her eyes as she walked past him with a light shove of his shoulder. "We weren't all born lucky enough to pee outside with ease. Who knows how long we'll be gone?"

Celeste nodded as she turned to follow. "She's right; it could be a few hours—or days."

"But didn't Pevelyn say we need to return the boat by tomorrow?" Noah asked.

Celeste chuckled and dismissed his comment with a wave

of her hand. "That was never happening. Father will get over it once we save our worlds."

"Are you sure you know—" Mark began.

"Wait," Luna called from behind. Celeste was immediately engulfed in a tight hug and tossed in the air. She gasped, the wind looking to be knocked out of her, and took a few steps back after Luna set her on the ground. "After being attacked, I wanted to say... be safe. I may think your mission is still half stupid and fake, but if it's something you believe in, then I believe in you."

Celeste smiled warmly. "Ever the way with words, Lu. Thank you. You better be safe, too. I'd hate to come back and find the place overrun with shapeshifters."

Luna smiled, pulling out four small, white packets that were sealed shut, and placed them in Celeste's hands. "If you're planning to meet the Ruler of the Deep—which is silly, by the way—then you can use these. They're called 'breathing bubbles.' Only open them when it's time to go underwater, though. They only work once."

They hugged again, and then Luna bypassed Mark and Katalina and stepped up to Noah. To say he was surprised would be an understatement. He thought he had offended her when they first met, staring her down because she was blue. It was still hard not to.

Luna held up her index and middle finger pressed together but with nothing held between them. With a smirk, she snapped her fingers, and a card appeared within them. She held it out for him to take.

He inspected the card, his eyes growing wide as a blush

spread across his cheeks. Written on it was a string of numbers so long it twisted around the card and started another row underneath, then another, and another. She leaned into his ear, her warm breath brushing against his neck. "If you're ever back on our planet, give me a call."

Noah raised a single brow and looked over at Celeste, who was deep in the middle of a conversation with Katalina, paying him no mind. He knew it wasn't logical to be so disappointed by this, but he was all the same.

As Luna walked away, Mark took up a spot beside Noah with his bulky arms crossed over his chest. "Wow. I never would've expected you to get *two* for the trip of one."

It was too early in the mid-morning for this.

22

THE CAVE WITH WINGS

THEY'D BEEN WALKING FOR EIGHT HOURS THROUGH A VAST AND uneventful forest made of two-dimensional pine trees, and now they were standing in front of a cave that was decidedly not two-dimensional.

It was deep and dark and silent aside from the soft patter of water from a source they couldn't see. It looked like a black hole surrounded by rock, another entrance into an unknown world, and he so desperately wanted to turn the other way.

The cave was surrounded by large, thick trees, a stark contrast to the two-dimensional woods they'd walked. The leaves were bulky and lush shades of oranges and reds.

Celeste gestured toward the opening with a bright smile. "Well, the only way out is through!"

"The only way out is in?" Katalina tried, and Celeste nodded eagerly with a finger pointed to match.

"Yes, exactly!"

Noah stepped up to the cave and examined the trees surrounding it. There was a ledge perhaps eight feet high before the treeline began, but he guessed they could have figured out how to climb it. His head swiveled from one way to the next. From a lush, beautiful forest to a dingy, damp hole. "And we can't go around because…?"

He trailed off purposefully, knowing Celeste would have an answer already lined up. "The forest won't take us there. There's only one way to the ocean and the boat from this direction, and it's this cave."

"Need we ask why the boat is so far away?" Katalina asked as she examined their surroundings further. "Wouldn't your family want to own one closer?"

"Ah, it's both close and far, depending on the day. The sides of my planet shift for no rhyme or reason. Only the cave knows the way to the correct side, so it's our fastest and safest bet. We could end up walking for eight more hours or days or weeks, otherwise! But the cave will—"

A roar rumbled throughout the walls, echoing off itself until landing in his eardrums in a horrid, incoherent thrum. He could hardly follow Celeste's absurd claims regarding the sides of a planet changing. What did that even mean?

Mark jumped back as he paled. "So there's only one way to go… and there's a monster inside?"

Celeste waved him off. "It's just an ecklweckl. It's probably tired—ecklweckls can read minds when they're sleeping, which means we probably just woke it up."

"I don't think you know when to use the word 'just,'" Noah said with a smile, his tone seeped in sarcasm. "Because I wouldn't start a sentence with it's 'just' a shapeshifter, or 'just' a man-eating monster named ecklweckl that's ready to eat us."

"Ecklweckls only kill mean people," she said. "It's in their nature."

Noah let out a soft gasp as he raised a hand to his mouth. To no one in particular, he said, "Mark's doomed."

"But all jokes aside, I'm not going in there," Noah added with a nod toward the cave entrance. The name of the creature was surprisingly cute, like a pet name given to a significant other, but its roar told a different story. Noah's stomach seemed to sink as his gaze remained locked on the black hole staring back at him.

Falling through the sky? Sure. Kissing a shapeshifter that looked like a bird in the name of survival? Okay. But an unlit cave with a monster inside? He was good to sit this one out.

"What if the cave gets narrower?" Katalina asked, inching closer to Mark for support. "And we can't pass through? Or if we get lost?"

Celeste patted Katalina on the shoulder. "Then the monster wouldn't be very big, and you'd have nothing to worry about."

Except getting stuck, never to see the light of day again as the planets exploded and all hope was lost. Right. Nothing to worry about.

"Come on," Celeste prodded, leading the way one slow step at a time. She grabbed Noah's wrist as though she knew he may try to run the other way if she didn't keep a close eye on him.

She was probably right, too; the thought was lingering in the back of his mind.

But, of course, he pushed forth. He was morally obligated to at this point.

When they first entered the cave, natural light poured in from the opening they'd come from—but then they got deeper, and the light faded along with everything else, and his heart couldn't help but rattle his ribcage.

"Are you sure about this?" he asked.

She chuckled. "Are you afraid of the dark?"

"No, it's not that. It's more so that I'm afraid of being crushed by falling rocks, or getting stuck in between two very narrow rocks, or starving to death surrounded by rocks, or getting eaten by a giant monster..."

"I find myself unsurprised by this fear," Mark interjected. "And yet surprised you're not afraid of everything else we've done."

"Pulling away from that shapeshifter after we kissed was a close second," Noah muttered, an added shudder rippling through his spine.

Mark snorted but refrained from making yet another snarky remark, which Noah was thankful for. Every nerve was on end, his hairs sticking up as the air became thinner—or were his breaths becoming shorter?

It was neither, evidently, and his chest felt like it may explode as intense, rapid breaths started escaping him. His hands were shaking. His throat was dry.

Oh, no.

He was having a panic attack. Again. Why was he always on the verge of panic?

"Are you okay?" Katalina asked, grabbing his shoulder from behind. "You're breathing incredibly heavy—"

Before anything more could leave her lips, the ground rumbled and shifted, and he lost his footing.

23

MARK'S DILEMMA

NOAH FELL ON HIS BUTT. HARD. THE GROUND WAS SMOOTH, BUT the landing was rough, and his tailbone paid the price. Worse still, panic continued to flow through him, but now it'd doubled.

The cave was filled with a cacophony of ripping and creaking as the ground rumbled once more. It was too loud and dark to decipher where Celeste and the others were, and his stomach dropped—had he lost them all?

Pockets of light began drifting in, breaking through small holes littering the foundation of the cave. The other three were surrounding him in various states of disarray. He spotted Mark first, who clung to the wall with Katalina pressed protectively against him, her arms wrapped around his waist.

"We could be playing kickball right now," Katalina yelled. "Our team was depending on us! But we're going to die, instead!"

Noah attempted to stand as his eyes found Celeste. She was leaning against the wall opposite of him in a half-squat. Her gaze was fixed on the ground, and he understood why—the moment he looked up, he became woozy and lost his footing once again.

"Goddesses, I miss kickball," Mark said. "But we'll have plenty more time to play after saving the planets... probably!"

"What's going on?" Noah called, ignoring Mark's strangely pessimistic optimism as nausea pulled him down further. He remembered Celeste's suggestion to hum whenever he felt sick, and so he did. It took a moment or two, but miraculously, he felt better.

"We're in the Winged Cave. Sorry, I should've mentioned it earlier," she yelled over the howling wind and growing chill of his bones.

"How do you keep forgetting to tell us this stuff?" Katalina cried, but her voice was lost in the wind.

Noah braced himself for another attempt at standing, and he found his footing—but then another bump sent his arms windmilling. Seconds from crashing to the ground, a hand caught him from the front of his shirt and pulled him forward. He and Celeste landed upright with her back against the cavern wall, his arms out on either side of her head. Their faces were inches from each other. All he had to do was—

"This should get us most of the way there," she whispered, and her eyes didn't drift from his, so he kept his where they were. Though he had to admit, the prolonged staring contest created a pang of heat within him. Noah shifted uncomfortably in his spot, the heat rising to places he'd rather avoid.

"Does everything here fly?" he whispered back. "Because you should give a warning whenever flying is involved."

Celeste nodded. "A lot of things do, so I think that's probably wise."

He found himself slowly leaning in to fill the small space between them. The cave was flying, and he was scared, and there was a monster somewhere inside, but all he could think about was her.

"Um," Celeste said, patting his shoulders before finally looking away. "They're staring."

Noah glanced over his shoulder to see Mark and Katalina staring back. He glared with a subtle shake of his head. Noah could've sworn he saw a flicker of something between him and Celeste, but then the moment was disrupted and disappeared.

"Sorry." He jumped back quickly, and his foot got caught on a rock. Noah clasped his eyes shut and when he opened them again, he was on the ground, looking up at Celeste with a twinge of utter embarrassment. It was a look he'd worn a lot the last few days and one he wore well.

"Why does the cave fly?" Noah asked, inspecting the walls further. There were thin cracks like veins running along them, and small holes letting in the light. They were still too deep within the cave to see an opening, but the amount of light pouring in was enough for now.

"How else would it get home?" Celeste asked. "And the ecklweckl needs a ride home, too."

As though it heard her, the ecklweckl—which was a name that felt incredibly silly to think, hear, or say—roared again. The vibrations were louder now, closer.

"Whenever he wakes up, the cave takes him home. And home is by—" She nodded for someone else to fill in the blank.

Katalina snapped her fingers. "The ocean!"

"And one point for Katalina! You're in the lead!" Celeste said with the thrust of a finger. Noah hadn't been aware there was a game to play and points to be won. The confused look on Mark's face confirmed this was news to them both, but Katalina bobbed up and down with excitement.

"Oh, good!" Katalina said, clapping her hands. "I love a good game of winning!"

"Women, one. Boys—"

"Men," Mark interrupted.

"Either way, you both have zero."

"We'll accept this challenge," Mark said before Noah could get a word in edge-wise, and suddenly they were shaking hands with Celeste and Katalina. There were no parameters as to how one got a point or when they would be given, yet a sense of adversarial tension fell over the scene.

Another screech echoed through the cave. It was different this time, a high-pitched wail instead of a guttural, primal roar, and it instantly forced him to a knee as he covered his ears. Wincing, he yelled, "Is that something else? Is something else in here with us?"

Noah felt faint, his breathing short and rigid. Celeste let out a nervous chuckle as she stepped up beside him and squeezed his shoulder. Somehow, it helped. It wasn't enough to stop the panic roiling through his body and mind, but it was all she could do, and it was enough. "It certainly makes the ecklweckl seem less daunting, doesn't it?"

"No, Celeste," Mark yelled. "Having *two* monsters instead of one isn't *less* daunting."

Another howl erupted, and Noah shrank away from the looming darkness. For the first time in his life, he was genuinely terrified—they could very well die here, and he would've chosen flight over fight if there was anywhere else to go.

As that thought passed, a steady clanking of hooves bounced off the walls. Katalina and Mark were off in the corner behind Noah while he stood in the center with Celeste. He gulped as a figure began taking shape in the dim light. The majestic beast looked like a fluffy white deer with two antlers twisting around themselves beside long, floppy ears.

Noah's shoulders relaxed as he scanned the beast. The eyes were deep brown and unassuming, and he determined it was likely nothing more than a harmless animal. They had nothing to worry about. They were safe.

The deer rubbed a hoof against the ground with a harsh huff. It lowered its snout, the antlers suddenly incredibly large and sharpened at the tips—and pointed directly at him and Celeste.

Noah's smile dropped as the beast charged, and he pushed Celeste out of the way. She let out a sharp gasp, and he wished he could check that she was okay, but he was too scared to look away.

His eyes remained glued to the deer as time slowed. Noah pushed himself to the side before he was impaled head-on, but a sharp pain erupted in his left arm. The deer burst past, an antler slicing through his skin. It was no deeper than a paper cut, but it drew blood, and it was slowly seeping out.

Noah yelped, pressing his other hand against the wound. Another pang of agony shot through him and his fingers were tingling, but he clenched his jaw and continued to maneuver away until he was pressed against the wall beside Celeste.

"Are you okay?" she asked, worry lining her voice. Noah sucked in a deep, trembling breath.

"That's a loaded question." He gave her a wavering half-smile, and she placed a hand over his. He winced—it was the wounded, tingling hand, but he didn't want to cause worry, so he breathed through the pain.

"One day it won't be."

He turned to look at her; her face was cast with both sun and shadow from the cave walls, her eyes shimmering from the light. She'd been so matter-of-fact that he nearly laughed. "How do you know?"

A shrill cry rattled the cave, and Noah let out a frustrated yell. Celeste had taken his stress away so easily, and life brought it back just as quickly. Noah's eyes found the beast, which had skidded to a stop after charging, and turned back around.

Noah gulped; he could've sworn the creature was staring directly at him. He was going to be impaled by a deer with a vendetta.

"It's only attacking me?" he shouted as he took off, sprinting deeper into the cave. He checked behind him only once to find his friends, but they were blurry as he ran, and their words were lost in the frenzy of his heartbeat and nervous breathing.

No, he couldn't be experiencing tunnel vision in a moment like this. Was he experiencing *another* panic attack?

He couldn't escape himself, could he?

Hooves continued to clank against the solid rock floor, and he hadn't a clue what to do except run and hope the ecklweckl got to him first. He wondered if this was a cruel test by the universe, designed to make him do the cardio exercises he always promised himself he'd get around to doing but never did.

"You got this, Noah!" Celeste yelled with a fist in the air as he ran past her and looped back around. The creature trailed behind, completely ignoring Celeste. "That's a derithia! It usually attacks the first target it locks eyes on! But you got this, you can beat it!"

"With what?" Noah called back. His unlucky streak continued to follow him wherever he went. "My fist in its antlers?"

"Well, when you put it like that"—she cut herself off with a gasp before adding—"Quick! Noah, Mark, I almost forgot! Take these pencils and draw a weapon!" Noah glanced back to see she was holding out two yellow pencils. Her other hand was around the original bag she'd brought with the watch and research notebook—was it truly disappearing and coming back when called to? He couldn't be certain.

"It will become tangible," Celeste yelled. "Even if you draw something from Sundar! Quickly!"

"Are you insane? I can't stop running long enough to draw a picture!" Cool sweat was trickling down Noah's face, and his breathing was notably heavier. He wouldn't be able to run for much longer at this pace, and when he glanced down and saw his blood, wooziness threatened to take hold. He tried to remind himself it was only a minor cut, but he was afraid of looking again. Glancing at even the smallest of paper cuts could send him into a bout of nausea.

"Why us?" Mark shouted. Noah couldn't afford to look back and see if Mark was drawing anything. Noah made his way further into the cave, fearing he might get lost forever before being swiftly killed by the evil deer.

"It's the gentlemen's duty!" Celeste called. "The cave isn't as progressive as our people yet! It thinks only men should slay the beasts!"

"You don't want to fight it," Mark accused while Noah focused on dodging to the left at the last second, effectively gaining more distance between him and the derithia. He circled back to where Katalina, Celeste, and Mark were huddled on the ground, each desperately trying to conjure a weapon. Relief washed over him. At the very least, his friends were there for him.

Wait—friends? Did he view Mark, Celeste, and his cousin as... friends?

"It's a mix of both," she admitted. "But I really can't conjure anything. Katalina, have you tried?"

"Nothing happened," Katalina agreed with a disappointed shake of her head. By now, Noah had made an extended U-turn and headed back in their direction, the glorified deer in tow. How hadn't the animal caught up to him by now? Was the derithia toying with him? A fun little chase before the kill?

"*Mark,*" Katalina's voice rang out forcefully. It was impressive, given how quiet she normally was, even when she was trying to be demanding. "Help him!"

"I'm trying," Mark yelled. Noah ran past as Mark drew on the cave floor. Noah couldn't make out what he was drawing—but he thought it might be a sword or a wrench. It looked a lot like a wrench, now that he thought about it, and that worried Noah more. "I'm trying, but I can't. I—I can't! Nothing is happening!"

Mark sounded desperate, and Noah felt that desperation in his core. "But I can—I can provide moral support!" He turned to Noah. "Whatever sport you played growing up, channel that energy and anger you felt toward the opposing team before a game!"

Noah was heading the way they came, and he wondered if he would accidentally run out of the flying cave and fall to his death. Wait—there was an idea in there, somewhere. He could try to trick the derithia into falling out of the cave's entrance—though there was a chance Noah miscalculated and fell out, too.

"What sport does it look like I played?" Noah called back. His heart was beating out of his chest, his mouth parted as he heaved. Sweat was threatening to pour into his eyes, and he felt like he was about to keel over. "Because the answer is obviously none of them!"

Noah blinked, and the world felt like it was tipping and folding in at the edges. His eyes snapped back open and the tunnel in his vision widened slightly. He stumbled but found his footing and yelled, "Guys? I need serious help here! I can't keep going like this!"

And by the goddesses, he needed water.

"*Mark!*" came Celeste and Katalina's cries in unison.

"Help him, Mark," Celeste begged again, drawing feverishly on the ground to no avail.

Noah's lungs were moments from bursting, and he gasped with each breath. Another blink, and he lost his footing, sliding against the smooth rock floor. He faltered, every inch of his body burning, but he hadn't the time to assess the damage.

He flipped himself over, but he wasn't quick enough.

The derithia advanced, and Noah released a shuddering breath at the size of it up close. Its snout was a dark brown, the mouth lined with rows of sharp, jagged teeth. The beast released a hoarse huff and placed two hooves on either side of Noah's body. No—six. It had six feet, three on each side, effectively trapping Noah with a hunk of fluff towering above.

"Now would be a good time to do something," he said, his voice riddled with terror and exhaustion. His eyes widened as the derithia leaned down to sniff his face, his body paralyzed with fear.

Why weren't they listening? Did his so-called friends *want* him to die? Was there nothing that could be done?

The derithia's eyes morphed from brown pits of despair to molten red and gray, and they seemed to flare as the beast breathed heavily on his face. The rancid, fishy smell that exuded from the derithia's mouth nearly made Noah gag, but he held it in for fear of moving and angering the thing.

"Noah, I conjured a knife," Mark yelled.

Noah crinkled his brows. "And are you going to use it?"

There was nothing Noah could do but stare. Could he try to push the derithia away from him? No—it was too big. Worse still, Mark didn't respond. His hesitation to act was evident in the silence that followed. There was no choice then, was there? Noah had to try pushing the creature off and crawl away as fast as he could. He couldn't lay here and let his demise happen; he had to at least *try* to live.

Didn't he?

Did he?

Maybe the world needed to end.

Maybe everything did.

His intent wavered, and he wondered if this was it. If this was the end before the end.

The derithia released a yelp as it was thrust to the side and off Noah's prone body. He stared up at where the creature had been and held his breath.

Turning his head, he saw that the beast had flown like it weighed nothing more than a pillow, landing a few feet away on its side in a stiff, toy-like manner. It was a sight that made Noah laugh in surprise; the derithia was menacing one moment, and unceremoniously nonthreatening the next.

Noah's eyes snapped to his savior.

Nearest was Katalina, of all people, with a foot outstretched. He continued to stare up at her, befuddled. "You... kicked it?"

She nodded. "It was the least I could do—since Mark was being completely *useless*."

"Another point for the women!" Celeste exclaimed, bringing back the game he'd forgotten they were playing, a betless bet the men were evidently projected to lose. Celeste pointed at Katalina with a nod of approval. "Women—two. Men—zero!"

"Hey, maybe I helped. Maybe, in a roundabout way, the cave

sees women should be able to conjure weapons, too," Mark retorted before squatting to meet Noah's gaze. He looked apologetic as he held up the knife he'd announced possession of and said, "I'm sorry I couldn't help you. I've never killed an animal before. I couldn't do it, but I'm happy you're alright."

Noah nodded before giving Mark a reassuring smile. "It's okay. I don't know if I would've hurt it, either, as weird as that sounds. Though it *does* give me a fresh perspective. Even a muscular, inarguably intimidating man can crack under pressure."

Mark tsked. "Ah, a backhanded compliment. You sound like my mother." Mark's eyes widened as the last word came out, but Noah had hardly registered why. His brain was in a fog, one where nothing could be deciphered for no particular reason. He did not react to Mark's joke or expression, and Celeste came to the rescue before the silence dragged on for too long and he started to think about it.

"Are you okay, Noah? You look like you're in shock," Celeste asked with brows crinkled in concern. Shock? He wanted to say something snarky in response, but the fog in his brain remained, and nothing came out. Celeste stood in front of him and grabbed his arms. Her eyes searched his, and he wondered what she saw.

What did he see?

Was she as lost as he?

"Derithia's induce fear, but I don't think it would've physically harmed you," she added.

"You don't think?" he asked, his complexion paling. Her words weren't as comforting as she seemed to think. Noah finally stood and brushed himself off, and when he checked the cut on his hand, he found it was no longer there. Had the derithia... healed him? "Have you ever asked yourself if saving the world is worth it without your brother here?"

"What do you mean?" Celeste's smile dropped, and he could tell he'd struck a nerve neither wanted pinched, yet the question slipped from his lips without a thought or care.

"Wouldn't it be easier to let everything be destroyed so you could see him sooner?" he asked.

She cocked her head. "Why would I want to see him sooner when I know I'll spend an eternity with him? Why not enjoy my time here while I can?"

Noah didn't respond, instead leaning against the cave wall with his head tilted toward the ceiling. A stream of sunlight poured into his pupils from a nearby crack in the foundation, and he took a deep breath as he absorbed the slight sun. It was still difficult for him to feel anything, and he supposed she was right and he was in shock. Would it pass, or would he be stuck in this limbo forever?

He could discern one thing—Noah felt as though he may fly away. The last note of a harp drifting on a soft breeze; the last call of a bird before night fell. Did he matter—did anything matter? Or was he nothing more than another blot on a horizon that never ended? They would save the worlds—but for what? What did he have to go back to? Maybe it was better for the planets to be destroyed.

They were trying to change the course of nature based on a series of hunches and myths. The pressure was insurmountable. But he was also experiencing impossible feats, and he'd been saved by a perfect stranger, and a flutter sprouted within him he'd never felt before. If there was one thing he longed to feel forever, it was the pang of *need,* of *want,* for her. He pressed his eyes closed and refused to open them.

This was the worst experience of his life.

He'd never had more fun.

24

ALONE AT THE RIVER

THE CAVE DESCENDED LEISURELY BACK TO THE GROUND AFTER another hour in the sky. When he stepped out, he was surprised to find they'd been dropped off at the edge of yet another forest. Though now, the trees were various shades of pastel and hot pink. Even in the darkness of their first night away from the city, the trees were exceptionally bright.

The ecklweckl remained in the cave, yet to be seen, and the derithia hadn't gotten up since it'd been kicked. It almost felt as though the creature had an 'off' switch, and Katalina knew exactly where it was. Though he'd inspected the creature extensively, and couldn't find a wound or reason as to why it didn't stand back up.

Night was rapidly approaching, and they collectively decided to stop for the evening a few feet from a bubbling stream. He was thankful for this, as was his body; their adventures were far too strenuous to keep going another minute.

Katalina and Mark set up the tents while Noah and Celeste were tasked with foraging for berries and collecting drinking water. Naturally, he was terrified of venturing into the woods alone, so the pair embarked together.

"I'm sorry for earlier," Noah said as soon as they were out of earshot of the other two—he didn't need Mark mocking him later on.

"For which part?"

His eyebrows rose at that. "I hadn't known there were parts... but probably for staring at you for too long back in the cave... and for everything else. I'm not exactly the best companion to bring on a world-saving adventure, and obviously, my long-lost family isn't much better at it, either."

Celeste chuckled. "If you're apologizing for all of *that*—even if it *is* completely unprecedented, mind you—then I suppose I should formally apologize for dragging you here with me in the first place."

"Why would you apologize? Without you, I would've thought everything in my life would forever be as it was. My thoughts were so endlessly dark that I thought I'd jump off the edge of Sundar—"

"Which, to be fair, you did," she added. He paused for a moment, losing his point along the way.

Noah tilted his head in thought before smiling. "True. I guess I did. But my intentions were far from saving the planet before we met. I wanted to save myself."

"So then... why didn't you jump? What stopped you?"

He chuckled, knowing how ridiculous it would probably sound. "My cat. Henrietta is too pure to be left all alone."

"And that's why you said yes to helping me save the planets, too? To save your cat?"

Noah blushed, fiddling with a piece of blond hair that kept falling into his eyes. He made a note of asking if there were hairdressers on Fortun or better yet, if she could cut his hair. At this point, he'd be surprised if she said no. Finally, he nodded, though the answer was *her,* and she laughed.

"Well, it's nice to know all of cat-kind can depend on you," she said.

"No, no. Not all of cat-kind. Just Henrietta... and I could add people with five percent 'hare' in their bloodline, too," he added, calling back to that rather odd tidbit of information she'd proudly provided prior.

She laughed again. "But you didn't have a passion or career path or something to work toward? Something to fulfill you?"

He gulped. She was asking the hard-hitting questions he'd rather not answer. "No. I'd worked in a kitchen for a few years, but nothing else was satisfying. I made money to exist, I guess."

"A kitchen, though? That's pretty cool—so you can cook?"

Noah sucked in a deep breath. He was always prone to downplaying himself for reasons he would never understand. He *could* cook, but he couldn't call himself *a* cook. "I was the dishwasher, but saying 'I worked in a kitchen' sounds better, doesn't it?"

"We'll find you a dream," she said, her tone hopeful, her smile soft and reassuring. "After all of this is said and done."

The conversation was lost; he didn't want to put her on the spot and ask why she was unemployed, too, and if he didn't clamp his jaw shut, he wouldn't be able to contain his true feelings toward her.

We barely know each other, Noah reminded himself, yet her words continued to ring in his head. *We'll find you a dream.*

Celeste went to collect water from the stream while he gathered a few plants she told him were safe to eat. All the while, he couldn't wait to get back to her. He'd been holed up in funeral planning and figuring out the will and selling the house and everything else that came with being the sole beneficiary. Now, he could finally have a life. He could finally talk to someone. Be *with* someone.

Noah had spoken to a few women in town, but no one made him feel much of anything. Until now. Perhaps it was the way her blackish-blue hair shimmered in the light, or how her eyes danced with excitement at every turn, or how she brought about a sense of calm and laughter and light. A sense of *home.* No one was as beautiful as her, for that he was sure.

A few minutes after foraging, he waited by the river until Celeste came into view, struggling to carry two jugs of water. Her knees were half-bent and her face was scrunched in a mix of pain, strain, and trying to look like she didn't need help.

"I got it," Noah called. He rushed to her side, quickly grabbing one jug, handing her the berry bags, and then grabbing the other. He wasn't particularly strong, but the jugs were so light he suspected she was pretending to struggle just to see how he would react.

He wondered if he had passed the test.

"Thank you. Wow, my wrists are *sore.* You have no idea how

harsh that current is! I could barely keep the jugs from being swept away!"

"Where'd you get them anyway?" he asked.

"The river supplies them, of course. No one knows how they're produced, but they float down with the current. Sort of like how I found those berry bags of yours and gave them to you, too."

He glanced down at the plastic bags in her hands filled with various shades of neon reds and oranges. He hadn't questioned where she got the bags, and it seemed absurd to suggest the forest supplied them with what they needed.

"And the tents?"

"I have a friend who's a friend of a friend of the Ruler of the Soil, and the Ruler owes said friend a favor. Basically, I'm lucky, and the Ruler of the Soil is a bit too nice. He used ants to send the tents through the soil."

Noah couldn't remember questioning where the tents had come from when they'd stumbled upon them, either. When had he started accepting the oddities surrounding him as fact?

The rest of their conversations were airy, and he couldn't help but feel like his words were dancing from his lips joyfully between flurries of laughter. He could've sworn their pace had slowed; surely, they would've made it to the campsite by now.

What a strange feeling. Here he was, utterly exhausted. A man who used to never want to see the light of day, now in this weird state where he wanted both life and death yet neither—but mostly he wanted to be by her side. "If you could go to any planet, which would it be?"

He knew, of course, that their galaxies were completely

different, separated by a thick layer of distorted time and space, and neither of them would know what the other was talking about. Still, he loved the idea of more planets, and he couldn't wait to hear how hers were described.

"I'd go to any of them, as long as you were with me."

Noah stopped walking, a blush creeping onto his features as his throat ran dry. She stopped a beat after. He'd never met someone so bold before, and he had to admit—he loved finally feeling *seen*.

He was so unbelievably flattered that his brain overheated, and all his thoughts were replaced with her delicate laugh at the look on his face. Somehow, he dug himself out of his thoughts and added with a chuckle, "Oh, my—are you flirting with me?"

She let out a full-bellied burst of laughter then, her head arching back as the breeze brisked through her hair. "Of course! It's only right since you've been staring at me so much, basically begging me to do something about it."

"And you want to?" he asked, his heart thundering in his chest. "You want to do something about it?"

"Of course. I wouldn't state my obvious feelings otherwise," she said before nodding for them to keep walking. Celeste led the way back to camp, where Mark and Katalina were putting the finishing touches on a small campfire they'd prepared. "But there's a time and a place. For now, go on and get some sleep. We'll be at our next roadblock by early morning."

He nodded with a slight smile, pausing once more beside the fire. It crackled, sending a shiver down his spine as the heat from the flames clawed at his face. They were standing shoulder-to-shoulder, peering into each other's eyes, and he thought there might be more, but she backed away and turned toward one of the two tents.

"Goodnight," he called as she disappeared inside.

She popped her head back out and said with a smile and a wink, "Goodnight, Noah."

Noah's heart skipped as his thoughts drifted to fantasies of them pressed together in bed. Katalina was sitting beside the fire using a stick to fix the kindling, Mark standing beside her. When she noticed Celeste wasn't coming back, Katalina exclaimed, "What? We made this awesome fire and you're both going to bed? Come on, stay up for a little longer!"

He shook his head, an involuntary yawn proving his point. "I need to rest for now. Long day."

Noah went into the other tent and prepared to sleep, curling up under a wafer-thin blanket on top of a mat barely big enough for his body. He vaguely questioned where they got all this extra camping equipment, but he chalked it up to either the Ruler of the Soil or this odd, bright pink forest.

As his eyes fell closed and sleep took hold, the lip of the tent's entrance shuffled open. Noah sighed as his eyes fluttered open. He turned, hoping to see Celeste, but was unsurprised to find it was Mark, instead. "Great. You again."

"Well, if you knew how to *stick* the landing"—Mark's mouth transformed into a wide smile at his sexual innuendo. Noah let out a snort before he could stop himself, though he wasn't entirely sold on the quality of the joke—"Then *I* would be with my fiancée. So it looks like we're both striking out tonight."

25

He thought he would dream of her after their conversation, but when he awoke, he found he hadn't dreamed of anything at all.

26

ROCK HOPPING

IT'D BEEN TWO DAYS SINCE THEIR JOURNEY FROM THE CITY BEGAN, and they were still venturing through uncharted land with no sight of the ocean or a boat to go along with it.

All the while, he couldn't shake the horror he felt as the derithia's blazing eyes bore into his soul. Flames seemed to erupt within molten reddish grey, pouring into Noah and melting away his core. Like the beast had taken part of his livelihood and stripped it from him.

His fingers no longer tingled, but something within him had gone numb. Was this what compartmentalization felt like? A feeling shoved so far down it wasn't felt anymore, though it was still there? Lingering. Waiting.

The trees led to a clearing, and his mouth dropped open. Spanning from left to right was either a patch of water or land that looked to be a mirror, reflecting each detail above with such clarity that it looked like a painting—a theme within this world, it seemed. The pink and purple wisps of the plump clouds and day-lit sky filled the entire ground and didn't seem to end.

The reflective ground was distorted only by rocks floating in space, much like the outskirts of his hometown. Katalina looked to have the same thought process because she peered over the edge where the grass disappeared and the reflection began, and asked, "Is this because of the gravitational pull of the black hole, too?"

Celeste shook her head as she stepped up to the ledge. "No, actually, this is a phenomenon that has popped up all over Fortun, usually near ocean shores. They say it's a pocket of time and space that has been created from desolation. No life was here for hundreds of years, so the land ripped away at itself and became a pocket like this."

"That makes no sense," Katalina countered with a raised brow. Noah almost argued that it was as nonsensical for Celeste to say as it was for Katalina to point out, but he determined it would be a moot point. "And isn't there plenty of wildlife around us now?"

"I'm probably not explaining it well. My brother was always much better at the science stuff than me, but I remember he mentioned these pockets both save and destroy where they end up. Because now, nothing will grow past this spot. But, on the other hand, wildlife always follows. The surrounding areas become overgrown."

"Interesting. A completely adverse reaction," Katalina muttered. Noah couldn't stop staring at the reflective pink and purple scene before him, and he didn't want to. It shimmered like a pool on a hot day, inviting him in, and he couldn't deny his body's need to drift closer. "What happens if you fall?"

"Please tell me we're done with the sky and falling," Mark said. "I think we've all hit our yearly quota."

"I second that," Noah added quickly, a hand raised.

"Quite the opposite. We'll want to take the floating pieces of land across. Then we should reach the ocean."

"And if one of us falls?" Noah pressed, sharing a glance with Mark that signaled neither of them wanted to put their lives in any more danger. He looked at Katalina next, whose prominent frown indicated she regretted following him all this way. Noah made a mental note that he still had to ask her *why* she had bothered to come.

Noah understood, to an extent, but there was no turning back at a time like this. Turning around meant being stuck on a planet they didn't know or understand. Turning around meant accepting that the world, and everything they'd ever come to know, was going to end.

"You fall in an endless loop," Celeste said. "It resets at some point, and then again and again until, well, I guess until someone catches you."

There was silence among them as he and the other two collectively shuddered. Mark placed a protective arm around Katalina's shoulder, pulling her closer as she leaned her head against his chest.

Mark said softly to no one in particular, "So we'll be jumping from rock to rock and hoping none of them flip over? That sounds rather dangerous to me. If we all end up falling, there's a chance we'll never stop ourselves."

Mark's grip around Katalina tightened. Would Noah ever hold someone like that again? Would he ever feel love to the extent his cousin and Mark did? He didn't dare look at Celeste for fear of jinxing himself.

"It *is* rather difficult," Celeste admitted. "I've only jumped through a full Reflectivscape once, and I admittedly fell. My brother saved me. I was hoping we'd find a way without one, but... it's almost impossible not to run into one along the shores these days."

"Is there anything you haven't done?" Noah asked, tilting his head in wonder before taking in the reflective landscape ahead of them once more. He would never get used to the grandeur of the magenta clouds, and he smiled to himself.

"It's hard not to when you live here. Our schools often bounced between countries and continents and landscapes. Every semester throughout college, we'd step out of our dorms and into a completely new place. My favorite was the Sky Kingdom by far." Celeste let out a deep, longing sigh. "'It's best to experience the oddities of life in a controlled environment before they can control you.' My teachers loved saying things like that. Deep, but at a surface level, you know?"

The statement befuddled him, as it was inherently contradictory—oddities, by definition, couldn't be controlled—but he also had to admit that he *did* know. He thought as much when listening to music with so many words that said so little. A message that was never really there.

Mark rubbed his hands together, disrupting the philosophy being untangled in Noah's mind. "Alright, if it means we'll be one step closer to saving our planets, then let's do this!"

Noah stared at him, dumbfounded, along with Celeste and Katalina. Mark's brows furrowed at the lack of an equally irreverent response. "What?"

"You're... being positive?" Noah asked, stunned.

Mark's fingers curled into fists as his smile instantly reverted to its natural neutral state. "Well, fuck me for trying, right?"

And just like that, he was back to his usual self, throwing up his hands in exasperation with a shake of his head for good measure. Noah stifled a laugh as Mark put his hands on his hips and began pacing.

"This is you trying?" Noah asked, poking fun at the man like he thought friends did, but it looked to be the wrong thing to say. Mark's eyes flared with newfound anger as his head snapped to meet Noah's gaze. Noah put his hands up in defense and, before Mark could get a word out, said, "Sorry—I was joking. Too far, I know. Too far."

"So you expect all of us to cut you some slack when you say douchy things because your mom died, yet no matter what I do, for no good reason, I'm getting hounded?" Mark asked. His voice echoed through the reflective scene as though the sky and the ground were walls of yet another cave.

Noah would've found it fascinating, if not for Mark's comment still ringing in his ears. Angry tears welled, threatening to fall, but he refused to let them. He would not let Mark's cruelty win, though it stung all the same.

The longer Noah stuck around, the more he understood why his mother didn't.

He gulped, trying to scrub any intrusive thoughts from his mind. Noah looked up at the wispy clouds and counted them by their swirls of color—five pastel pink, six purple, three blue. Calmness washed over him, and soon he could look Mark in the eyes—but he still hadn't a clue what to say.

So he brushed past Mark with a shoulder bumping into his and stopped with his toes pressed against the ledge between land and where the reflection began. Two sturdy boulders were floating about two feet away. He assessed them for hand and foot placements before deducing he had better odds with the one to the left.

The top was flat, as they all were, and the lack of solid ground was incredibly terrifying. If he didn't jump now, he never would. His feet were already begging for him to turn the other way.

Noah took a deep breath and jumped.

He stuck the landing with a grunt as he wobbled atop the rock, crouching to maintain his balance. With his arms out on either side, it looked like he was surfing in the air. He waited a beat longer to fully stabilize the floating rock and then he righted himself.

"Good job, Mark," Katalina hissed, somehow loud enough for Noah to hear, and it only made him angrier. He'd committed a rather brave and incredible feat, yet pity took hold of his image yet again.

Noah preserved what little pride he had left and kept his eyes ahead, though he desperately wanted to check if Celeste was close. Did she feel sorry for him, too?

He took another deep breath before jumping to the next rock, then the next. Noah eventually checked over his shoulder to spot Mark was the closest behind, with Celeste taking up the rear, and he regretted starting without her and leaving her so far behind.

Up and down all looked the same, and if he didn't keep his eyes ahead, he would start to feel lost in an endless sky. The others must've felt the same because they were all silently jumping between rocks and maintaining their balance.

A gasp escaped from behind him, subtle yet profoundly frightened in a single breath, and he spun around quickly. Katalina had slipped, and now she was desperately clinging to the rock she'd been standing on. Her fingers were turning white as she held on for dear life, the rock tipping sideways, then flipping over and over. She somehow held on with both arms and legs contorted around the rock as she screamed.

"Hold on, Katalina, I've got you," yelled Mark, bending as low as he could before reaching for her.

Noah jumped between two rocks in quick succession, landing beside Katalina on the other side of Mark. He took up the same position Mark was in, both their arms outstretched. Noah grabbed Katalina's rock, gripping it with all his strength until she finally stopped twirling in circles.

Then came Mark, who grabbed Katalina's foot and pushed one of her wobbling legs all the way up onto the flatter surface of the rock. She swung her second leg over, and suddenly she was stabilized on her stomach, with legs bent sideways to fit onto her limited platform.

Katalina kept her eyes on the bottomless ground; magenta clouds and sky stared back with a faint reflective sheen. Her hands were shaking, but she was okay.

Mark said what they were all thinking, "Thank the

Goddesses, Katalina. Who knows what we would've done if you'd fallen?"

Noah nodded as the stress of the situation evaporated, and his discomfort towards Mark's words went along with it. "Ain't that ri—"

He pushed his hand off her rock and slipped, his balance instantly lost. His body flung forward as he scrambled to get a solid grip on the rock. There was none to be found. His fingers loosened, and then he fell.

27

ENDLESS LOOP

Celeste told them anyone who fell would fall indefinitely. An endless loop of constant stomach-dropping, nausea-inducing movement. Although she may not have gone into that specific of detail, he still expected as such upon the initial pull of gravity.

His assumptions were wrong. Whatever he was experiencing could hardly be classified as a fall at all. Instead, it felt as though he were almost completely still, hovering in the center of an expansive universe. The reflective ground made way for a galaxy speckled with stars and bright auras of golden-blue and purple and pink hues. No longer were there rocks to hop from, or family to argue with.

Noah was alone.

He was always alone.

He was breathless, completely and utterly shrouded in glorious, sparkling light as he remained suspended stomach-first in the air, his arms outstretched on either side. There was a slight breeze, though it didn't align with how motionless he felt, or how slowly the three blobs below came into focus.

There they were, staring up at him on a rock big enough for three. Mark knelt in the center to keep their collective balance, while Celeste and Katalina stood on either side. Celeste held out an arm, fingers separating with strain as she struggled to reach him.

Close, but not close enough, and he slipped by, his eyes catching hers at the exact moment they passed each other, a split second between only them. Her eyes were big and beautiful and bright—and worried. They'd traveled together for almost two weeks, graduating from strangers to friends somewhere in between, yet the notion of her worrying about him was still surprising.

Noah's lungs begged for him to call out to her, but words did not come. After another failed attempt, he was left with only one choice—to enjoy *this.* A long, narrow galaxy swirled off in the distance, transforming from green to blue to purple in a mosaic of twinkling lights and stardust. There were planets upon planets, big and small and everything in between—some with rings and moons and craters, and others with nothing at all, a perfectly smooth plain devoid of obstruction or life.

A tear slipped up his temple and trailed past his hairline, drifting into the cosmos behind him as he fell. Was it still considered falling if there was no apparent end or beginning? At what point did falling become nothing more than existing?

Another tear slipped, then another and another, until he was certain that if he looked over his shoulder now, he would see a stream of droplets floating behind him. The brightness of the stars, the vastness of everything; the universe wasn't just a universe. It was one stacked upon another, which was stacked upon another. It was *endless.*

Why, then, did life have to be what ended?

A sob remained lodged in his throat. Because, of course, the first person he would tell about something as extraordinary as this was his mother. And, of course, he finally met someone who she would've been excited about on his behalf. She always gravitated toward those who were bubbly and presented themselves as happy, even if she wasn't. As though she could take a piece of their joy if they just stuck around long enough.

Why did she leave him behind? He would ask himself this over and over again, and come to a million conclusions, but he would never truly know. There was no note, or letter, or message passed along by another. All he knew was that she was so fed up that she needed to go.

And by the Goddesses, did he want nothing more than to show her this right now. He looked over, and he could swear he saw her beside him with her reddish-blond hair whipping in the wind, their fingers interlaced. Their eyes met, a smile painted along her features.

He blinked, and she was gone.

A forceful jerk of his body brought him back to the present, and he released a loud *oof* as he was pulled on top of something and next to someone. He expected it to be Celeste, but it was Mark, and now Noah was lying with an arm wrapped around Mark's neck and a leg around his torso.

Noah scooched away, temporarily forgetting they were

floating on groundless ground. The rock wobbled, and he quickly readjusted himself so he didn't fall again—though he wouldn't mind a second go of it.

The galaxies were replaced by the reflection of the bright magenta sky and puffy clouds stretching as far as any of them could see. A few feet away, the other side was waiting, a patch of grass and trees and sand mixed into one.

Celeste and Noah exchanged a final glance before he jumped over the endless sky below and onto land. His legs stung, but he hardly noticed from the ache of everything else. He was officially physically and mentally exhausted. Behind him, the others followed, though he did not look away from the grass beneath him.

His chest grew tight, and he clutched at it desperately as he dropped to both knees with a sob. It was a guttural, half-suppressed howl full of agony, and it rattled within his ribcage as sorrow took hold.

Noah bent forward, his lips contorted in horrified misery; the way one looked when sadness consumed them whole, and all they could do was let go.

Celeste knelt in front of him, but he was too embarrassed to look up and meet her gaze, so he kept his head lowered. It was too much—too much to feel this powerfully in front of others about things he didn't fully understand. With any luck, she would turn around and wait until he settled before she realized what a mess he was.

What a lost cause he was.

A gentle hand grazed his cheek and lightly guided his green gaze up to meet hers. He must've looked terrible—his eyes stung with fresh tears, red-rimmed and half-sealed shut, and his mouth was still parted as sobs escaped. He sniffled, rubbing away at the tears trailing his cheeks.

"This probably isn't the best way to see me," he said with a soft chuckle despite himself.

Celeste smiled, a hint of sadness and understanding reflected within her gaze. Then she pressed her forehead against his, her eyes closed. They knelt in silence; the birds chirped overhead as the grass rustled in the distance. "Every way is the best way. There's no need to sell yourself short."

He leaned into her hand, feeling the dampness of his tears soak into her palm. Celeste's words washed over him like a waterfall of cascading comfort, and warmth filled him. Even if nothing more came of their time together, he was thankful for it. Kindness was so easily lost in life, and she somehow always knew how to find it.

Noah kept his eyes clamped shut, brows drawn together as he tried to suppress the sobs threatening to break. His shoulders bobbed while she silently rubbed her thumb in light circles over his cheekbone.

Warmth continued to spread along his back as someone hugged him from behind, and then a third pair of hands wrapped around his torso. He opened his eyes in surprise to find that Mark and Katalina had joined.

His embarrassment morphed into gratitude. Just this once, he was heard. His pain was recognized and accepted instead of pushed down. Words didn't need to be spoken, because everything was already written.

Noah did not ask Celeste if it got better, if the pain eventually went away, or if the grief dissipated with time, as with everything else. He knew, somewhere deep down, what the answer would be. But the sadness could be managed, he supposed, if he had something or someone to help. Here, he had three someones, all ready to offer a hand.

Why was he not enough for his mother to stay?

The tears fell harder as he closed his eyes and his cries rang out, "I'm sorry. I'm sorry. I'm sorry."

The words left his lips over and over as Celeste whispered sweet niceties in his ear. He could sense a hint of sadness in her voice, too, and if he were to look up, he would see fresh tears streaming down her cheeks.

Noah wished he could pause time and stay in this moment forever. Here he was seen. Here, he may have been stuck with his thoughts, but he was no longer trapped, because he had them.

"THANK YOU."

28

CALM TIDES

THE SHIP BOBBED CARELESSLY ON THE EBBING WAVES. AFTER three days of docile weather, they'd yet to spot another landmass or ship or even sea creature. The seacraft was on the smaller side, with enough room for ten people, but nothing more. There were two small triangular sails side-by-side in the center, facing away from the wind, yet billowing ferociously.

Noah was astonished they were staying afloat, but knowing the mechanics unnerved him more than not knowing, so he opted to do what he'd been doing since they stepped foot on this planet and just let it happen.

While Katalina and Mark were in the lower compartments to sleep before their night watch, Noah and Celeste remained on the top deck. He'd taken his leave to use the bathroom, and when he returned, she was leaning against the railing ahead.

"What was it like growing up here?" he asked, stepping up and leaning beside her. Peering ahead, his mouth fell open—

there was something there, disrupting the horizon. The pastel pink and purple clouds were gradually dimming as night neared.

He could feel her gaze from the corner of his eye, but the conversation was lost as they grew closer to the blot on the skyline. He grabbed the railing and pulled himself half-over, as though a few extra inches would make the image before him any less shocking. "Oh. *Wow.*"

She chuckled. "That seems to be your go-to phrase here."

"I can't help it if everything here wows me." *Including you,* he thought. The words almost left his lips, but he kept them to himself for the time being.

Ahead of them now was an entire city of skyscrapers built right there, in the middle of the ocean. The buildings must've started underneath the water because there were no doorways or walkways to speak of. Most of the buildings stretched so high they disappeared into the clouds. Waves beat against and in between the city, but the structures stood strong.

There were still no other boats or people or species in sight. It was disconcerting to see the makings of a civilization empty.

"A Mertropolis," Celeste's soft, knowing voice cut through the stilted breeze. "One of many. You'd be unsurprised by the amount of ship-related deaths that happen in a Mertropolis in the dead of night."

A grating gong sounded, and his attention snapped to a particularly pointy building that ended a few feet above the water. A long, horizontal platform slid out from the side; at the end sat a woman playing the piano. She was performing an intricate and fast-paced melody, leaving him speechless and luring him in—

"It's a siren. But you're lucky; she isn't calling for you today. I believe today is shark day." He cocked his head, and she clarified, "Everyone gets a turn with the siren."

"Oh?" Her ominous response only left him with more questions, but he didn't want to ask and be led down dark tales of such a grandiose planet.

The music traveled through the air as physical notes, much like the flower that'd grown at Celeste's house after he dropped the Remembrance Well water. But unlike that flower, these notes didn't bring about a sense of despair or dread, and instead of hopefulness. It was refreshing to hope.

"It seems like it'd be a wonderland," he added, trying to steer the conversation back to her and what Fortun was like. He needed to know more—anything and everything—and, secretly, he hoped she would respond with something playful, as she was prone to do.

A pang of desire pulsed through him and he turned his head away quickly, his cheeks growing hot. There was that feeling again. *Hope.* Was it the song, or was it her? Or, perhaps it was this planet, and everything that came with it. But really, it was probably her.

Celeste raised a brow, reaching out and grabbing one of the floating musical notes. Her fingers slipped through, and the note evaporated into smoke before finding its way back together. "At what point does wonderment turn stale? Is it when the mundanities of life hit? When the routine strikes and suddenly every morning and night is painstakingly unchanging? Or perhaps the wonderment is lost when you realize that no matter where you go, people are all the same."

He stared at her for a moment, deciphering her long-winded message. "Have you been rehearsing that? Because it was astonishingly beautiful and not at all what someone would say on a whim. But I understand your point—life gets boring."

"I'd prefer my point to be that stability is important, and nothing is stable here."

"I don't think I would call a crumbling planet stable..."

"But you have a sky without a kingdom, soil without gifts, oceans without cities built inside them. Sundar has structure. You can build a foundation somewhere *and it stays.*"

"Nothing stays," he said before wincing. "I sound like my mother."

His eyes widened with surprise, and he shuffled in his spot. This time, he could blame no one for bringing her up but himself. It'd been so lonely since his mother passed that he hadn't had a chance to talk about her to anyone else without being put on a display laced with pity.

But, at the same time, he regretted putting his heart on his sleeve; it was embarrassing, and Celeste had been upbeat until now. His sudden negativity brought him back to when he listened to his mother's endless woes throughout his childhood. She'd always wake up with a long list of complaints about her life that he would constantly have to combat, and sometimes he wondered if her negativity was ingrained in him, too.

"I—I'm sorry. I don't know what came over me." Noah ran his fingers through his hair. "I think maybe—I think all this talk of her lately, and with the world ending, I've been on edge. Like now, I nitpick every little thing until I find a reason to be upset. Does that make sense?"

She nodded along. "Of course, it makes sense. I see me in you, after all."

Noah blushed. "Shouldn't it be the other way around?"

How could he be cowardly one moment, yet so bold the next?

A single, sharp laugh left Celeste's lips, one of glee captured and then released in a sole sound. He gulped at the way she tilted her head upward and her hair danced along her back. "I mean, you're right. Nothing stays, but doesn't that make everything that much more important to cherish?"

Noah allowed silence to fall as he took a deep breath and peered down at the waves lapping against the ship. He wanted to ask how she could exude such positivity, even when saying something rooted in devastation, but he thought that might lead to too heavy of a conversation.

"You know," he said. "Despite a few mental breakdowns while being here, I've felt surprisingly unsad these last few weeks. I would dare say I've been happy."

"Well, right now, it feels like a vacation. A spectacle. But if you stay in one place long enough, it all feels the same—"

He wondered then if she used positive affirmations to hide her true feelings. As though if she could convince him to be happy, then she would become so, too. But occasionally her mask slipped, and he was reminded that she was sad, too.

"Doesn't it depend on who you're with?" Noah asked, and he swore her cheeks reddened. He chuckled lightly. Maybe they could convince each other. "I never thought I'd leave you speechless... or see you so down. You seem so... happy."

"Can't I be both?" she asked. "Can't I be overjoyed one moment and tragically devastated the next?" A beat of silence passed before her frown gradually rose at the edges and her brows crinkled in faux confusion. "I think you just... cheered me up."

He laughed. "I guess I owe it to you after... well." It was his turn to blush as he wrung his fingers together at the thought of his breakdown after falling through the endless loop. "So does that mean you feel it? That pit in your stomach? That feeling of utter despair each time you think about the ones you loved being lost to you forever?"

Her brows crinkled further, and this time, they appeared to be of genuine confusion. "What kind of question is that? Of course, I feel that way about my brother. Altair was my closest friend, and I miss him every single day. But I choose to acknowledge this feeling, and nothing more. I don't need to dive into the pool of sorrow every day to know he loved me, and for me to know I loved him."

"Do you think you find it boring here because he's gone?"

Celeste nodded, her eyes widening the tiniest of amounts, though she was quiet for a moment more. "I've been thinking about him a lot since we started sailing. Our family used to sail together often; this boat has been around since before either of us was born. The memories we made here as a family... it's unbearably... bearable."

Her eyes were glued to the water below as she let out a shuddering breath. The sense of wonder she brought about inside him each time they were together was unparalleled, and he desperately wished he could say the right thing to make all her pain go away. She was tired and sad and broken, but she was beautiful and kind, and she'd decided to save the planets all on her own.

"You asked me what it was like to grow up here," she stated, finally breaking the slow build of tension that'd been accumulating. "For me, it was... loud. Everyone always had something to say, but their words always meant nothing. I had a lot of half and step-siblings and we all lived... very close together, though we hardly got along most days."

He raised a brow—he couldn't relate. His experience was quite the opposite; he was the only child of a dead mother, with a father who left when Noah was six and never looked back. Noah supposed too much of anything wasn't healthy, whether it be too little or too much family. Though he preferred the latter because, at least then, there was someone to talk to, even if they weren't the nicest. "But not anymore?"

"My dad and stepmom have been together for years now. My mother was around, but distant, for a time. Once Altair died, she couldn't handle it. So she left, and all of my siblings left too, except Luna. I haven't seen Mother since. Sometimes I wonder what she's doing out there, or if she has a completely new family somewhere else."

He inhaled sharply. Noah had never known his father enough to care about his absence, yet he could empathize with the way her words came out as a sigh, and her eyes welled with tears. He hadn't expected to see her cry. It was jarring, and he winced at her words. He'd made her feel better, only to bring her back down in the same conversation. Nice.

Noah wrapped an arm around her neck and pulled her into a side hug, resting his head atop hers. "Life has a way of pulling people apart. I had no clue Katalina and I used to play together when we were younger, for example. For years, we lived separate lives, barely speaking, but life brought us back together."

He smiled to himself. "If Katalina hadn't reached out that day to meet for dinner, you and I wouldn't have met. I would've stayed home to sulk, gone to sleep early, and woke up late the next morning for more interviews. Just another day."

Celeste huffed, but he could hear the smile underneath it. "What are you getting at?"

"Well… maybe these things that led us here—maybe it was the universe pulling us together to protect it. What if some things *don't* just happen?"

"Maybe there's both, maybe there's neither," she said with a hint of resignation.

"I mean, what are the odds we were both at the same place?" he pressed. "And I'd tell you to stop running, and you would? I'm happy for whatever made this happen, either way, but it seems far too… choreographed to be a coincidence."

He didn't know what response he was expecting, or if he was expecting one at all, but his lips parted as she said, "Me, too."

Noah could've sworn his heart stopped. Celeste raised a hand to her mouth as she released a light yawn. It was nearly time for her to go to sleep. Mark would take her place for two hours before Katalina took Noah's—but Noah didn't want this moment to end. He didn't want any of their moments together to end. Ever.

But they always did.

He sucked in a deep breath and held it, forcing himself not to think about how one day the planets would either end, or he would have to go back to his.

"Last question, I promise," he said, pulling away from her and leaning against the railing with his arms crossed over the wood. "And then you can go wake Mark and take your nap."

She yawned again with another nod and a stretch before turning and leaning her back against the railing.

"What do you plan to do… after we save the worlds?" Noah asked, almost slipping and saying the word *if.* Their clear-cut path was now muddied with the ever-expansive ocean and a note in her brother's research to 'look where no one else is looking.' Look where and at what, they hadn't a clue, but the horizon held no answers.

Her silence became tormenting the longer it lasted, and the increased thumping in his chest was impossible to decipher. He'd never felt such a thing before; to want to be around someone all the time, yet fear everything that came out of his mouth because he wanted to impress her.

"That's a very sudden and specific question."

"For a very sudden yet specific woman," he quipped, and he damn near thought his heart was going to explode. The things he said truly baffled him sometimes. He'd never pegged himself as a flirt, yet it came so naturally when he was with her.

"I find plans to be useless. My world has a funny way of turning everything upside its head. One day, I could be sailing the sea as a lone pirate, the next—a dancer in a ballet! Which I did once, two years ago. I was the lead."

"You were in a ballet?" he asked. "That's incredibly impressive… I can't say I've seen or been much of anything."

"You shouldn't talk about yourself like that—"

"You love birds done yet?" Mark called from behind. Their heads turned to find him walking up as he stretched his arms and rolled his head. His eyes were stained with red rims, but he arrived at his post ten minutes early. A dedicated man.

"Missed me so much you showed up early?" Noah asked. "I'm touched."

Mark pointed a thumb over his shoulder. "I can leave if you'd like. I'll happily sleep for the rest of the night."

With that, Celeste nodded and gave Noah a last little smile before briskly taking her leave. She waved as she walked away with a glance over her shoulder. "Night, boys. See you in a few!"

"*Men,*" Mark grumbled. He leaned against the railing beside Noah and pulled out a box from his jeans pocket labeled 'Lights'—smokable sticks that gave someone a light-headed, euphoric head high.

"Now, don't tell Katalina," Mark said. "She thinks I quit months ago. Which I did—until I relapsed. I wasn't going to use them while we were here, but, I mean, the world is ending, and we're on a completely different planet, so I think I deserve to have one." He lit it without hesitation and offered the box to Noah, who waved his hands in dismissal.

"I think this planet is a trip enough as it is," Noah said with a brow raised. "I feel inclined to tell Katalina, too." Mark gave him a glare that Noah couldn't peg as a joke or real, so he added with his hands up in defense, "Or we'll keep it between us. That works, too."

"I knew I could count on you." Mark brought the light stick to his mouth. As he inhaled, the paper started burning away at the end, transforming into light blue fluorescent bubbles. They varied from humongous to incredibly small, and they floated high into the sky until they disappeared into the clouds.

Mark brought the light stick away from his mouth with a look of confusion, and when he exhaled, more bubbles arose from his mouth instead of smoke.

"Ah man, the black hole must've messed up my lights!" He chucked the box into the ocean and slammed a fist onto the railing while grabbing a fistful of hair. Mark released grunts of frustration—careful not to be too loud and accidentally wake Katalina, alerting her of his hidden habit.

Though there was still a looming pit of sadness and confusion in Noah's belly, as there often were these days, he couldn't help but laugh.

29

THE CREATURE COMETH

TWO MORE DAYS OF CALM TIDES PASSED AND THEN, IN THE DEAD of night, the ship swayed so harshly that he tumbled out of his hammock. He landed on his stomach with a groan, his cheek pressed against the ground as he collected his bearings. One moment he was dreaming of going out to dinner with Celeste, and the next, his entire body was radiating in immense pain.

He used the wall as leverage as he stood, but it wasn't enough to stave off the harsh jolts caused by the waves. His footing was lost, and gravity shoved his shoulder against the wall nearest his hammock. A groan escaped his lips as he slid to the ground, keeping his back pressed firmly against the wood to keep from being tossed around.

A small, circular window rested above his head, the wind howling and slapping against the glass. A strike of lightning temporarily blinded him, though there was no rain to speak of.

Could a thunderstorm cause such destructive waves? No—this must've been something else, something more. But what?

Noah crawled along the floorboards before righting himself at the open doorway. Footsteps pounded from down the narrow hallway, and Celeste skidded to a stop when she noticed him. She turned, their eyes meeting as she prepared to speak, but another jolt sent her stumbling forward. Celeste caught herself with a rough shoulder slapping against the wooden wall before pushing long, blueish-black strands out of her face.

His heart sank. "Are we being attacked?"

"I don't have a clue, but I hope it's not a rainstorm," she shouted, shaking her head frantically. "They're beautiful, but if you stare at the rain for too long without special glasses, you'll get uncontrollable hiccups for five hours—or more!"

"The rain does that?" he asked in horror, following her through the hallway. It was easy to avoid looking directly at the sun, but the rain was rather pervasive in its need for attention.

Celeste ran up the stairs leading to the main deck, and he followed, bracing himself for thick droplets and heavy thunder, but there wasn't a cloud in sight.

"What's going on?" Katalina yelled as she ran up from her nightly post on the deck with Mark close behind.

"We're figuring it out," Noah called. "And don't look at any rain!"

Noah stopped in surprise; Celeste turned in circles, staring up at the sky. "Something's not right."

She rushed to the other end of the boat, her hands tightly clasped on the railing as she peered over the water. Noah hurried to her side, pulling on her shirt from behind—if she leaned forward anymore, she'd fall—and her feet landed securely back on the floorboards. She turned to him with a nod of thanks and pointed.

Noah followed her finger, but couldn't see anything beyond the treacherous waves. "Wh—"

The ship shook again, disrupting his words as he grabbed onto the railing to avoid falling over. He gulped; directly ahead, the water parted to make way for the head of a beast. It had scales like a draegon, but instead of wings, it had large, sharp spikes along its back. It stood on two legs with four smaller arms on either side of its torso. The creature appeared to have no eyes, yet it snarled at them, displaying jagged teeth.

It was also incredibly large—at least thirty feet tall, and as thick as their boat, if not more. Noah fell backward; Mark took Katalina's hand and kept her behind him, using his body as a shield against whatever this *thing* was.

The beast bent forward, its rotten breath a concoction of heat and fish. The noxious scent made Noah hopeful—maybe humans were off the menu. This thought evaporated rather quickly as the creature grabbed onto each side of the ship. Noah gulped, fearing the worst. They were in the middle of an empty ocean, with not another creature or Mertropolis or landmass in sight.

There was no escaping the inevitability of death. There never truly was, but he'd hoped he had more time here, alive, with her and with them.

Katalina may have been a know-it-all mouse of a woman, and Mark may have been the nicest jerk Noah had ever met, but there was a sense of comradery. The kind that could exist during and after this experience—if they survived.

Celeste released a gasp as the creature kept its claws wrapped around the ship and lowered its head. Was it trying to get a better look at them? He squinted, looking once more for the eyes or ears of the creature, but there was none to be found. The entire top half of its face was smooth and reflective, like black marble.

"Do you think it's trying to decide on who to eat first?" Mark called.

"It's the nevelo," Celeste yelled, as if that meant anything to the rest of them. "We'll see if it thinks that far ahead. I've only ever seen a drawing. There's reportedly only one or two of its kind left alive."

Noah's heart dropped at the sight of the nevelo opening its mouth. He could've sworn it was twisting into a salivating smile. "Are we about to be eaten?"

He was certain the creature was preparing to have a midnight snack, but it released a series of whines instead. The sound reminded him of telephone wires buzzing with electricity. The waves shook harder, and the other three were forced to the floorboards, too.

"What's it doing?" Katalina cried. She and Mark were the furthest from the creature, and closest to the stairs leading below deck.

"It's a cry for help," Celeste shouted back. "I think!"

"Great!" Mark yelled, pushing Katalina down a few of the stairs, though she seemed hesitant, her eyes glued on Noah and Celeste, who were still out in the open.

"Should we hide?" Noah asked. "Or should we try to fight it?"

His heart sped up at the thought; the creature was *enormous.* He was tired of fighting surreal beasts he had no shot at defeating. Maybe this was one reason Celeste preferred Sundar, too.

"We have to 'look where no one else is looking,'" Celeste said. "That's what Altair's research said to do."

She was standing in the center of the ship now, securely planted in place despite being tossed around moments ago by the battering waves. Noah pushed himself upright and found that he was no longer wobbling, either. Was it because of the nevelo's steady grip on the boat?

It was no matter—he stepped up beside Celeste and took her hand. "I want to let you know that if we die today—thank you. Thank you for seeing me. Thank you for understanding. I can die now, knowing I tried to live."

She looked up at him with her mouth agape before she shook her head. "Don't say that. No one's dying today."

A shout came from behind. He turned to see it was Katalina, her hands cupped around her mouth.

"You're right! 'Look where no one else is looking,'" she yelled over the rushing wind. "The eyes, Noah. We can all see every body part except the eyes."

"How are we supposed to find the eyes?" he asked. A face devoid of eyes only made the beast more terrifying; it could make up for its lost scent by enhancing others. "How do merpeople survive here?"

"They multiply like fish," Celeste stated as if a monster wasn't attacking their ship. "A lot of them die, which is why people like my stepmother and sister come up to live on land."

Perhaps paradise wasn't as perfect as it seemed from the outside, after all. But man, how he wished it was.

Noah scanned the ship, his gaze stopping on the sails. They each had a thick pole leading to the top, and a set of metal bars were attached to the sides as a ladder. The question was—did he have the upper arm strength to commit such a feat? He could hardly hold Celeste up when they'd saved the draegon.

Noah supposed he had no choice but to try. He dashed for the mast, and the nevelo must've understood Noah was up to something because it started shaking the ship again. Noah stumbled along the way, careful not to lose his footing. Then he climbed, losing his grip only once. When he looked down, Celeste was staring up at him with a wide smile. She gave him a salute of support, and he gave one back before continuing his ascent.

It was incredibly difficult to see much of anything when the ship was tilting every which way, but he could identify floppy, dark black ears on either side of the creature's head, made evident by the dash of pink underneath. Now he had to find the eyes...

Noah's heart skipped a beat when the creature tilted its neck slightly, revealing the back of its head. There—a hint of a green, round eye. Then another, both with skin furrowed above like eyebrows. Noah stared at the eyes as best he could, despite the thrashing of the creature's head and the shaking ship. It was all he could think to do.

Nothing happened.

"I'm looking where no one else is looking," he shouted down to the others, thinking they'd understand the situation was dire and there was nothing more to be done.

The nevelo stopped its shrill cry before the ship ceased shaking altogether. The waves settled. Noah remained at the top of the ladder as he watched in awe, the creature lowering them back into the water. The creature seemed to split down the center and open like a set of double doors outward. There was nothing grotesque about the scene, however—instead, its insides were blacked out like a wall, and on the other side of the opening was more ocean.

"A portal inside a creature?" he whispered to himself as their boat passed through the nevelo. The sky morphed from night to day, from magenta to pastel green, with fluffy cotton-candy-colored blue and pink clouds, and a pastel blue ocean. Everything felt as though it were slightly swirling. The waves curled a little more than they had before, and the clouds turned inward like smoke.

It was gorgeous.

Noah reached toward the sky, and his fingers breezed through a cloud, a coolness washing over him. Celeste released a celebratory 'whoop' below, followed by a laugh. He looked down to see she had a fist in the air and an ecstatic grin.

Katalina and Mark drifted away from the safety of the stairs hesitantly before Celeste engulfed them both in hugs. Then she looked up at Noah, and their eyes met, and his heart stopped. She cupped her hands around her mouth. "Come down here and celebrate! We did it! We figured out where the Ruler of the Deep lives!"

Noah did as instructed, hopping down the last two rungs, and Celeste threw her arms around him before his feet hit the deck. He laughed, her joy seeping into him. He pulled away and looked around and at the sky above. "Have you been here before?"

She shook her head vigorously, her smile never wavering. "The last thing described in my brother's research was the nevelo. I don't think... I don't think they made it this far."

"Hey," he said, looking at her as they stood side-by-side, their noses inches from each other. "We made it. We're going to save the planets together."

There was a moment where she stared into his eyes and then glanced down at his lips and another moment where he did the same. A quell of need shot through him, heat drenching his entire body in desire, and he placed a hand on her cheek, his eyelids drooping closed.

He leaned forward slowly, their lips meeting halfway. Noah held his breath as his tongue guided hers thoughtfully and seductively, his pace hesitant and slow. Her lips were smooth as they brushed against his, and everything else seemed to melt away. The breeze on his back, his cousin and her fiancé watching a few feet away, the pastel sky above. It was all gone, replaced by their lips pressed together.

He wanted to explore her more, feel every inch of her mouth as his tongue danced with hers—but it was short and simple, and over too soon.

When he pulled away, his eyes were glazed over, his mind in a frenzy, wanting only one thing. Noah was thankful he was facing away from Katalina and Mark; he couldn't hide the lust burning within him as it spread throughout his body.

Their mouths remained inches apart as she asked softly, a mischievous twinkle in her eyes, "Better than the shapeshifter?"

His smile brushed against her lips. "Definitely."

30

HOW WERE WE TO KNOW?

AFTER THEIR KISS, CELESTE WENT UP TO STEER THE SHIP LIKE nothing happened. Steering toward what or where remained unclear. After traveling through the sea creature—which was still a mind-blowing thing to think—he would've thought there was nowhere else left to go.

Noah was outside, taking up his usual spot in the corner against the railing, though now he was sitting with his back pressed against the wood while looking up at the pastel-green sky. There was no telling when they would be thrust from this environment and into the next, and he wanted to relish in it for as long as he could.

The clouds danced in a sea of swirls before drifting off into shapes. They held no significance, at least not to him, and remained largely in the realm of standard squares and circles, with the occasional rhombus to add a splash of variance. His cat would probably think the clouds were toys because of how fast they changed into something new.

He noticed Mark heading down to the lower cabin from the corner of his eye; Katalina was waving goodbye to him. They were always dramatic when they left each other's company, waving and saying 'I love you' or hugging. As though any moment together could be their last, and they had to celebrate their limited time.

Katalina approached Noah slowly, and he only looked at her once she was close enough to block the clouds. "Hey. Mind if I sit with you?"

He shook his head, patting the hardwood floorboards. "This incredibly comfy spot is all yours."

She chuckled and took up residence beside him, though she did not continue the conversation. His brows crinkled—there wasn't much to converse about, so why sit with him? He was rather enjoying the quiet, his thoughts drifting to Celeste and her lips brushing against his...

Noah suddenly wished Celeste had come over and joined; she and Katalina got along so well that he could avoid talking to Katalina altogether. He never knew what to say, and he wasn't in the mood to rehash their adventures thus far or talk about their lives outside of this. While he was thankful for his cousin, he preferred to stay at an arm's length away.

"What was your mother like?" Katalina asked, finally breaking the silence, and he couldn't help but clench his jaw. Of all the things to talk about. Hadn't he already told her he didn't want to talk about his mother?

Why was it always on him to repeat himself, instead of on

other people to listen? A sudden anger coursed through him. Born of sadness, yes, but a fury that needed to be unleashed, nonetheless.

"Not like you've ever cared before," Noah said under his breath. It left his lips with little thought attached, and although he certainly felt that way, he probably shouldn't have voiced it —now or ever.

"Excuse me?" Katalina asked. "When will you stop? I see that sour look you give me from time to time. Like you want to make peace, but you're still so... so angry."

"It was a joke, Katalina," he said, unwilling to admit to the slip of his tongue. Should he *have* to apologize for how he genuinely felt? "And you could simply not ask me about her when I've said I don't want to talk about it."

"And for the love of the Goddesses, *why* on her birthday?" he added, the anger bubbling over and spewing out. "*Why* her memorial site? Did you not think that would hurt? It's barely been three months since she passed."

Katalina's eyes widened as she covered her mouth. "I-I thought it would be sweet. A celebration of her."

He shook his head. "No. For the next time a family member dies—*no.* I don't enjoy visiting her tombstone. It's sad, Katalina, and so is talking about her unless *I* want to talk about her."

Truthfully, Noah could've kept going. There was so much noise in his head, so many things to unload, and things he'd never thought he'd say. It was dark in his mind, and he didn't know how to make it stop.

He noticed someone approaching, and his heart leaped

with the hope it was Celeste, only to find it was Mark instead. Noah's shoulders dropped in disappointment.

Mark stopped in front of Katalina and Noah and peered down with furrowed brows and hands on his hips. To either or both of them, he said, "You look angry. What's going on?"

Noah threw a hand out at Katalina before rising to his feet. "She's being disrespectful. I don't need to talk about something traumatic if I don't want to, so leave me alone about it. It's not like you had any interest in my mother when she was *alive.* I don't know how many more times I can—"

"With all due respect, Noah, you need to stop feeling sorry for yourself," Mark interjected. Noah's mouth remained parted as he met Mark's blue gaze. "You claim you're sick of receiving pity, yet you're constantly moping about. Did you ever reach out to Katalina, huh? Be honest—you didn't think about her before the funeral, either. You either didn't remember or know she existed. Do not blame her when you were equally distant."

Noah stared, unable to form a response that didn't end with him looking like a fool. He clenched his jaw and said through gritted teeth, "I asked not to talk about my mother on multiple occasions, and yet Katalina brought her up once again. What did you think my response would be?"

"You can't expect people to tiptoe around your feelings," Mark said. "She was Katalina's aunt, too. It's still sad for her."

"Neither of you knew her; what gives you the right to be sad? And, no, I don't expect people to tiptoe around anything, but I expect the bare minimum of being *listened* to. Because when you're asked not to do something, and then you do it, it pisses the other person off! Like fuck, is that something that went through your head *at all*?"

Now, Noah wasn't one to swear in his day-to-day life, but these circumstances were so far beyond anything he'd ever known that swearing was the only way to adequately express the anger he felt.

He was tired of expecting the bare minimum and getting nothing in return.

Noah thought Celeste might chime in on his word choice, filling the silence between a heated moment with a light-hearted joke, but her voice did not come. The quiet settled like a heavy blanket on his shoulders, threatening to crush him.

Katalina stood with a nod before turning her head away. Looking toward the skyline, she whispered, "I'm sorry."

Her fists clenched, her lower lip quivered, and then she was off, performing an awkward half-walk, half-run toward the stairs leading below deck.

Now he was alone with Mark. Great. Mark had already reached a point of yelling, and there was no telling what stage came next in one of his blow-ups. But when Noah turned to him, Mark was merely shaking his head in disappointment. He stepped up beside Noah with a hand on his shoulder. "People make mistakes. Patience, my friend, is key."

Noah was far too baffled to respond. Of all the people to lecture him on patience, it was the ticking time bomb? Instead of anger quelling within Noah, he simply watched Mark walk away in stunned silence.

Strangely, he felt like he lost. Was this how Mark felt every time he yelled? Noah couldn't help but feel slimy from it all, and he wished the conversation had gone differently. And yet—

He turned to the ocean, peering over at the calmly crashing waves. He and his mother had gone to the water on Sundar together once. It looked similar to this sea, but much smaller and a darker blue. They'd danced around the sand singing some song she wrote when she was younger. They were both smiling, then.

Noah felt a familiar quell of unequivocal sadness at the memory, but it did not simmer over. Instead, he forced himself to smile and practiced what Celeste suggested—he chose not to stare into the darkness. He may have said some things he regretted and ruined their last evening before meeting with the Ruler of the Deep, but it was nice to be reminded that there were good memories of him and his mother to look back on, too.

The memories before he knew something was wrong.

The memories before he could see the signs written on the walls.

He tsked. Why did Katalina have to bring her up?

31

AM I WRONG?

Noah eventually made his way up to Celeste, who hadn't left her post at the steering wheel after his horrid interaction with the other two. There was still a twinge of hurt in the pit of his stomach, the kind that came after a verbal match.

He tried to turn his attention to Celeste and away from his worries; her eyes were glued on the sparkling water ahead, the wind nudging her loose, black strands. What good did steering do when they didn't know their destination? There were also many instances where no one was at the wheel, so it seemed rather pointless to steer, but he didn't want to ask for fear of offending her.

When she noticed him, she said, "That sounded like an ordeal."

"It was," he said. "So you heard it?"

She nodded solemnly. "Every word. Want to talk about it?"

"Not particularly." Noah sighed, looking at her as she

looked ahead. The sky was still a vibrant green, and it occurred to him then that it'd been hours, and there was no sign of the daylight changing, nor a sun or moon to replace each other.

"Do you think I'm overreacting?" Noah blurted, scared to see her reaction but forcing himself to look. Would she lie to appease him, or tell the truth?

His breath hitched as she shook her head. No—he didn't believe her. "Why not? I understand why they're mad at me. I would be, too, if our roles were reversed, but I can't help how I feel any more than they can."

Celeste appeared to consider this extensively before saying, "I guess because I've been where you are. I've gone through the same phases. There will be a time when you wake up and no longer feel like the world is against you. Because it isn't. Why would it be?

"One day you'll realize that's life—everything goes through a cycle, and while things and people and places may come and go, you'll stay for a while longer and then you'll go, too. One day you'll realize it wasn't the time you have, but the time you had."

Noah remained silent, soaking in each word. He wished he could write down every little thing she said so he could remember it all forever, but ingraining her words in his memory somehow made them all the more special.

"I think you just started me down a path toward a midlife crisis," he said jokingly, rubbing the back of his neck with a trembling hand. He wasn't entirely joking, though.

"Katalina and Mark don't understand yet," she continued. "They think you can talk about it whenever, wherever, to whoever. And one day, you *will* be able to. Just not yet. But I hope we can save the planets so you can experience the freedom of living."

He prepared to thank her, but she stuck an index finger out between them with a shake of her head and quickly added, "*But,* even though they don't understand, you shouldn't lash out at them. Like you said—without Katalina reaching out, we never would've met. Remember that. Write it on your hand or something if you have to."

Noah nodded abashedly. She was right, of course, but he wasn't ready to admit it yet. He needed to sit with the anger a little longer before he could think about apologizing.

"One day... will the void go away? I swear—I swear some days I don't feel anything at all," he admitted. "But others, I am so overwhelmed with sadness, or anger, or discontentment. But here... here I could almost escape it. At least longer than I ever could back home."

Because of you, he wanted to say, but he held it in. Why? He flirted so effortlessly one moment and then bit his tongue the next. He wondered how anyone else could know him if he didn't know himself.

"I distinctly remember telling you this is how a vacation feels. You're on a new planet experiencing new, exciting things. Eventually, it'll pass and become—"

"Yeah, I don't think it's the planet." Noah turned to her, and while she kept her eyes ahead, a light-hearted laugh erupted from her lungs and dissolved his nerves.

"To answer your question—yes, I think your emotions will level out at some point, but the pain never goes away, either." Celeste continued. "Sometimes you'll be picking out milk at the store, and a memory will strike and the tears will fall. It could be two years later, or ten. That's the thing about grief. You learn to accept that it will never go away and that you have to live for them. You need to find the good in what you have, and in yourself."

"How long did it take for you?"

She shrugged. "Who's to say? I can't pinpoint an exact date, but last summer, I remember traveling to your planet made it better. Knowing my brother's research was real, knowing there was such endless beauty in this galaxy and universe and everything beyond and in between. Knowing that life isn't against anyone. It simply is."

An inexplicable lump formed in his throat. Noah tried to gulp it down, to no avail. In about two minutes, he was going to break down and cry, and he'd cried too many times in front of Celeste to be seen as enduring or sexy. Of that, he was sure, so he looked for a quick exit. Noah desperately wished to stay, but there were times to grieve together and times to grieve alone.

"Thank you, Celeste," he whispered. Her fingers were still wrapped around the helm, but her gaze had drifted from the horizon to Noah, and she gave him a light nod. She must've seen it in his eyes.

"You don't need to keep thanking me. Although it is boosting my ego, I must say," she said with a smirk. "I should be thanking you for saying yes. Without you, my shapeshifter could still be impersonating me! You're more useful than you give yourself credit for."

"Am I?" he asked before sheepishly turning away. "I think

I'll head down to sleep one last time. Since we have a busy day ahead of us tomorrow."

He made it down two steps when she called his name.

"Noah!" He turned to face her, one hand resting atop the railing. "Tomorrow we'll be meeting the Ruler of the Deep. We'll have to go underwater for it."

"Yeah," he said with a chuckle. "I could've guessed that. Is there something else?"

Her face was scrunched in a goofy concoction of embarrassment and determining if she should say what she was about to say. Celeste nodded. "Yeah—yes. Yup. Uh. Well."

He'd never seen her so flustered before—it was unrightfully adorable.

"I didn't want you guys to think less of me, but... I'm terrified of swimming," she finally said, the words coming out like a fresh sigh of relief as her cheeks reddened.

Noah crinkled his brows in confusion. "That's it? I'll help any way I can; I'm a decent swimmer."

She shrugged, looking away. "There's one more thing. I left this out because I didn't want to scare you, but... well, there's also a chance that if the Ruler of the Deep doesn't like us, he'll force us to stay underwater and drown."

Oh.

That *was* terrifying.

32

BREATHING BUBBLES

The next morning, he found Celeste drinking from a teacup while overlooking the ocean. It turned out there wasn't much to do on a ship except watch the waves. Mark and Katalina were maintaining a distance from Noah for the time being, conveniently leaving the upper deck shortly after he came up.

If that's how they wanted it, then so be it. "I didn't know we had tea on board."

She held up the teacup with a smile; the design was made of tiny, pink flower petals. "It's water. Care to have some? I brought a bottle from the Remembrance Well with us."

Noah waved her offer away. "I don't know how you can drink that stuff. But, uh, anyway, I thought we should talk about that fear of swimming you have before we dive in later. Maybe we could also circle back to that 'forced to drown' part. Did something cause it? You don't have to answer, though, of course."

Honestly, he shouldn't have been surprised after the sea monster they'd encountered. There was no telling how many more were lurking below, and Celeste's stepmom and stepsister *left* their home in the ocean because of how dangerous it was. The most his world dealt with were sharks and a waterfall leading off the edge of the world.

"He was pushed off a boat." The way her voice wavered as she said it, the way her eyes darted away from his—he'd opened a wound. She had a reason far beyond a terrifying sea creature or a shipwreck, and he was exactly like his cousin, asking things that shouldn't be asked.

"But the report said he fell," she continued. "Isn't it interesting that every single person on his research team fell off the same boat, but with no storm or monster in sight?"

"I'm—well, you know the bit. I'm sorry." A half-smile crept onto her features. There weren't many things to say when presented with a devastating truth. Even as someone who experienced a recent loss—he never knew what to say.

"Do you think someone had him and his team…" He couldn't get himself to say the word 'killed.' "I mean, do you think there are people and creatures, like those shapeshifters, out there who want the planets to be destroyed?"

Celeste shrugged. "Perhaps there are more people than we think who see this as the Goddess' Hand."

His brow raised at that. "You worship goddesses on Fortun, too?"

"No, only one. It's said the Ruler of the Sky is a descendent of the Goddess, but there is no proof in our Holy Texts."

"Oh. Do you think it's the 'Goddess' Hand?'" Noah asked, though he hadn't a clue what he was asking. There was no such thing on Sundar. Celeste cocked her head, and he realized then that he clung to each pause while mindlessly gravitating closer to her.

"I don't know," she finally said with a shake of her head. "I feel like our civilization is too young to be squashed by the hand of the Goddess, though."

Noah shuddered.

"What about you?" she asked. "Do you believe it's the end of days? Your Goddesses passing judgment and exterminating your species?"

"I'm partial to believe humanity errs on the side of sucking, and people do bad things for what they think are good reasons, even if they have no real reason at all."

"But there were other creatures on our trip that caused an equal amount of trouble as humans do," he added as an afterthought. He didn't know what his point was, but she nodded in agreement before they fell silent. It was a peaceful, comfortable quiet, one between two people who shared mutual respect and understanding toward one another.

"Did they?" she asked after a while. "These creatures—they act on instinct. Though, I guess some out here have a higher level of consciousness like us—mermaids and cats, for example—"

His ears perked at that. "So Henrietta would have the same level of thinking if she was here? Would she be able to talk?"

"Naturally. Do you want to hear what your cat thinks about, though? Or is she better off looking cute?"

He'd have to think about that.

"Anyway, there are other species that show compassion, like draegons and ecklweckls, but most are primal. They might kill, but out of necessity. Humans, on the other hand, have choices, and they tend to choose wrong."

"Maybe it's human nature," he pondered.

Noah searched her gaze, though he didn't know what he was looking for or what he saw, as she said, "No—humanity is good, but they also stink." She stuck out her tongue. "There are always some bad bunches, but overall—we're good. So are the merpeople. It's the bad who are the most prominent in our minds; we remember them the most."

"Why don't you find merpeople trustworthy, then?" he asked, remembering her side comment weeks ago regarding merpeople being unhelpful.

Celeste raised a brow and looked him up and down while biting the inside of her lip. "Because I told Luna I liked you, and she still gave you her card."

He blushed, the heat insurmountable. Noah patted down his pants and slipped his fingers into his pockets, but he must've lost the card because it wasn't there. He hadn't thought much of Luna since leaving the city, and he hadn't thought Celeste cared either way. "You noticed?"

"Of course. That's only one example of many, but I don't want to paint my stepsister in a worse light. *In general,* merpeople tend to be more jealous than humans. I'll just say Luna always tries to take what's mine."

His brows rose at her words. “I’m yours?”

Celeste faltered, and he had to admit—she looked adorable when put on the spot. He would gladly be hers, but it was fun to make her squirm about it.

“Are you guys ready?” Mark asked, approaching with a stretch. Katalina stood behind him, nervously fiddling with her brown braids and looking anywhere but at Noah. Mark had a way of interrupting Celeste and Noah’s conversations that sent a twitch to Noah’s eye, and this time was no exception.

“Alright,” Celeste agreed, nodding for them to follow her to the front of the boat. They huddled together, and then she pulled out four white packets from her pants pocket, holding them out in the center of their group. “Take a packet, but don’t open them yet. These are the breathing bubbles Luna gave us. We’ll jump into the water first, and then open and attach the bubbles to our faces.”

Mark raised a hand. Celeste pointed. “Yes, Mark?”

Huh. Raising hands was new.

Mark cleared his throat. “What should we do if we lose the packet? Or attach the bubble incorrectly?”

“Well, if you lose the packet, you can live with the fact you’ll have to stay behind and be docked points in our bet and as a world savior. To answer your other question, the breathing bubble is foolproof. You put it over your mouth and nose, and it’ll do the rest.”

Katalina raised her hand next, and Celeste pointed again. “Do they run out of air at some point?”

Celeste nodded with her eyes closed and mouth contorted in an apologetic half-frown. “I was hoping you wouldn’t ask, but yes. They will only last twenty minutes, give or take, and they'll get smaller depending on how many breaths you take per minute. Unless you're seriously panicking, they'll last a full twenty."

"That's not a lot of time," Noah observed aloud.

Celeste's gaze shot to his. "You forgot to raise your hand."

He looked around with a look of confusion. "This is a ship, not a classroom."

She raised a brow. "Can it not be both? You learned how to raise the sails according to the wind, didn't you? I think anywhere can be a classroom if you open your mind a little and learn."

Mark released a chuckle. "Did she just call you close-minded?" He turned to Katalina with a goofy smile. "I think she did."

"We're veering off track," Celeste said with a clap. "Now, is everyone ready?"

"No," said Noah.

"Absolutely not," Mark agreed.

"Yeah, me neither," added Celeste.

They all turned to Katalina, waiting for her to tack on how she felt. She shrugged with a blush and averted gaze. In an almost whisper, she said, "I like to swim."

Celeste cocked her head before handing out the packets. "Once we activate our breathing bubbles, we'll head down. Remember to think the following phrase *very* loudly—'Show me the Ruler of the Deep.' If we all think it, the Ruler should come."

"Should?" Katalina asked.

"He can be judgemental," Celeste admitted. "Supposedly. From what I've read, it's mostly folklore."

"Celeste," Katalina said again. "I'd like to take it back; I think I'm scared."

Celeste's sharp, determined eyes held Katalina's gaze. "Me, too, but following Altair's research is the only way. Do you believe in me?" Katalina nodded, and Celeste provided her with a reassuring smile. "And I believe in you. So there's nothing to worry about! Plus, Mark would share his breathing bubble with you if need be."

"I don't think that's as reassuring as you think it is," Noah said as he scratched the back of his head with an anxious half-smile.

Celeste moved to the nearest railing and glanced down at her packet; the other two followed without so much as a glance Noah's way. They were avoiding him, alright, and the tension somehow lingered in his muscles until there was a lump in his throat.

Part of him still felt ashamed for lashing out, but he couldn't back down and apologize when he was right. Celeste may have pointed out the flaws in his logic—as in, others were flawed—but he was still right and that was that.

Suddenly burdened with frustration at the tension he didn't think needed to be there, he took to peering down at the water below. The drop was only a few feet, but a sharp stab of nerves shot through him. It would be cold. There were likely going to be sea creatures or sea people of some sort. He wasn't prepared.

Noah watched as Celeste began removing her shoes and socks. Then she pulled out a rubber band and pulled back her hair before handing one to Katalina. "Our clothes will have to stay on. I suppose packing swimsuits would've made a bit of sense, huh?"

"Don't worry about it—it is what it is. I *love* swimming in layers. Feels like a damp and heavy hug," Noah said sarcastically, attempting to ease the air.

He received three blank stares in return. He chuckled to himself awkwardly. Well, that joke didn't land.

Instead of reacting, Celeste pulled herself onto the railing with a grunt and swung her legs over, her fingers turning white while keeping a tight grip to maintain her balance. Her messy ponytail swished in the breeze as she turned to Noah. "Ready?"

He mimicked her motions, prepared to hang on next to her, look her in the eyes—maybe give her a quick kiss—and then jump in with their hands clasped together.

But after he threw his second leg over and tried to lean like her, he lost his balance and fell.

His body hit the waves like a bag of bricks, and he was engulfed in the freezing depths instantly. Noah kept his eyes clamped shut, and the packet secured in his hand as he propelled himself back to the surface with frantic kicks. His fingers went numb, and after another minute of swimming, he realized he still hadn't cracked the top, and his lungs were burning.

Noah opened his eyes.

It felt like a thousand needles were stabbing at his pupils. He stopped swimming for a moment, releasing a sharp *ah* at the pain. Water rushed into his mouth, filling his lungs as bubbles of air escaped. Somehow he had yet to lose the breathing bubble packet, but he couldn't open it with the world fading in and out.

Noah gasped, and a fresh wave of water filled his mouth, his body convulsing. This was it—this was the end. And yet, his life didn't flash before his eyes. Neither did Celeste, or Mark, or Katalina, or even his mom. All that remained in the darkness of his vision was an orange and white cat sitting in front of his bedroom window, gracefully licking her front paw. Henrietta glanced up and tilted her head with a meow.

His last memory would be of his cat.

He supposed he could live—or die—with that.

As the darkness seemed to take hold, something crashed into his head. Suddenly, the world was bright and pastel green again, and he could expel the water from his lungs. Which he did, bobbing and treading and coughing with heavy gasps in between. Celeste was at his side, patting his back. "There, there. That's it. Get it out."

He coughed until his throat was hoarse and his desperate gasping ceased. Looking down, he noticed he'd stopped treading, and a muscular arm was wrapped around his waist. He looked over his shoulder to see it was Mark, holding him upright from behind. Protected by a man he'd insulted and hadn't spoken to since.

Noah reminded himself that Mark deserved it. But he still felt bad as he coughed and coughed with the support of Mark. He'd probably been the one to fish Noah out, too.

"I—see—why—you—hate—swimming," Noah said between gasps, catching Celeste's galaxy-speckled eyes in the light. She was a head bobbing in the water, her blackish-blue wavy hair slicked down to her scalp with the hair tie loosely clinging on.

The pastel blue water was nearly transparent. He tried to squint and make out something, anything, indicative of what they were looking for, but there was nothing. He couldn't see the ocean floor, but he could see tiny orange fish darting around his toes and happily swirling through the water. When he wasn't drowning, he supposed the ocean wasn't so bad.

But man, did his lungs *burn.* His head was throbbing, and his eyesight was still blurred. When his coughing settled and the air felt fresh again, he said, "I thought I was about to die."

"Oooo, did your life flash before your eyes?" Celeste asked, her eyes twinkling with intrigue.

"Thank you for your ongoing concern for my well-being," he said with a raised brow. "But no. Just my cat."

Celeste gave him a goofy grin and a light shove on the shoulder. "Aw, that's cute!"

Then she held up her packet, and her face grew serious. "Everyone still has one?"

The packets were raised; the heads were nodded.

They were ready to begin.

33

BELOW

"GOOD." CELESTE HELD UP A FINGER AND ADDED ONE WITH EACH rule she listed off. "First, you'll submerge your face in the water —with eyes *open*—then rip open the packet and secure the bubble around your mouth and nose once it drifts out. But remember—don't talk. Do. Not. Talk. The bubble could pop, and we may need all twenty minutes to go down and up."

"I thought you said these were foolproof," Mark grumbled.

Noah gulped and nodded along despite Mark's grievances, his chin hitting the water as he bobbed. He was now across from Mark, treading on his own. Glancing around, he could tell Katalina was tense; she was notably far quieter, and her mouth was contorted into a half-frown. Not a question to be had, when usually she had the most.

He looked at Mark next, who was already staring him down with creased brows. When their eyes met, Mark held Noah's gaze with a squint, the intimidation he exuded palpable.

Usually, Noah made it a point to maintain eye contact when being stared down, but today he briskly brought his attention back to the packet in hand. The three did as instructed with no complaint, which was another rarity. Everyone was nervous.

Noah submerged his entire body underneath the water, his blond hair lazily floating around him in loose strands as he opened the packet. The sting of salt water bit at his pupils, but the pain was no longer excruciating. Now he welcomed it.

A flat disk floated out of the packet before inflating into a bubble big enough for him to wrap a palm around.

Noah grabbed the bubble gently from behind and guided it toward his mouth and nose. It was transparent yet fluorescent, shimmering in the reflection of the waves. The bubble jiggled the entire way, and when it reached his mouth, a warm sensation fell over the area it covered.

He took the deepest breath he could muster, nervous he miscalculated and it would pop or detach from his face at any moment. But when he inhaled again, the bubble remained intact. Exhale. Inhale. His eyes widened—it worked. He was breathing underwater.

A smile crossed his lips, and it took everything within him not to shout with joy. This contraption *worked*, and they were *doing it*. They were getting closer to saving the planets. He could hardly believe it.

His smile slowly fell as he realized that, aside from the tiny fish at his feet, the ocean was vast and empty, and the bottom remained unseen. The challenge was far from over.

Katalina and Mark attached their bubbles, and then Celeste waved a hand for them to follow. The blue highlights in her hair seemed to glow ever-so-slightly in the dim light underneath the surface. He had to keep his eyes ahead to avoid getting distracted.

While Noah didn't consider himself the best swimmer, he could've sworn there was a current pushing against him as they went further down. Curiouser was the growing brightness the lower they descended, as though the sun could reach unfathomable depths. Or was it something else that was causing it, like a Mertropolis?

Noah's arms ached, but he couldn't look weak in front of the woman he was trying to impress, could he? Or was it too late for that? His thoughts had a way of wandering away from the task at hand, anxiety coursing through him about every little thing all at once. It was a tumbling wave crashing into his chest as he took another breath.

Finally, something came into view and disrupted his swirling thoughts—a boat cracked in half, barnacles and seaweed growing along the rusting metal.

In the center was a garden. A full-fledged garden of flowers and fruits and vegetables. None that he recognized, of course, but the array was bright and beautiful, with green vines and splashes of purples, pinks, and oranges. Bright blue pops of coral were sprinkled throughout, and he couldn't tell if the display was beautiful to look at, or nauseating.

He trod closer to inspect the garden, reaching out to pluck a violet flower made of tiny petals when the ground released a low rumble and shifted. Sand from the ocean floor created a haze above the garden, and Noah jolted back with a sharp intake of breath; there was a crack opening in the center. Noah's heart plummeted at the idea of being pulled into the ocean floor, never to be seen again.

At one point, he may have found comfort in that thought. Now he was terrified of it.

Whatever was happening, he didn't want to be a part of it. He twisted his body around to swim back up to the surface when the sound of gurgling bubbles erupted from below. He didn't dare look down, but he knew he wouldn't be able to swim away fast enough if something were to attack. What to do—

The phrase! He and the other three had to think of a phrase, and the Ruler of the Deep would come... but what was it? Noah wracked his brain, but he couldn't remember, and now the bubbles were engulfing him in a strange, cold heat. He was sure his breathing bubble would either pop from the friction of the surrounding water or his frantic breathing, and he was becoming oddly sleepy despite the adrenaline coursing through him.

It started with an 's'... 'say?' No, that wasn't it—

His eyelids were threatening to close from the fatigue washing over him. No, he had to keep thinking—

Show! Right—it was 'show!' *Show me the Ruler of the Deep.*

A bright light erupted from the flowers and coral, engulfing the entire boat in a blinding white. He squinted, covering his eyes as the bubbles from below seemed to dissipate into small, watery bursts. His vision cleared, and he spotted Celeste a few feet away. Noah swam toward her frantically, reaching out to graze his fingers against hers; he found comfort in being close.

A creature arose from the ground slowly, a long snake-like beast with slicked-back, curly blue horns to go with its blue scales. The eyes were black pits, and its tongue was pointed outward at the end, like the tip of a pencil.

You were quite tasty. A voice popped into his head, and Noah nearly jumped—if not for the fact he was underwater. A chill climbed up his spine; the voice was a deep hum, a laugh resting underneath it.

Noah checked himself for bite marks or wounds but found none. It took him a moment to realize the creature was referring to the bubbles. The Ruler... tasted through bubbles? The thought was... surprisingly unmenacing for a sea creature named 'the Ruler of the Deep.'

I would be careful about who you call unmenacing, the rumbling voice said.

There was something deeply unsettling about a newfound voice reading his thoughts, and he couldn't say he liked it. How much could the snake hear? Was the subconscious involved? Because Noah did not want anyone venturing *there.*

He looked at Celeste and attempted to converse with her via his thoughts, then Mark and Katalina, but it was no use; only the creature could hear him.

Terrified and ready to be breathing air above the surface again, Noah tried to speed the process up and direct his thoughts toward the Ruler. *I know we are nothing more than mere strangers, but please, help us. Our worlds are ending. If you know of a way to... to reverse this process somehow, please help. Please.*

The Ruler's eyes narrowed, bubbles sprouting from his nose, his thin line of a mouth curved upward in a smile. His bright blue scales shimmered against the dark sea as he twirled around Noah quickly.

The Ruler stopped circling with his black, devoid eyes set on Noah—was he about to be devoured?

I may or may not have the answers you seek. Whether you have the right questions, however, is up to you.

34

RULER OF THE DEEP

Who are you? Each word from the Ruler dragged out in a comically slow way, his slithering shape shimmering in the sea light as he swam around the others. Noah was still struggling with the concept of breathing underwater, and now he had to deal with a talking eel, too?

Sea serpent, it said, *and I'm not an 'it.'*

Noah nearly shrieked; there was no adjusting to a creature listening to every thought that popped into his head.

Looking up, he couldn't tell how deep they were, nor if up was truly up. Celeste had every right to be scared here; some monsters opened up to an entirely new landscape and sea serpents could read minds.

Don't look so surprised. All the rulers can. Now I ask again, who are you?

Little did the serpent know rulers like kings and queens never existed on Noah's planet outside of fictional novels, so he didn't know the true extent of their abilities here. But now was no time to argue when presented with a giant snake who could eat him at a moment's notice.

The Ruler let out a low grumble of a laugh. *Like I'd want something with such little meat to their bones.*

Noah glanced down at himself. It was true—Noah was incredibly skinny, probably because of his lack of a sustainable diet and genes. Of course, he didn't want to be eaten, yet he found himself disappointed he didn't look more appetizing.

More bubbles erupted from the Ruler's mouth, garnering a cocked head from Noah. He deduced the creature was releasing another laugh, the gurgled rumble in Noah's thoughts confirming it. *The Ruler of the Sky would enjoy you.*

Although Noah desperately wished to inquire, they had other business to attend. He pointed a thought directly at the Ruler of the Deep—*Don't you have other minds to read?*

More bubbles erupted from the Ruler's mouth as he swam around Noah and Celeste before moving on to Mark and Katalina, pushing the four closer together like he was herding cattle. *None that are interesting. Two are fascinated by me, and one is blocking me out of her thoughts completely.*

Noah turned to Celeste, who was staring at him with wide, worried eyes. Her bubble was even smaller than his now. She must've been silently panicking, which meant they had to wrap this up quickly.

It was comforting to know she was as big a mystery to her world as she was to him.

How am I any more interesting? Noah asked. The Ruler of the Deep circled back around Noah and Celeste, his tongue tickling

Noah's cheek as he whizzed past. Noah jerked his head away, mildly terrified of being deceived and devoured.

Noah could've sworn the Ruler was smiling as it said, *Good. You should fear me.*

That was less comforting.

And, sure, the Ruler of the Deep continued, *one is incredibly smart—she's already deduced we're conversing, so she's keeping an eye out for danger, instead. The guy is very angry about nothing in particular, but anger is often bred from insecurity, and I'm not interested in that, either.*

So are you saying I'm not smart, and that's what makes me interesting? Noah asked.

Not particularly, but many aren't, the Ruler admitted. *But you're viewing me differently than the rest.*

Enlighten me. Noah genuinely hadn't a clue what the sea serpent was talking about. Noah *was* like the others—amazed yet horrified that a shiny thing was swimming around and reading their minds. Though by now, they shouldn't have been so shocked; this entire planet was a piece of decaying art.

The rest fear me because they want to live. You fear me because you want to live and *you want to die.*

The Ruler of the Deep darted toward the dark depths below, his voice becoming distant.

Which one will you choose, I wonder?

The blue light radiating from the Ruler's scales gradually dimmed, as did the blinding light from the garden. Sudden despair washed over Noah; the Ruler was leaving them to drown, just like she said.

The Ruler of the Deep abandoned them so abruptly that

Noah hadn't a chance to collect his bearings. There and then gone with a thousand more questions and no answers. He and the others were back where they started, only this time in the deepest depths of the ocean as they ran out of oxygen.

No. Noah couldn't let it be.

But what was he to do?

The light wasn't returning, and he couldn't see a thing. He was alone in the immeasurable nothingness of cold water. Noah reached out to where he thought Celeste was, but only water slipped through his fingers.

Panic consumed him as he reached for her again. Again, no one was there. He could tell his breathing bubble was running low by the constricting of his lungs, and he had no choice but to swim up to the surface or stay here and drown.

He was taking too long. There wasn't a chance he could make it to the surface when he didn't know which way to go. Had Celeste already reached the top? Were Katalina and Mark already up there, too, swimming toward their boat with a string of swears and heavy gasps?

Should he try to make it? Was there time?

Was there a point?

Everything he loved was either dead or would someday die. Why put everything he had into his survival if it meant nothing at all?

He'd be able to see his mom again, and she'd be warm instead of cold, and they could both finally be at peace. He'd be able to feel whole, away from the constraints of everyday life.

Celeste flashed through his mind, then Mark and Katalina —then Henrietta. He couldn't give up when his friends and family were in danger. He couldn't leave entire species behind knowing the worlds were going to collide in a matter of weeks. Mostly, though, he wanted to see where things went from here, and that meant doing everything in his power to stay alive.

Noah kicked feverishly, despite not knowing which way was up. There was no time to think; every ounce of effort was dedicated to holding his breath and kicking.

A shimmer of light shone from below, slowly climbing toward him. He stopped and looked down—the light was coming too quickly for him to dodge. Noah could do nothing but brace himself for impact and hope he wasn't eaten or crushed or burned alive.

A whizz of bubbles and swirling water engulfed his body. He opened his eyes to find a brilliant yellow light shining around him; a smaller and shorter sea serpent was circling him. Then another and another. Dozens of eels—*sea serpents*—appeared, though they were smaller than the Ruler and made up of yellows and oranges. Their faces were also notably different, with thin mustaches trailing each side of their thicker, smiling lips. Their mouths remained open, teeth pointed.

Giggles from multiple sources erupted in his head, though he still couldn't spot Celeste, Katalina, or Mark anywhere. Was the giggling from the sea serpents, then? Did they all come with the power of reading minds and broadcasting their thoughts?

He supposed it made sense for sea serpents to communicate telepathically since they lived in such a large underwater terrain.

Very good, a feminine, high-pitched voice said with another giggle. *The ocean is so infinite and dark and empty and full. Sometimes we go months, years, lifetimes, without seeing each other.*

How do you keep going? Noah asked, his heart wrenching. He had already gone months, and soon it would be years and the rest of his lifetime without his mother. It was a miracle he was keeping his breathing in check. *If you never know if you'll see those you love again, how do you keep going?*

Another giggle rang through his thoughts before a voice full of childlike wonder sounded next. *There are always new souls out there to meet, and new adventures to be had. Why wouldn't we want to keep going?*

He bobbed in the water silently, his thoughts too muddled for even the sea serpents to understand. His one and only friend on Sundar had always doled out similar platitudes about how there was more to experience, to live for, but he'd never understood what those experiences could be. He waited and waited for something to change, but nothing ever did.

Until Katalina walked into his life.

And then Celeste.

And suddenly he *knew*.

Noah looked around frantically, his hair flowing in the water with each turn of his head. As if understanding his dire need to find his companions, the bubbles engulfing him slowly faded. Light returned, and his heart leaped from his chest when he saw Celeste a few feet away. A neon purple sea serpent was lazily creating a loose spiral around her. Behind her was Katalina in Mark's arms, with a yellow serpent as their captor.

Celeste must've felt his eyes on her because she turned and met his gaze. With a smile distorted from her breathing bubble, she pointed toward her mouth. Her bubble had grown bigger. He reached up and grazed his bubble with his fingers. Though he couldn't see it from this angle, it felt noticeably plumper. Relief washed over him—the Ruler of the Deep wasn't leaving them for dead after all.

Noah didn't know how to communicate with the others, but he figured he'd try, anyway. With Celeste, Katalina, and Mark in mind, Noah asked, *Is everyone okay?*

He jumped at the sound of Katalina's voice almost immediately. *All good over here.*

I'd like to kindly ask the Ruler of the Deep if we can leave now, Mark thought next. *It's a bit too cold down here for my taste.*

Wow, you've refined your complaints. Almost sounded professional, Celeste's voice joined in, and Noah blushed at the way her words made him want to laugh. To think she could evoke such a feeling—and oh, man, he needed to stop thinking about her before she read his mind—

Mark laughed heartedly. *Shocker, the guy finally leaves his house, and he gets a crush on the first woman who talks to him.*

Noah's blush deepened against the coolness of the water. His skin was pruning along his fingers and toes, creating an uncomfortable chill.

I'm sure he's talked to other women, Katalina argued, and he half-expected Celeste to say something, or at least laugh, but she was silent. Somehow, her silence was worse.

A luminance washed over them, his vision instantly filling with black blots. He squinted against the light, a shape emerging. Noah held his breath, hoping for the best but expecting the worst. He smiled when the Ruler of the Deep came into view, his blue scales illuminating the ocean for at least a mile each way. Yet at the very edges, darkness still loomed.

You've asked for my help, said the Ruler of the Deep. *Usually, that means I ask for something in return, but that seems a little silly, considering there would be nothing to return if I didn't help.*

Noah clung to every word. Was it possible for a fish to have the answer to saving their planets?

The Ruler of the Deep stopped speaking and turned to him with a glare. Noah gulped, swiftly offering up profuse apologies.

Do you know how to save our planets, dear Ruler? Celeste asked, somehow broadcasting her thoughts to everyone when she'd been keeping them hidden a moment ago.

The sea serpent nodded and the smaller serpents dispersed, swimming toward the light below. Their giggles became distant the further they swam until his thoughts finally grew quieter. It was a relief to get them out of his head.

I am aware of a way, the Ruler of the Deep proclaimed calmly. *Though I've told your people I will not share it.*

Why not? Celeste asked, her voice lined with shock.

They are greedy. They want the world for them. I was even offered money. Ha! I let the children pick away at him.

Noah gulped, realizing once more that he could easily become food. The Ruler looked at him, their eyes locking as the Ruler said, *No, I already said I wouldn't have you eaten. No point—too thin. But that man, on the other hand...*

Who? Me? Mark asked before his inner voice became increasingly louder. *No way! You are not talking about who you'd eat and picking me?*

Will you tell us? Noah asked, turning the conversation back to the topic at hand. *We want to save the planets. Our intentions are good.*

The serpent released what could only be described as a sigh. *Yes, I suppose I will. But only because you passed my test, and only with a condition—bring me back the blue star.*

I thought you weren't going to ask anything of us?

That's the thing about sea serpents—we have fickle minds. Consider our contract amended. Do you accept these terms?

Noah looked between the other three for confirmation before he made the last call. They all nodded, and the sea serpent burst around them quickly and efficiently, starting from their heads and moving down to their torsos and feet. Another cocoon of air bubbles formed, but it felt different this time. Instead of extra padding against his limbs, he couldn't help but feel like he was being forced upward.

You must find the stars above the hill. A star the shade of hope awaits. There, you will find what you seek.

But what will this star do? Celeste asked, treading closer to the serpent as if doing so would make the Ruler of the Deep more willing to help. She was scared, Noah guessed, or eager—or both.

There was no answer. Noah directed his thoughts toward the others, but he was met with silence; he was back to being alone. His surroundings were becoming hazier as more bubbles formed, and suddenly his stomach felt as though it were flipping in on itself, water whizzing around him. Were the bubbles… taking him to the surface?

It's a shame the crumbling planet will go. I will try to help you, but know that our planet always remains.

Noah hadn't a chance to decipher what the Ruler of the Deep meant; the rush of adrenaline that came was intoxicating as his body shot through the water. Seconds from hitting the surface, the sea serpent said,

Remember—the stars hold more power than you may think.

35

UP, UP AND AWAY

THE SKY BURST INTO VIEW IN A BURNING BRIGHT HAZE THAT instantly scarred his retinas, yet he forced his eyes to stay open. A thick stream of water hit his back at an impossible speed, like a water hose lifting him into the air. He could feel the bruises forming with each thrum of pain, yet he welcomed it.

The water pressure stopped, and there was a brief moment where he was peacefully hovering in the air. The pastel green sky was replaced with the familiar purple and pink hues glistening like strokes of paint against a canvas. He felt oddly at peace despite the drop of his stomach as he free-fell backward. His back hit the ocean with a *smack*, and he was beneath the waves once more.

He gasped for breath when he reached the surface, temporary shock rushing through him. The waves here were harsher, and he struggled to find his way back onto their ship—which had somehow been spat out of the Ruler's realm as well, albeit a tad more gracefully.

Finally, he found his grip and climbed aboard. When he turned around, he caught the last glimpse of the four-armed monster they'd gone through to reach the Ruler of the Deep. The creature was whole once more, slowly walking backward while lowering its head into the sea until there was nothing but a ripple in its place.

Noah bent down to catch his breath with hands on his hips, and eyes fixed on the ground. Was it possible to have terribly great luck? He almost drowned—twice. But they'd also found the Ruler of the Deep and got their next clue toward saving the planets.

"Katalina," Mark yelled, rushing to her side. She had no noticeable scratches or an unusual cough or wince of pain, yet Mark slid against the ship's floorboards and scooped her into a tight hug. She let out a surprised huff as their bodies remained pressed together. "I thought I lost you."

Her mouth parted in surprise, but she clamped it shut quickly, a small smile painting her lips. Then she wrapped her arms around him and squished him as hard as she could. His blue eyes bulged as he let out a constricted laugh. Still, she remained secure around him. "Never. Even if I were to go, you would never lose me."

Mark stared down at her, his eyes glazed over with infatuation. Noah found it nauseating, though he couldn't deny his want for a relationship full of so much passion. "I love you so fucking much, Katalina. You're crazy for dragging us down here, but without you, I wouldn't experience anything at all. I'd be home on the couch, sleeping or running or doing... absolutely nothing every day. Simply just existing. But with you, life is simple but far from just existing."

"Practicing your together vows already?" Katalina asked before pulling him into a kiss.

Noah went to stand beside Celeste with his arms crossed over his chest, watching the romance unfold as Celeste stood at the helm. Her mouth was a tight line as she overlooked the horizon. Once again, he was tasked with wondering how necessary steering the ship was.

"Their love is beautiful," she said, but her voice didn't show she thought so. Something was wrong. They'd found the Ruler of the Deep, they had a lead on where to go next, and yet something was wrong.

"I'd make a strong case against it," Noah said. "He's too angry; she's too quiet. It's odd."

"Is it? Or does he stick up for her while she cools him down?" Celeste asked. "I think they're perfect."

He grimaced. "Yeah, they are. I just didn't want to admit it."

She playfully rolled her eyes. "You could get it over with and apologize to them."

"That would be too easy."

She cracked a smile, and he wished he could add something more to make her laugh, but he was fresh out of jokes. His thoughts were fleeting after the events of their day. Being submerged for so long—it felt incredibly unnatural to stand up here instead of bobbing in the water. "Did he talk to you at all? The Ruler of the Deep?"

"Yes, in the beginning. He told me I was interesting, and that you were blocking him out of your thoughts."

Celeste nodded. "Something Luna taught me how to do. Anyone can learn how, but it's easier for merpeople, of course. I've trained a bit with her, though. Otherwise, she'd know what I'm doing and thinking all the time!"

"No comment on why he thought I may be interesting?" He thought she'd be surprised by this tidbit.

"I already know why—it's because you're you," she said. It was his turn to crack a smile. "Let's go celebrate, and then we'll see if there's any nearby land so we can rest and eat and get off the water for a bit."

"Do you have any idea where we are relative to where we started?"

"No, not really. But that's the thing about life—you tend to end up where you need to be without knowing how you got there."

He declined to comment on how both their closest family members ended up in the ground, and rather recently. Instead, Noah followed, his heart a pitter-patter of nerves at the thought of facing Katalina and Mark in a celebratory nature. Their little argument from earlier had yet to be hashed out, and this fact wedged itself in the spaces between them.

The air grew thick as Katalina and Mark went from speaking in their normal tones to a whisper until they fell silent. Noah and Celeste stopped once they reached the other two, and Celeste raised a fist in the air with a beaming smile. "We did it!"

"Hazzah!" Katalina yelled, a blush quickly overtaking her

features after doing so, eyes darting around at Celeste and Mark abashedly. She was careful to bypass Noah completely, and he was okay with that. It appeared they all equally did not want to talk about it or apologize.

Celeste grinned from ear to ear and raised another fist. “Hazzah!”

Mark chuckled, patting Katalina’s head. “Nice to see someone get along around here.”

Noah couldn’t help the *tsk* that left his lips. Only Celeste acknowledged the noise, glancing over at him with brows pinched in worry. He refused to give in, however.

“You should follow her example,” Celeste said as she glared at Mark, and Noah’s head snapped up to face her in an instant. If he’d been drinking water, he would’ve spit it out. Had she defended Noah by… insulting Mark?

She was perfect.

But something was clawing at the back of his mind, and it was only growing louder and clearer the more he thought about it. The sea serpent had made a comment that startled him, and while Noah tried to push down the unease, it was no use.

“Did you guys hear the Ruler of the Deep’s comment about our planets? Wasn’t what he said odd?”

The other three shook their heads, and he was left baffled. The Ruler had made it apparent he favored Noah, for whatever reasons, but Noah would’ve thought this comment was meant for all of them.

“He said, ‘It’s a shame the crumbling planet will go. I will try to help you, but know that our planet always remains.’ And I thought that was incredibly odd, seeing as your brother's research predicted your planet was going to—"

Noah cut himself off.

He was merely sharing an observation, but the look of panic in her eyes was enough for him to know. His heart crumbled in his chest as he sucked in a deep breath of betrayal.

In a crashing wave, the question he feared an answer to came tumbling out, "It's not your world, is it?"

36

THE TURNING POINT

"IT'S NOT YOUR WORLD THAT'S GOING TO BE COMPLETELY destroyed, is it?" he asked again, hurt flashing across his features.

Noah's brows crinkled in the way they did when he cried, but instead of tears falling, his fists curled. His knuckles turned white as he pressed his nails into his palms until he drew blood. Celeste stood tall, yet her demeanor shifted slightly, and she pulled away from him like a wounded animal.

"No," she said with a gulp. "It's not my world."

His eyes bore into her, and she shuffled uncomfortably in her spot. "You aren't smiling."

Words appeared lost on her. "Come again?"

"This entire trip, you've been smiling, but now it's gone. Why? Because you lied to us? Or because you know the knowledge that no one on our planet cares enough to save everyone is too much to bear?"

She blinked. "The second one."

"Why keep it from us?"

"Wait," Mark interrupted with his hand out, his voice surprisingly calm despite the disastrous information piling atop itself. Noah, however, felt as though his next words would erupt in a shout. He suppressed the rage from boiling over, but barely. "So, you're saying that *our* planet is the one that's going to be destroyed, and *you* get to keep seventy-five percent of yours?"

Celeste nodded slowly, carefully avoiding everyone's narrow eyes.

"But," Mark started, running a hand through his hair. He was shaking, and his voice grew notably louder. "But, by Goddesses, that's *everyone*. I mean, *everyone* can't die! W-we have a kickball team!"

"I don't think gravity cares about anyone's friends or family," Celeste murmured, sending a chill through everyone's bones.

"The Ruler of the Deep said he'd try to help us," Noah said under his breath before clearing his throat. "Our planets, one way or another, are doomed unless we find these... stars. Because when the black hole sucks us both in, we'll have no way to stop it."

"There *has* to be a way," Katalina sobbed. "I told my parents and sister I'd be back after dinner, Noah, and now it's been almost a month since. I can't—I can't stay here knowing they'll die so soon and without a goodbye."

"We'll continue with the plan as it is now," Noah reassured, before turning toward Celeste, his tone softer along the edges. Tired. "Why did you lie?"

She stood her ground, though he could tell she'd prefer to shrivel away by the way she stepped back and glanced around the ship.

"Why, Celeste?" He'd never said her name in such a defeated tone before, and it made him wince—he wouldn't be able to take back his disappointment later.

"*Technically,* it doesn't matter that I lied, because we'll save the planets either way, right?" Her voice was but a mere whisper. "It doesn't matter."

"Of course it does," he said. "It's the principle. It's the fact you could look me, and all of us, in the eyes and lie. Who's to say what else you have or will keep from us?"

"But why would it matter—"

Noah threw his hands out in exasperation. "How can you possibly be so positive all the time? I don't *get* it. I don't get how you can know an entire planet will be destroyed and be so *happy* about it and act like it doesn't matter that *everyone is going to die if we fail.*"

She shrugged. "It's a gift."

"Are you sure?" he asked, knowing how it sounded—condescending and annoyed—yet standing his ground, regardless.

Her fingers curled next, and a burst of air escaped from her lungs as she yelled, "Of course, I'm not happy about what's happening. Of course, I'm scared. But there are two ways to go about the knowledge of imminent death—which we all face every single day. You either stare at the horror and sit in it, spouting platitudes you don't truly believe, or you start to believe the platitudes until one day, it's not so bad anymore."

He clamped his jaw shut.

"I understand your negativity, Noah, but that doesn't make it right."

Noah looked away. "I'm sorry. It's all I've ever known. I don't know how to turn it off, either, honestly." He folded his arms. Somehow, she'd turned the fault on him, yet the tension still left his shoulders. "You shouldn't have lied, even if you were trying to protect our feelings."

Celeste nodded as she took a sharp breath in. "I'm sorry, too. I didn't want you to worry any more than you already were, but I promise, that's all I've lied about. We can save *both* our planets, and everyone will be okay."

"If you truly believed that, then you would've told us the truth from the get-go," Katalina said, her body shaking as her brows furrowed. She looked between Noah and Celeste. "You two are real pieces of work, you know that? A liar and a jerk. Perfect for each other."

Katalina stormed away; Mark watched her go before turning to them. "This storming off has been happening too much lately. Get it together."

And then he followed his fiancée down to the hammocks below deck. Celeste sighed, leaning against the railing with her head in her hand. He felt inclined to follow. Though he was still upset, Mark's words rattled him enough to put her deceit on the back burner. After all, the chances they all died from the planets colliding—or at the very least being sucked through a black hole—was high the entire time.

Still, he made a note of this moment as a reference point if another lie were to come about. There was a record now; he was entering at his own risk.

"I meant to ask when you'd said the sides of your planets move—what shape is your planet?" he asked, and she looked at him like his question was absurd.

"Square."

Her face was so serious he had a double take.

"Square?"

"Yes, square. What do you mean? What other shape would it be?"

For his planet, there were two widely accepted theories—Sundar was either round or flat. It'd long since been debunked as round, however, with a corner of it quite literally crumbling off into space. Well, it wasn't completely flat, as there was also a sizeable chunk of dirt and roots and whatever else lured beneath the surface, ending in a jagged point below.

Scientists knew this because they tried to climb down the side of Sundar—but the gravity was different and they just sort of drifted off and froze. Naturally, scientists also deduced the sun and moons were flat, too.

But square?

"How do we know when we're on another side of the planet?"

Celeste shook her head. "It's hard to figure out, but there's only two sides with an ocean, so we're on at least one of them. The planet feels circular, but from the Sky Kingdom, you can see it is indeed a square."

"Huh. Neat." He did not have kingdoms in the sky or otherwise to boast about. "Did you know in our world, we've invented a hotdog with chili and cheese on it? Can you picture that?"

Her nose scrunched. "Is that good? It sounds... not worth the trouble, eating a dog."

"Oh, no," he said with a laugh. "They aren't made from actual dogs, and they're delicious! We'll have to try some sometime... it's better than that Remembrance Well water, I can tell you that much. The ice cream here is a close contender, though."

Celeste smiled and finally found the courage to look him in the eyes. The gentle breeze from the oceanfront rustled her blueish-black strands. "I'm really sorry, Noah. A lie slipped out because I wanted you to stick around, and I was afraid knowing the full truth would make you... implode, as it would anyone else. I mean, you saw how they reacted."

She gestured toward the open doorway where Katalina and Mark had made their descent. "It seemed fun to bring someone with me, and I'm happy I chose you, but I never should've lied."

He nodded. "That is true, but I accept your apology."

"That was fast." Her eyebrows rose as though she couldn't believe his words. "Are you lying to make a point?"

"I used to hold many grudges and resentments, but I've learned that life is too short. You had your reasons, and I think you feel bad and know not to lie again. We're all human—I've told a lie or two in my lifetime."

"Have you ever lied to me?" she asked after a beat of silence.

"Not that I know of, but I understand. Take it or leave it—I'm going to go take a nap." He chuckled to himself before walking away.

"What're you laughing at?" she asked, taking a step closer and grabbing his wrist to keep him from leaving.

"To think, all this time, you were all only a fall away. I guess I find it amusing."

Her mouth remained parted as if she was waiting for him to say something more, but then her lips met in a closed smile. "Well, it's a bit more complicated than that, wouldn't you say? For example, if we'd truly fallen and hadn't jumped, we'd have exploded. Same with if you aren't holding the hand of someone who definitively knows where you're going. Thankfully, you all listened."

"And you didn't mention that before?" he asked, mouth agape. If he, Katalina, or Mark's legs had failed them, or if they hadn't heard the demand...

He shuddered, unable to finish the thought.

"I didn't want you to worry."

He gave her a light glare, but there was a smirk forming on his lips to indicate he wasn't upset. "Jeez. Like I said, no more lying. I mean it. It's better to get the truth out there quickly. Like ripping off a bandaid. But... I forgive you for that one, too."

Noah took his leave and headed toward his small room with a hammock. Halfway there, Celeste called out his name. He turned; her eyes were full of tears that did not fall, her smile bright yet wavering as she said, "Thank you."

37

APOLOGIES ALL AROUND

After a week of smooth sailing, they docked on an island that appeared remote. It was perhaps the size of a large city, except with tall trees instead of skyscrapers. The sand was a light tan against dark blue water, and he almost felt like he was home.

Though it was implied Noah felt bad and forgave Katalina and Mark, he wanted to apologize formally—their ongoing feud was becoming a ghost left unacknowledged each time they passed.

The couple was currently sitting under the shade of some orange palm trees along the shore, whispering to each other as Katalina picked at the sparse blades of grass. When he approached, they looked up at him with neutral expressions. Well, that was better than anger, he supposed.

"Hey," he said.

"Come to insult us more?" asked Mark.

"Laying it on there thick, honey," Katalina said with a pat on Mark's shoulder. "Let's hear what he has to say first."

She was a natural conflict defuser most days, which meant what Noah said earlier must've been pretty nasty for him to be ignored for so long.

"You've both been so kind to me while we've been here. Mostly." Noah gave Mark a pointed look before turning his attention back to Katalina. "And it was so thoughtful of you to reach out to me. I'm sorry for the way I've been acting."

Apologizing always brought about a feeling of both shame and relief, but he was happy to get everything out. Now he wouldn't have to worry each time he walked into the same space or looked their way—in theory.

"Thank you," Katalina said with a soft smile and a nod. "I accept your apology!"

Noah held up a finger. "I have to ask, though. Why did you choose to reach out to me after my mother's death and not before?"

"And why did you agree to be dragged down here on this mission in the first place?" Mark added with a squint. Something told Noah that Mark had been pressing Katalina extensively about her reasoning on this very issue, and she had yet to budge.

Katalina continued to pick at the grass as Noah towered above.

"Does it have something to do with why my mother cut yours off?" Noah tried, knowing it was a long shot. The question had been burning within him since it'd popped into his head days ago. His mother had always been elusive regarding the 'why,' and he was never supplied with a phone number or address to reach out to. Katalina had told him they'd played together when they were younger, but he must've been too young to remember.

Katalina nodded. "Well, I only know my mother's side of the story, but Aunt Relma wasn't fond of how my mom was raising me, so they got into a fight. I guess when I was a baby... my mother would leave me in my stroller outside while she shopped, or leave me at home, alone. She used to hurt me, which is why I carry gauze around with me everywhere... I love her now, but I would probably speak up if I was Aunt Relma, too..."

She took a deep breath. "My mother is deeply regretful now, Noah. She prays every day, and she is ashamed of how their relationship transpired and how she treated me. She'll never get to say goodbye or reconcile with my aunt, and it's her fault. How sad must that be?"

"And that's the real reason you reached out to have dinner with me?" he asked. "To reconcile?"

Katalina provided another nod. "I was hoping we would get along, and then you would agree to meet with my mother. I think she'd like to know her nephew."

"For the record, I don't forgive you—" Mark began; Katalina tapped him on the stomach rough enough to garner an *oof* and Noah could get a word in edge-wise.

"I don't accept yours, either, Mark. What you said was pretty messed up, too."

Mark stood and went nose-to-nose with Noah, as though he may start a fight, and they had an awkward staring contest where Noah didn't completely understand what was happening. Mark finally backed away and put his hand out for Noah to shake.

Noah glanced down at his offer skeptically. He saw Mark's lips move and heard him say something, but his words were too muffled to understand. Noah leaned closer as he asked, "What was that?"

"I'm sorry," Mark raised his voice, but it cracked halfway through. He cleared his throat while averting his gaze. "I was out of line. You asked us to not bring the... thing—"

"My dead mother, you mean? That thing?" Noah asked, allowing Mark to squirm for a moment before giving him a soft smile. "I'm giving you a hard time, but that'll be the last time I do, I promise."

Mark's cheeks darkened. "You told us not to bring her up, and we didn't respect your wishes. For that, I'm sorry."

Noah nodded, satisfied. "I didn't mean to make Katalina feel bad, either. It was something that slipped out, but that doesn't make it right."

Mark waved away his words. "That's history now. But I'll add that sometimes your jokes are a little much."

"Your anger is a bit much, too, but sometimes we deal with things we don't like about the people we love."

"Or we grow to change," Mark retorted with a flat voice.

"In due time," Katalina interjected. Then she clapped and rolled her shoulders before hopping up and engulfing Noah in a tight squeeze. "I think we need to pause and party! We're so much closer to saving the planets!"

Mark glanced around. "Not much to party with here... and Noah doesn't strike me as much of the partying type."

He looked Noah up and down, and Noah couldn't help but feel the need to defend himself. "Hey, I'm a partier. I party. I know all the songs they play at parties and—"

"You've said the word 'party' too many times for me to believe you," Mark said with narrow eyes and arms folded over his chest triumphantly.

"But what will we do?" Noah asked, opting to let Mark win and change the subject altogether. "After the planets are saved and the celebrations are had—where will we go?"

Katalina and Mark exchanged a worried look, and Noah took to inspecting the tree branches full of lush leaves drenching them in shade.

"Well, life would go back to how it was, I suppose," Katalina said slowly. "And we could finally get that dinner."

Noah smiled, though he couldn't help but feel unequivocally torn. They had a kickball team to go back to. Parents. Siblings. He had a—

"Can a cat from our planet fall through and land here, do you think?" he asked suddenly.

Katalina's smile wavered. "You're thinking of staying?"

He scanned the area for Celeste; she was standing a few feet away from the boat, barefoot in the shallow water. Her hands were clasped behind her back, and she was fidgeting with a blue bracelet around her wrist.

Noah spoke to Katalina from over his shoulder. "I don't know. Maybe. But it's too early to tell."

Was it possible to escape forever?

38

IF YOU STAYED

"What would you do here, though?" Mark asked, scratching his chin. "The job market back home is tough enough, and you don't have experience in this world."

Noah shrugged. "I have a degree in finance. How hard could it be? That's like a universal skill."

"Uh, the money system is completely different here!"

He recalled the money Celeste gave Mark and Katalina back in the city. "I can learn it easily enough. It can't be too much different from the basic math we use."

They stared at him, dumbfounded. After a moment more of the uncomfortable silence, he snapped his fingers. "You never told us why you wanted to come, Kat. Can I call you 'Kat?'"

Katalina smiled warmly, but it was shrouded in something else, something sad. There was a truth she was desperately hiding. "That works. As long as you don't call me 'Lina.' I hate that nickname."

"Noted," Noah said. He'd have to ask her again another time; for now, they deserved to celebrate.

"Why are you so desperate to avoid that question?" Mark asked, shaking his head in disapproval. He didn't appear to care about ruining the jolly mood any more than he usually did. "Is it because of me?"

Her mouth hung open. "No, of course not. I'm... tired, I guess. Every day has been the same. I can only play so much kickball and go on so many hikes and cycling competitions from one end of Sundar to the next."

Was everyone secretly unhappy with the mundanities of life?

"I know," Noah said suddenly. "While you guys talk about this, I'll ask Celeste about the cat thing. It'd be neat to bring Henrietta here, and it's good to keep my options open after we save the planets!"

He prepared to jog toward Celeste when Katalina grabbed his wrist. He turned as she said, "Do you think it's smart to stay here for a girl? A girl you met a little over three weeks ago, who you just found out lied to us?"

"It's been four weeks, actually. That's almost a month." His thoughts soured at that—they only had one more month before the planets collided. "And it's not like her lie mattered much, anyway. We're being sucked into a black hole, Katalina. Do you think Sundar can sustain that, with or without being completely obliterated?"

Katalina shook her head. "That's not the point. If you broke up, you wouldn't know anyone here. You wouldn't have anyone to lean on if things fell apart."

"Now, now. For someone who has found true love yourself, you don't have much faith in my romantic endeavors, do you?" he asked jokingly.

"You're a sad person who is still healing. I think you're hurting and you want to do everything in your power to escape, and this would be the *easy* way to do it. But is it the smart way? The right way?"

He held his chest as though she'd wounded him, but he wore a goofy half-smile as well—a sarcastic dagger through the heart. Although, if he were to be honest with himself, her words did sting a bit.

Before he could comment further, she added swiftly, "You'd have us. I know you think you have no one, and maybe you didn't, but you could. You do."

Katalina gestured between her and Mark. He gave them both a small nod, his joking demeanor slowly drifting into square shoulders and a clearing of his throat. "Thank you, Katalina. I guess we'll see when the time comes."

With that, she let go of his wrist, her hand dropping to her side. He jogged toward Celeste, slipping off his sneakers and socks before splashing through the shallow waves and stopping beside her.

The initial contact with ice-cold water was always the worst part—or perhaps the lead-up was—and he shivered as soon as his toes hit the water. The ocean foamed along the edges before receding into itself, sand shifting beneath his feet leisurely.

Her wavy blueish-black hair was flowing in the breeze behind her as she tossed rocks into the waves. They bounced along the top of the water, creating ripples before disappearing underneath.

"Enjoying the detour?" he asked, crossing his arms over his chest as she tossed another flat rock.

"You did well today," Celeste said, her voice sugary sweet. "With spotting this island. I didn't think I could stay on the boat for another second."

He nodded. There was still a lingering tension between them, though he couldn't pinpoint why. They'd both apologized and forgave, so what continued to cause discontent? Was it the kiss that bothered her so?

He'd made up with Mark and Katalina; he could crack Celeste's shell, too.

"We couldn't—and wouldn't—have done it without you," Noah said. "You should thank yourself. Or... we could thank my mom and your brother for dying. They are, oddly, how we met."

Knowing his joke would either be taken lightly or fall flat, his shoulders relaxed when she chuckled. "That's true. Maybe they were conspiring in the afterlife for us to meet."

Noah snapped his fingers. "That's it."

A blanket of silence fell before he added, "You mentioned what happened to him."

Maybe he shouldn't have kept going.

"I should do the same, I think. My mom, uh... well. She was a very sad, sad person. Sometimes she held it in well enough, and maybe for a month or two she would be fine—or at least appear to be—but then you would see... cracks. Like her eyes would be all red and puffy when she came home from work, or you'd hear sniffles in the other room. And I think, one day, it was too much."

A tear rolled down his cheek. Then another. "I can't... I can't say it, but there was no letter or anything. Growing up, I always used to wonder if I was enough." He took in a shaky breath. "Turns out the answer is no."

Noah avoided her gaze, unable to bear the sadness and pity that'd be staring back. He thought he was ready. He thought, after all the crying he'd done the last few weeks, that he had no more tears left to shed, and he could say it.

But he couldn't.

His heart felt like it was being crushed in someone's hand. He needed to get away—he couldn't talk about her. He couldn't. It was too sad. It was too sad how alone she felt, and how alone she truly was when Noah moved away. She was alone when she died, and no one noticed except her supervisor and her son.

He hadn't a key into her house, and by the time authorities agreed to go in, she was long gone. Gone and alone.

Noah needed to get out of here.

There was nowhere to go.

Celeste turned to face him head-on and clutched his shoulders. "Noah, listen to me. Whatever her fight was, it had nothing to do with you. All that negativity, hatred, and despair she felt was directed at herself and the world and others, but not you. And if she felt a sliver of that toward you, well then, that's not very nice, now is it?"

Noah smiled. Even if he didn't fully believe her, her reaffirmation was enough to soothe his nerves. He had become so overwhelmed with emotion that he'd forgotten to ask about the logistics of getting Henrietta through the black hole and into his arms.

Celeste rested her head against his like she had at the endless loop, and his racing heart found a steady, comfortable pace. He'd have to save his question for another day.

39

HOME

THE FOLLOWING MORNING, HE AWOKE FROM RAINDROPS PRICKLING his skin. Droplets slipped up his nose and into his eyes, and he snorted, his body jolting upright as he gasped and gauged his surroundings.

His shoulders relaxed at the sight of the other three curled up under the thick leaves of the trees above. They'd found a nook beside a large, mountainous cliffside at the other end of the island, the trunks long and the branches big and bright and full. Except now, in the fresh dawn, a blanket of gray clouds overtook the sky, and a drizzle had started.

Until now, he hadn't thought this world had dark days, yet weak sunlight filtered through the leaves. Looking up, he noticed one leaf above the sleeping trio was teetering with too much water, and before he could get a word out, the leaf lost its structure, and a bucket of water fell on Mark's head.

Mark sat upright with startled gasps, water spilling from his mouth and nose. He gagged on the air feverishly, his face turning a deep shade of red before he finally caught his breath. Katalina awoke next, her head on a swivel. Celeste was last, waking slowly with a leisurely stretch and a yawn.

And then her eyes widened, and she hopped up. "Don't look at the rain!"

His heart sank as he remembered her words from weeks ago —staring at the rain caused uncontrollable hiccups.

"Why not—" Katalina began, but before she could finish her question, she hiccuped. She gasped and covered her mouth with both hands.

Celeste grabbed her shoulder apologetically. "It's okay. It usually only lasts five hours."

"Only," Noah exclaimed, clamping his eyes shut and holding out a hand. "I'm not taking any chances. Someone take my hand and lead me out of here."

Katalina responded with a suppressed hiccup, her shoulders bobbing along.

"It's fucking freezing," Mark remarked with a final wheeze before his breathing leveled out. "Why did we decide to sleep out here again instead of on the ship?"

"We unanimously voted that it would feel like a fun little sleepover," Celeste called over the rain. "Which it was until now."

The temperature had dipped considerably since the clouds rolled in, and when no one took his hand, Noah rubbed his forearms to keep away the chill. A pair of hands eventually grabbed his shoulders from behind and led him toward a dry patch of ground formed along the edges of the cliffside. The rough rock was jagged and frozen to the touch, and his teeth chattered, but at least they would be away from the rain.

"Here," Katalina called with another hiccup. She was a few feet ahead, pointing to a crack in the rock. They followed; it was damp and cramped—which made him woozy with paranoia—before opening up to an enormous cavern. Blue and green crystals lined every inch of the walls, glistening against the reflections of each other.

"Oh, wow," Noah said, finally opening his eyes. His voice echoed despite its initial soft tone. It was notably warmer in the cavern, and though the rain was loud, they could still hear each other better than they could outside. "Why didn't we come in here before?"

In the center of the ceiling was an opening in the rock, where rain cascaded like a waterfall. There was another hole, this time leading below, and the waterfall descended further. Though he presumed it was rainwater, it did not cause hiccups, and plumes of steam spooled out from below.

There was also a telescope set up a few feet away from the waterfall, facing up to the sky. Celeste inspected it with a raised brow, making a full circle around it before finally looking through the eyehole.

Time stood still as he watched her tuck a black strand behind her ear and close one eye, pushing the other toward the lens. Noah stepped up beside her, unable to wait a single second for a chance to look through the telescope; he hadn't looked through one in years. "What can you see?"

She pulled away, brows crinkled in confusion. "Nothing."

"Nothing?"

Celeste moved aside and gestured for him to look for himself. When he did, he found she was right. "Well, it is cloudy this morning—and raining."

She shook her head. "These types of telescopes can see through clouds. It appears the stars have disappeared. Moon, too."

"How—*hiccup*—does—*hiccup*—never mind," Katalina said, waving a hand in defeat. Noah was increasingly thankful he hadn't accidentally looked too hard at the rain. He was lucky.

"I think she's trying to ask how that happens," Mark said. "Did they burst? Die out?"

Celeste shook her head. "No... no, I think it's none of the above. I think they moved."

The dots were formed in his mind before being connected swiftly. "They're underneath the hill."

"Yes, I think so."

"And that's the only description the sea monster gave us? 'A hill?' Have you seen how many hills and mountains we've passed so far?" Mark asked, throwing out his hands.

Celeste sighed. "Am I to have all the answers?" She shook her head. "Something must've activated their movement, but what...?"

Noah could see that look in her eyes—that longing for answers. People went their whole lives longing for answers they'd never find. But what were her questions?

Katalina hiccup-whispered something to Mark and then,

acting as her mouthpiece, he proclaimed, "But that's not how stars work. They can't be moved. And how do we find them?"

"There's only one person I know who can move astral objects, but I don't know if she could, or would want, to move all of them," Celeste said, conveniently leaving out the 'who' of it all. "And she's not a cheerful person. Honestly, I'd rather avoid her altogether if we could."

"Please don't tell me it's another fish," Mark said.

A small smile crossed Celeste's lips. "No, no, quite the opposite. The Ruler of the Sky."

Noah's ears perked at this. Another one of the four rulers? Celeste had warned that none of the rulers were particularly personable, but a ruler of the sky sounded more whimsical than scary. And, if he remembered correctly, the Ruler of the Deep mentioned the Ruler of the Sky would 'enjoy' Noah. Whatever that meant.

"Wait," Celeste said, throwing out her hands as if she were stopping two people from fighting, though she stared directly ahead at no one as she spoke. "I need to check something."

She burst into a full sprint the way they came, and the other three were inclined to follow.

"What is it?" he yelled after her.

"A hunch," she called back with a bright, excited smile on her face.

They ran outside a moment later; the rain had dissipated, the cold smacking his cheeks and inducing a red hue. Noah stopped beside Celeste with hands on his knees, gasping for breath as he looked at the mushy dirt below. When he finally caught his breath, he looked up to find her spinning around frantically, searching for something in the sky.

"Aha!" Celeste pointed toward somewhere off in the distance. Noah followed her finger toward a darkened sky, and he was about to ask what she was pointing at when he saw it. He squinted long and hard to find it, but there was the faintest glow of light. His gaze snapped back to hers with a smile already creeping onto his features. "There. I think that's it."

Noah nodded enthusiastically. "It has to be!"

"I've never noticed a light off in the distance before..." Mark trailed off as the other three nodded in agreement. This was it —this was the way to the stars above the hill. Giddy bubbles burst inside him as he engulfed Celeste in a hug, burying his face in the crook of her neck and twirling her around. When he set her down, he was going to kiss—

"What are we going to do?" Katalina's voice disrupted his moment of joy, the hiccups incessant.

Noah pulled away and cocked his head. "We follow the light and save the planets, of course. Why? Were you thinking of giving up now?"

As he asked, he noticed Mark was holding a photograph of their... kickball team? His hand was over his mouth, brows furrowed as he stared down at a group wearing matching red shirts and khaki shorts.

Noah's mouth hung open, baffled. Were they... thinking of conceding? He tried to think of a comforting statement, but he came up short. Noah didn't have any other close friends; he didn't fully understand their need to be there instead of here.

There was only one solution, of course, the obvious solution

—they would find the source of salvation, the way to freedom of life for both planets. A way to save everyone, including themselves. He didn't know if he could live with himself if he didn't at least try, and it shocked him the other two wouldn't feel the same. After all, they needed Sundar more than he did. As long as he had Celeste, he had everything he needed.

Selfishly, he wanted to curl up on this elusive hill under the stars with Celeste and let the worlds collide. But, of course, nothing was ever so simple. To live in ignorance was one thing, but to live with *knowing*—he wouldn't be able to bear it.

Everything and everyone—*and Henry.*

"I'm going to help Celeste, and I think the two of you should, too."

"But what if it doesn't work?" Katalina asked. "And we're never able to say goodbye? If we fail... I don't think I could stomach not saying goodbye to my parents and sister..."

"What if it *does* work and we save everyone, and you won't have to?" Noah quipped back.

"And"—he took a deep breath, finding Katalina's gaze—"I'll respect you as a person if you help."

Her eyebrows shot up, and a smile slunk onto her features almost immediately. "Really?"

Noah smirked at her eagerness to win him over, which transformed into a bold grin after he noticed Mark's twitching brow. Mark took a step forward with a hand outstretched in front of her. "We were always going to help. I'd rather save everyone than a sliver of them."

"Wow, Mark. I'm proud of you." Noah tapped Mark on the

shoulder and laughed; he'd never seen someone look so disgusted by such a gesture.

"I'm not a complete heathen, you know."

"I don't know," Noah challenged with a sly shrug. "After the draegon and shapeshifter we encountered and the way you hit them, I don't know what to call you anymore. And while you chickened out and forced Katalina to save me from the derithia, *I* got us points for convincing the Ruler of the Deep to help us."

Celeste gasped. "He's right. Women have two, and now men have one point. Too bad; maybe you'll catch up next time."

"'Next time...'" Noah said with a brow raised.

"He's not a heathen, but he is *hot*," Katalina added boldly, though her timing was incredibly off. Then, under her breath, she added, "Even when he's an ass, he's hot."

"Mumbling insults doesn't make them any less insulting," Mark grumbled, looking away with a pout.

"It was a compliment hidden within an insult, honey. Trust me, you'll look back at this in five years and laugh," Katalina said, chuckling at her joke before the realization struck that five years might be nothing at all.

"So it's settled, then? We're all going?" Noah asked, looking around the group and meeting the eyes of each person with an added nod of encouragement.

First was Katalina, who nodded hesitantly before averting her gaze. Then Mark, who gave Noah a light glare as his head bobbed in agreement. Finally, Celeste, who simply held his gaze with her galaxy-speckled eyes. He smiled, and she smiled back, and the flutter in his stomach sent him into a whirlwind of eager anticipation. He wished he had an excuse to kiss her again.

Celeste took a step forward and pointed toward the faint glow of the sky, proclaiming loudly, "Onward, then. To the stars!"

Noah, Katalina, and Mark mimicked her pointed finger and called in unison, "To the stars!"

For the first time in years, he felt like he was home.

IF YOU ENJOYED THIS SERIES, PLEASE CONSIDER LEAVING A REVIEW TO SHOW YOUR LOVE AND SUPPORT!

CHECK OUT THE PAPERBACK EDITIONS:

TURN THE PAGE FOR A SNEAK PEEK OF THE EPIC CONCLUSION OF THE WORLD BEYOND DUOLOGY

THE STARS ABOVE THE HILL

THE WORLD BEYOND DUOLOGY
BOOK TWO

~

1

"YOU MEAN TO TELL US FISH CAN FLY HERE?"

Mark's voice rang out against the ample chatter of the crowd. He and Noah trailed behind Katalina and Celeste through a section of Mermain City full of skyscrapers and fish swimming through the air. No rhyme or reason; no thoughts or feelings. They simply existed, flickering out of existence when they hit a building, only to reappear on the other side unharmed.

Noah glanced up at Mark as they paused in the center of a busy walkway, noting the man's once-short black hair was now beginning to curl around his ears. It'd been a month since they'd jumped off their crumbling planet of Sundar and landed on Celeste's, and their journey was nonstop from there. It was made apparent by everyone's physical states that they all needed long naps and showers.

"The fish don't fly; they swim," corrected Noah. "And I thought I told you this weeks ago when we first came here?"

Noah combed his fingers through his dusty blond hair; it felt notably longer, though they hadn't been somewhere with a mirror for him to check. He feared the length didn't suit him, and though he knew there was no point in fretting over something he couldn't change, Noah wanted to look his best for Celeste.

He knew, however, that the grime splattered across his black shirt and his tattered jeans did not suit him. Not one bit. Celeste and Katalina were dressed in once colorful jumpsuits—pink and olive green, respectively—that were now various shades of muddied brown. Even Mark, who Noah considered handsome, had a damp maroon shirt and hair stringy with sweat.

Mark was easily two inches taller and stared down at Noah with piercing deep blue eyes and a cocked brow. His mouth remained agape in shock, exposing perfectly straight white teeth, as he turned to Celeste for confirmation. "In the air?"

She nodded, arms folded over her chest. "In the air."

"Is your house close?" asked Katalina. Noah's cousin was the shortest of them all, and the long, intricate dreads cascading down her back were two shades darker than her ebony skin.

"Isn't coming back here a waste of time?" her fiancé added with a stretch, glancing Celeste's way. Her disgruntled, pinched eyebrows twitched at him as she glared, and Mark gulped with hands up in defense. "I mean, I love seeing fish outside of water, flying in the sky and everything, but weren't we on the side of your planet we needed to be on and now we're, uh, not?"

Celeste's planet, Fortun, was shaped like a cube, and the

sides shifted at random. The moment they docked their ship and broke free of the desert leading to the city, the sides of the planet changed. They could no longer go back the way they came; the ocean was no longer behind them, the dazzling stars no longer ahead.

The stars once littered the entire sky, but they'd been moved by something—or someone. Evidentially, they were instructed to retrieve two of the stars, which they'd decidedly gone out of their way to not do.

"I'd like to see my family one last time, in case we don't make it," Celeste said. "Thank you very much."

"We don't get the same luxury, you know." Mark trailed off as he looked at Noah, the guy whose mother passed away long before they knew of the planets colliding. Noah spared Mark a chiding for obviously pitying him and instead turned his attention to Celeste. She would never say goodbye to her brother, Altair, either. There were hundreds of others who sat with similar sadness, and he would stop at nothing to save them all.

Though a thought rested in the back of his mind—even if they protected everyone and everything, one day, nothing would remain. Nature always found a way back to its own demise, and if not nature, then man surely would.

"If we could give you that chance, we would," Noah said with hands on his hips. "We're going to save everyone, anyway. This is just a cautionary goodbye."

"Wow. Since when did you become so positive?"

If only Mark could hear Noah's endless, and frankly, dreadful, thoughts.

"When I realized that's all I've got." Noah's eyes flickered to

Celeste. Positivity and *her*. She was perhaps the only thing holding him together, aside from the limitless marvels her planet presented. "Though I'm worried about those shapeshifters that attacked us."

Katalina rubbed her chin in thought before snapping her fingers. "What if they've impersonated one of us again and we can't tell until it's too late?"

"Why would you suggest that now?" Mark asked, bewildered eyes bulging from their sockets.

They were in an odd predicament. A group of shapeshifters were after Celeste, determined to stop her from saving the planets. They'd not only attacked her family but also impersonated her and her stepmother, nearly tricking Noah completely.

Shapeshifters were terrifying, gangling, bird-like creatures. The thought of them made him shiver, and now their group was going back to the one place they'd met the monstrosities. He couldn't piece together why anyone would want the planets to end, and that terrified him most of all.

Noah's thoughts quickly delved into a vat of anxiety, the city of swimming sky fish drifting in and out of focus as he attempted to figure everything out.

It was a game of mental gymnastics, and he was losing. All his thoughts pointed back to something the Ruler of the Deep said. While the ruler proved to be helpful, giving them insight on the next step of their journey, the sea serpent made it abundantly clear he didn't extend help to anyone else. *They were too selfish.*

Perhaps the shapeshifters wanted the worlds to collide

because selfishness plagued their societies, and there was no longer any hope of civil survival.

"On our planet, fish *stay* in the water, you know." Mark's voice shocked Noah out of his relentless rumination, and Noah's gaze drifted to Mark. When their eyes met, Mark stammered, "W-What's on your mind, there? That look in your eyes is scaring me."

Celeste took a step forward, head cocked, as she examined Noah from head to toe. "I'm inclined to agree."

He took a deep breath before exhaling a string of fast-paced words. "I'm trying to figure out why the Ruler of the Deep told me everyone who visited him before us was selfish. I mean, how is it selfish to want to save humanity?"

"How isn't it selfish?" Celeste's tone was matter-of-fact and airy, as if it was silly to even suggest humanity could be selfless.

"Are you saying the inherent desire to live is selfish?" Katalina asked, astonishment lining her voice. "That's absurd. It's merely human nature."

"Exactly."

Before the debate could go on, Noah pointed ahead. They'd reached the part of the city separating the swimming fish from everything else. It looked to be a wall of nearly transparent blue jelly. When he reached a finger out to touch it, a ripple began like a slim rock skipping atop the water.

A swath of coolness washed over him when he walked through the barrier, the tension evaporating from his shoulders. A small, nervous smile stretched across his lips. If he'd been told this was where he'd be a year ago, he would've laughed. He would've called his prophet delusional. Oh, how thankful he was for such a delusion.

On the other side was a bustling, urban-looking city. Every building was black, accented with neon pinks, and purples, and blues. Celeste's family was somewhere on this side, living in a pointy yet quaint house not too far from where they stood.

There were no modes of transportation on Fortun, aside from paved paths big enough for pairs to walk side-by-side. The walkways were surrounded by patches of teal grass speckled with bright bushes, flowers, and trees. Occasionally, a series of benches or tables would appear, often populated by humans and merpeople alike. Other subspecies drifted in and out of sight, from two-legged fish heads to human-sized snails slowly sliding down the pavement.

"Uh, are you guys seeing what I'm seeing?" Noah asked, his jaw falling open. A cat sat upright and stretched on a small cloud drifting by. Three kittens followed on their own individual tiny clouds.

Katalina shrieked with delight, a hand over her mouth. "That's the cutest thing I've ever seen. *Cloud kittens?*"

Celeste nodded. "They cannot be tamed, though. They are not pets."

"Good. We would *not* adopt a cat. You promised," Mark warned, wagging a finger at his fiancée.

Katalina's shoulders slumped. "Aw, I wanted to take one back to Sundar with me. For science, of course. Are you sure they can't even be rescued?"

Celeste gently squeezed Katalina's shoulder with a look of solemn understanding. "It would eat you alive."

The group went silent after that, instead storing that chilling information deep in the back of their minds and marveling at the cute animals along their walk. Eventually, the city skyscrapers tapered out into suburban land made up of picket-fenced homes.

Celeste led them to an uneven house painted black and riddled with jagged edges, stopping in front of a red door. Her knuckles rapped against the metal with a hollow bang. At first, there was no response or indicators of life on the other side.

Noah became tense at the sound of turning locks and clanking chains. The first time they'd visited, Celeste's stepsister, Luna, answered the door, and he expected to see the familiar blue-skinned and gill-covered merwoman again.

His heart dropped at the sight of a short man with a thick, bushy mustache. The man was balding, and what little was left of his thin, gray hair was parted to the side. A bright grin grew on Celeste's features and she jumped into his arms while exclaiming proudly, "Dad!"

Oh no.

Noah was running on two hours of sleep and he hadn't showered in days, his scent that of dried saltwater and sweat. He wasn't ready to meet her father.

- Continued in book 2, The Stars Above the Hill -

ENJOY THE WORLDS OF FORTUN AND SUNDAR?
CHECK OUT MORE BOOKS BY ANGELA FUNK

THE FORSAKEN DESTINY TRILOGY

FIVE STRANGERS.
ONE DEADLY EXAM.
NO ESCAPE.

A DARK ACTION ADVENTURE FANTASY

ACKNOWLEDGMENTS

I am unbelievably thankful that I have had the privilege of time to work on my novels and can now say I have a second series under my belt! Not only that, but to make a special hardback option is truly so surreal and so fun!

This duology particularly hit close to home as I have dealt with anxiety and depression for as long as I can remember, and Noah struggles with many themes I think a lot of us can relate to at some point in our lives. I am lucky enough to be surrounded by amazing friends, family, and artists throughout this writing and publishing journey and my life to give me the courage I need to keep going.

First, thank you so much to my beta readers and close friends, Hayley Whiteley (Author of *Ink & Ore*), and Ashleigh Carter (Author of *The Variance*). We have worked together to give each other advice and support, and I am so thankful to have gotten to know you both! You are so talented and I can't wait to continue to do great things together! I am also super thankful for my soon-to-be husband's grandmother, who gave editing advice and a final read-through. You have been a substantial support throughout this process, and I am so thankful to have you in my life!

There are so many incredible artists to thank, from my cover designer to the character artists. Thank you to my amazing cover designer, @OnyxCatArt on Etsy, who I worked with to make this story come to life. She was incredible to work with, and she created covers for both of these hardcover editions!

I would also like to thank the amazing Akar (@akarstudio) over on Fiverr, which is a group of artists based in Indonesia. I gave them loose clip art ideas, and they made a masterpiece far surpassing what I envisioned regarding the planet designs! They truly made the planets in my head come to life! You can also find their work over on Instagram (@akar.std).

The gorgeous artwork of Noah and Celeste was done by @SYKOSAN. I couldn't be happier with the result. Thank you so much for your amazing work! While @Azukiarts and @shinkxart are not featured in this book, I am so amazed by the work they did on my characters, and character art they've made for Noah and Celeste are located over on my Instagram and their respective pages.

Of course, I would not be where I am without my husband, Caleb. He has been my biggest and brightest support and he has given me the confidence I need to grow. I am so lucky to have you in my life and to have someone to travel with and do such amazing things together. Thank you for reading my novels and for being the best support anyone could ask for. I love you!

My family has always been an amazing support in my life and with my writing career. I'd like to thank my father, Jon, my mother, Tasha, and stepmom, Kristen, as well as my half-sister, Emily, my grandparents, aunts, and cousins, have been incredible supports throughout this journey and I'm continuously amazed and blessed by the support you have all given me throughout the years. Liz, Sam, Ben, Sophie, and Izzy are amazing cousins and stepcousins and I'm so thankful to have you all in my life!

My best friend, Carissa, has always bought my books and has been a great maid of honor and lifelong friend! You know she's a bestie for life when she stays in the ER with you until 6:00am! All my other closest friends—Ryan, Amanda, Katelyn, Omar—have been great supports throughout my journey, along with new friends—Zach, Lewis, and Preston. Thank you so much, every single one of you is awesome!

Thank you to all my ARC readers and to everyone who has bought my books thus far. I am so grateful to have this gift and the means to share these ideas, and for the community of readers and fellow authors. I'm astounded by the amazing people I get to meet every day because of this craft and community, and I would be nowhere without you, the readers, and the community over on Instagram and TikTok!

Last, but never least, thank you to all those who have read and bought this book. As a reader, I rarely ever read the acknowledgments, but if you're here, know that I could not be here without you. To have someone read this outside of my friends and family is something I will cherish forever. It is truly a magical experience to touch even one life with a book I've written, and I hope it helped you escape the world for a little while. Life is short, so I'm forever grateful that you've taken some of your time to read this book. God is good, and I am so lucky!

ABOUT THE AUTHOR

Angela Funk is the author of the action-adventure fantasy, the *Forsaken Destiny trilogy*, and the sci-fi romantic comedy, *The World Beyond Duology*.

Her love of reading and writing came at a young age, and she was often found with her nose in a book. Before publishing her debut novel, *The Heroic Facade*, she graduated from the University of Iowa with a B.S. in Therapeutic Recreation. She currently lives in Iowa with her cat, Rory, and her fiancé, Caleb. Outside of writing novels, Angela works full-time with children with autism and enjoys hiking, playing Mario Kart, and watching anime.

Author Website

https://www.angelafunk.com/

instagram.com/authorangelafunk

goodreads.com/angela_funk

www.ingramcontent.com/pod-product-compliance
Lightning Source LLC
Chambersburg PA
CBHW020458310726
48979CB00016B/2712/J